# THE HIDDEN CORPSE

The drive home took less than five minutes and as soon as she hopped out of her SUV, Hope slipped off her pumps and wiggled her toes in the grass. She couldn't believe she used to wear high heels every day to work. She grabbed her latte and purse. Barefoot, she crossed the lawn to the front porch.

All the relaxation she felt after her facial was wiped away by her run-in with Norrie and the weird thing at the newspaper. Why would Milo want to suppress an article on his wife's business? Why did the editor agree to it? What happened to freedom of the press?

Bigelow's loud and piercing bark jogged Hope out of her thoughts. He was always excited when she came home, but there was something different in the tone of his bark she couldn't identify.

Her eyes darted around as she climbed the porch steps with a keen sense of alertness. She was looking for something out of the ordinary. And when her gaze landed on her front door, she found something out of the ordinary.

She crept forward. A torn sheet of notebook paper was nailed to her door. The block lettering read: PLAY WITH FIRE AND YOU'RE GOING TO GET BURNED. . . .

**Books by Debra Sennefelder**

*Food Blogger Mysteries*

THE UNINVITED CORPSE

THE HIDDEN CORPSE

*Resale Boutique Mysteries*

MURDER WEARS A LITTLE BLACK DRESS

**Published by Kensington Publishing Corporation**

# The Hidden Corpse

## Debra Sennefelder

**KENSINGTON BOOKS**
**KENSINGTON PUBLISHING CORP.**
www.kensingtonbooks.com

KENSINGTON BOOKS are published by

Kensington Publishing Corp.
119 West 40th Street
New York, NY 10018

First Printing: April 2019
ISBN-13: 978-1-4967-1593-7
ISBN-10: 1-4967-1593-4

ISBN-13: 978-1-4967-1596-8 (eBook)
ISBN-10: 1-4967-1596-9 (eBook)

10 9 8 7 6 5 4 3 2 1

Printed in the United States of America

*For my husband, George.*
*When you found out I wanted to write a book*
*all those years ago you bought me my first computer*
*and since then you've always made sure I had*
*whatever I needed or wanted.*
*Thank you for everything.*
*Love always.*

# ACKNOWLEDGMENTS

Writing a murder mystery means I am quite often asking very curious questions. Luckily for me when I was plotting *The Hidden Corpse* I had someone very knowledgeable and happy to answer all my questions. An added bonus: I didn't have to go too far to ask questions about food photography because right across the hall from my former office was the test kitchen of a food magazine where Scott Phillips worked as the staff food photographer. Scott graciously allowed me to shadow him for a day and answered all of my questions. Thank you, Scott, for your patience, your expertise, and your enthusiasm for my story. I've more than once reached out to my niece, Dr. Sarah Kuhlmann, for answers regarding medical situations, whether it be an injury or treatment of a poisoning. I don't think it's every day a doctor gets questions from her aunt about murderous scenarios. I can just imagine the stories she'll tell one day about her writer aunt. Thank you, Sarah! Thank you to my agent, Dawn Dowdle, and to my editor, John Scognamiglio, and to Arthur Maisel, Claire Hill, and the whole team at Kensington for bringing *The Hidden Corpse* to publication. Thank you, Ellie Ashe, the best critique partner a writer can have, for helping shape Hope's second murder mystery into the book it is today. A big thank-you goes to all of my readers for your support, your kind words on social media, and for buying my book! THANK YOU!

# Chapter One

*"Still missing, no new leads on Lily Barnhart."*

Hope Early stopped scrolling on her tablet when she came to the article. Her interest piqued by the ongoing saga about how the forty-one-year-old architect went missing three weeks earlier, after last being seen by her husband when she left for work. Hope shook her head in disbelief. How could the police have no new leads? A woman simply didn't vanish.

Lily disappeared on a damp, rainy day. Hope remembered because it had been a perfect day for baking. She'd spent hours in her kitchen testing banana nut bread recipes. The first three attempts resulted in so-so breads, but with the fourth try she had perfected the recipe for her blog, *Hope at Home*.

When she worked on recipe development, she blocked out the world around her. It was just her, the recipe, and the ingredients. So, it wasn't until later in the evening when she'd settled down for a cup of tea and a slice of bread that she'd learned Lily had gone missing. By morning her hometown of Jefferson, Connecticut, was abuzz with speculation, and the fear for Lily's safety was palpable.

"I can't believe she just vanished." Felicity Campbell sat

down next to Hope at the long table that was set up for the four students attending the food photography course.

Hope looked up from her tablet. She met Felicity when they both auditioned for the reality television show *The Sweet Taste of Success*. Hope was chosen as one of the thirteen bakers to compete for the grand prize, while Felicity was encouraged to audition for another season. Hope left the show as the first runner-up with a small monetary prize and a broken marriage. So maybe Felicity had won after all.

"It's scary, isn't it?" The thought of leaving her house one morning and never returning sent a shiver down Hope's spine.

"Since you live in town, did you know her?" Felicity's auburn hair was pulled back into a loose ponytail and her makeup was heavily applied, which was a bit much for a food photography class. She was known for posting selfies on her blog, *Felicity Cooks with Style*, so Hope figured she always wanted to look camera ready.

Hope doubted any of her readers wanted to see what she looked like when she was in the midst of cooking. Her shoulder-length dark hair was usually pushed back in a headband, her face was makeup free, and she preferred to cook in her comfortable lounge pants and loose T-shirts. She hardly looked camera ready when she was in her kitchen.

"Not really. I saw her a few times in town." Hope closed the website and set her tablet on the table. The last thing she wanted was her photography instructor peering over her shoulder and seeing an article about his missing wife.

"This must be a nightmare for Cal. I thought for sure he would have cancelled this class." Felicity raised her cell phone, leaned in closer to Hope, and angled the phone down toward them. "Selfie," she cooed. Within seconds she was tapping a message to accompany the photo of them on her Facebook page. "I tagged you."

"Thank you." Hope was glad she opted to apply a little blush to her usual mascara and dusty rose lipstick for her class.

Felicity finished checking her Facebook page and set her phone down. "I've been so excited about this workshop for months. I'm really glad he didn't cancel. Though, I'm not sure if I was excited about being taught by Cal Barnhart himself or finally seeing his studio. It's awesome, isn't it?"

"Yes, it is." Hope looked around the large space where Cal worked when he was home in Jefferson.

A dozen floor-to-ceiling windows allowed for natural light to flow in and brick walls gave the expansive space character. Baker's racks were packed with props and a fully functioning kitchen was tucked into the corner for food preparation. His photography class used real food and, from where Hope was sitting, she saw Cal's assistant working in the kitchen.

"This place is awesome." Louis Maddox pulled out a chair and sat across from Hope. The thirty-something writer behind the *This Man Grills* blog was dressed in a short-sleeved plaid shirt and khakis. He wore dark-rimmed glasses that kept sliding down the bridge of his nose. "Barnhart's cool factor is off the charts. Especially since his wife disappeared and it's an active missing person case."

"What a terrible thing to say." Elena Voss approached the table. She was the main recipe developer behind the *Two Chicks and a Stove* blog. Upon meeting Hope, she quickly listed all of the magazines her recipes were recently published in. Hope was impressed by the woman's professional pride and the ability to ramble off multiple titles without taking a breath.

"Really? Tell me you ladies don't think he's even hotter now that there's a hint of scandal around him," Louis challenged.

Felicity nodded. "He's right. Cal is hotter now."

Elena let out an exasperated sigh as she sat down next to Felicity. "What about you, Hope? What do you think?"

She'd always admired Cal's work, but now that he was in the midst of a scandal, there was an air of mystery about him. And mystery could be, as Louis said, hot. Not that Hope would ever admit that to anyone, especially the three bloggers surrounding her.

"Okay, let's begin. Everyone take a seat." Cal Barnhart's voice boomed as he entered the studio, clapping his hands. He got everyone's attention; even his assistant stopped what she was doing to focus on him. He was tall, lean, and ruggedly artistic, a potent combination for any woman to take in and Hope understood Felicity's assessment of him. He wore his trademark black, his dark hair was peppered with flecks of silver, and his deep blue eyes cast a sweeping glance over his students.

"How do you create sexy food photography that your readers can't get enough of?" Cal asked, his intense gaze landing on Hope.

She shifted in her seat and the studio suddenly seemed warmer than the cool May morning. This wasn't college, and she wasn't a silly freshman who flirted with instructors. Especially one with a missing wife.

"Your goal is to entice your readers with your photographs. Make them stop from clicking off of your website. Grab them. Pull them in. Keep them. If your photography is lackluster or substandard, I guarantee your reader will be off your blog before you can say Google Analytics."

His students chuckled.

Hope lifted her gaze and found Cal had moved over to one of the tables set up for their class. He now was looking at the whole group, not just her.

"Shouldn't our recipes be enough to keep our readers on our blog?" Elena asked.

"If you believed that, you wouldn't be here," Cal replied dryly.

"I'm all for learning how to create sexy food photos," Felicity gushed in a breathy voice.

"I doubt any of my grilled bratwursts will ever be considered a sexy photo," Louis quipped.

"You can make any food look delicious and appealing. That's *your* job. And the reason why you're here today. We're going to begin with lighting. Then we'll cover styling, editing, and angles. Angles are easy. I have two preferences." Cal picked up his digital camera.

"I wouldn't mind being angled by him," Felicity whispered as she leaned over to Hope. "Come on, you have to be thinking that too."

"Actually, I was thinking of why he chose that lens to use." Hope pointed at the camera Cal held. She'd invested in two lenses when she purchased her digital camera for her blog, but he was using a different lens. She was curious to find out how the lens performed compared to the two she owned.

Felicity rolled her eyes. "Boooring."

"We'll begin with shooting bowls of oatmeal and fruit. What we want to accomplish is snapping a photo that will go viral. Everybody and their mother will want to make your recipe. So, let's get started. Everyone to their table." Cal clapped his hands again.

Cal's assistant had set out a bowl of oatmeal and berries with a gingham napkin and a spoon at each station to be photographed to death.

Hope grabbed her camera bag and walked to one of the tables. There wasn't anything fancy about Cal's setup. Its simple functionality gave the space a cool, hip urban vibe. Each station consisted of a four-foot table topped with a thick board. She ran her fingers over the rough surface and had some serious prop envy.

Stacked against the wall was a stash of boards in various sizes and finishes. Hope had a similar growing collection, but Cal's selection was huge. She spent weekends scouring flea markets and home centers for creative backdrops, trying to find a mix of wood boards, laminates, and stone to get just the right photograph.

She pulled out her camera and attached one of her lenses, all the while keeping an eye on Cal. Countless questions ran through her mind, probably the same questions everyone in town was asking. How was he able to live a normal life with his wife missing? Was she dead or alive? Did she take off with someone or did someone take her? Cal's head turned and he caught her staring. He flashed a smile and she wanted to crawl under the table. She broke their eye contact and returned to adjusting the focus on her camera. He moved to Elena and assisted her with setting up a soft box to diffuse light, giving the photographer more control over the shoot.

"Flirting with the teacher?" Felicity whispered as she passed by Hope on the way to her table.

Hope cleared her throat and returned her attention to her camera and bowl of oatmeal. How Cal was dealing with the disappearance of his wife wasn't her concern. She was there to improve her photography, not to stick her nose into his private business. No matter how curious she was.

The workshop ended at three. For over five hours, Hope was standing and, even though she wore sensible shoes, the same ones she cooked in for hours, her lower back ached. The pain probably was due to the various angles she contorted her body into to get hundreds of photographs. At one point she even used a three-foot ladder to get overhead shots. A nice long soak in her tub would go a long way in easing the tension that spread across her back. But she had one stop to make on her way home. Drew had texted her right as class ended and asked to meet for coffee.

She pushed open the door of the Coffee Clique and found a midafternoon rush of desperate caffeine seekers. A long line at the counter snaked around carefully laid out posts, while two harried baristas whipped up fancy coffees. Her shoulders sagged. The last thing she wanted was to stand in line for a coffee she desperately needed. A quick glance around the coffee shop revealed every table was taken, but then she saw Drew waving her over. Bless him. He'd grabbed a table for them. She passed by the line of customers, smiling at familiar faces. When she reached the small table, she draped her purse on the back of the chair and sat. In front of her was a large coffee cup and a pastry.

"Luckily, I got here before everybody else in Jefferson started jonesing for a coffee. I ordered you a hazelnut and the cinnamon bun. I know they're your favorites." Drew gave a big smile as he stood. He looked like the picture of cool casualness in a turquoise-colored polo shirt paired with pleated dark blue pants and two-toned blue sneakers. Hope glanced at her simple outfit of a floral top and khaki capri pants. She seriously needed to up her fashion game. Drew gave her a peck on the cheek and then returned to his seat.

Something was up. She knew Drew too well not to be suspicious of his doting. He'd been her closet friend since grade school. They'd grown up together, went through breakups together, and shared the ups and downs of their careers. While Hope went off to New York City, he stayed in Jefferson and worked for the *North Country Gazette* newspaper.

"Thank you. I'm starving." She took a sip of her coffee.

"I know you've had a long day in class, so I didn't want you standing in line for your coffee." He glanced over at the counter. "They really should get more help."

Hope bit into the cinnamon bun. The layers of sweet, soft dough melted together with the heavenly sugar glaze topping and bursts of cinnamon exploded in her mouth. She needed to figure out a way to make cinnamon buns a food group required at every meal.

After she swallowed, she wiped her mouth with a napkin.

Now it was time to find out what Drew wanted. "You're being very kind to me."

"Well"—Drew waved his hand in a dramatic gesture—"it's my pleasure. After all, you're my best friend."

Hope nodded as she chewed another bite of the pastry. "I am."

"And best friends are happy to do things for their best friends."

"I suppose."

"So, it was my pleasure to make sure you had your favorite coffee and pastry." Drew leaned forward and rested his arms on the table.

Hope wiped her mouth again, discarded the napkin, and then took a sip of her coffee. While she was confident something was attached to her afternoon treat, she had to admit she was enjoying being taken care of for a change. She couldn't remember the last time someone fussed over her.

"What do you want?" she asked.

Drew grinned. "That obvious?"

Hope laughed. "Yes."

Drew took a long drink of his coffee before confessing his ulterior motive. "I want every detail of what happened today."

"Since when are you interested in food photography?"

"I'm not. I'm interested in Cal Barnhart. More precisely, his missing wife."

Hope shook her head. She should've known. Every reporter from local newspapers to the wire services wanted an interview with Cal. During the five hours she was at Cal's studio, which was located on his home's five acres, he never once mentioned Lily. When they broke for lunch, they all gathered around a picnic table outside under a majestic maple tree and ate a catered lunch his assistant picked up. Their conversation revolved around photography and blogging and a bunch of photos were snapped for everyone's social media platforms.

"There's nothing I can tell you. He didn't talk about Lily during the class. We weren't there to discuss his missing wife."

The workshop cost Hope an exorbitant amount of money, so the only thing she wanted to talk about was photography. Food blogs that earned decent money had great food and awesome photographs, reason number one to sign up for the class. The other reason was to up the ante on her camera skills because she'd been approached to contribute to a cookbook being published by *The Sweet Taste of Success*. Along with the recipes, she needed to include photographs.

Drew slumped and his face twisted with frustration. "I've been trying to land an interview with him since Lily disappeared. He's shut out all media. I can't even get a 'no comment' out of him." Drew reached across the table, broke off a piece of the cinnamon roll, and chewed it.

Hope couldn't blame Cal for staying away from the media. After her loss on *The Sweet Taste of Success* and her subsequent divorce, she was on the receiving end of some negative coverage in newspaper gossip columns and on celebrity websites. In the past couple of weeks, she had seen Cal receive some of the same treatment. But his case was worse, since husbands were always the first person the police looked at when a wife went missing.

"I need that interview. I need an exclusive." Drew rubbed his temples and exhaled a deep breath. "You know him personally."

"Barely. And only through blogger events and some work at the magazine years ago. What's going on?"

Drew set his hands on the table, then laced his fingers together. "Remember what I told you a few weeks ago about budget cuts at the newspaper?"

Hope nodded. The newspaper's publisher had gathered

the staff together for an impromptu meeting to announce that the *Gazette* was in financial difficulty and would be looking at ways to reduce expenses, including layoffs. To recover from the stunning announcement, Drew showed up at her door that night with a bottle of wine, a container of ice cream, and a list of movies he wanted to watch.

"You're very good at your job, Drew. I don't think you have anything to worry about," Hope reassured.

"I have a lot to worry about and she has a name."

"Norrie?"

"You got it! The new shiny star of the *Gazette*. She ran out of the office today because she landed an interview with Lily's secretary. If I don't get something exclusive or juicy, I'm out! Out!"

Hope reached out and covered his hands with hers. "Drew, calm down. You're overreacting."

Drew harrumphed.

"You're not going to get fired."

"Not if I can get an interview with Cal Barnhart."

"Reach out to him again," Hope suggested.

"He'll just turn me down, *again*. But I bet you can convince him to give me an interview."

Hope shook her head. "I'm not going to do that."

"But we're best friends and you did ask what you can do for me."

Hope swiped her coffee cup and stood. "You're right, we are best friends. Next time the coffee and pastry will be on me. I have to get going."

Drew sighed.

"Good grief," Hope muttered.

Drew pouted.

Hope sighed that time. "Fine. I can't promise anything."

Drew smiled. "You're the best."

Hope turned and headed out of the coffee shop, shaking her head. She had no idea how she'd approach Cal about Drew.

*My friend Drew is a reporter and would like to interview you about your missing wife.* Not a bad start to getting herself kicked out of class. Hope pulled open the glass door and stepped out onto Main Street.

Maybe something more direct. *Would you like to set the record straight that you didn't kill your wife and dispose of her body?* Hope winced. Too direct. She walked toward her car, which was parked down the street.

Lordy, how did she allow Drew to manipulate her so easily? Guilt. He knew her too well. At least she had three more days of the workshop to figure out how to approach Cal about an interview with Drew. She'd figure something out.

# Chapter Two

Hope's kitchen door swung open and she was unexpectedly greeted by her sister, Claire Dixon. She had one hand propped on her hip and her nude-colored lips were pursed. "Where have you been? Your photography class ended over an hour ago."

*Uh-oh. Claire is channeling our mother.*

"Sorry I missed my curfew." Hope walked past Claire and dropped her bags on the table. She'd had a long day and just wanted to collapse on the sofa, but with the stern greeting she'd received, she doubted there would be any relaxation.

She turned just in time to brace herself for the excited onslaught of her adopted dog, Bigelow. His ears flopped and his tail wagged and he bounded across the antique pumpkin pine floor at record speed to welcome her home. She rubbed him enthusiastically. Having a dog wasn't on her to-do list when she moved back to Jefferson, but when his owners could no longer keep him, she jumped at the chance to take him.

"It's good Bigelow was here to keep you company while you waited."

Claire gave the dog a sideways glance. She and Bigelow had a complicated relationship. He liked jumping on people and dragging his dirty paws on their clothing, while Claire preferred not to be pawed by dogs.

"Some company. He's been sleeping." Claire walked to the counter and picked up her protein shake bottle and took a sip. "I finished at the gym early so I thought I'd come by to see you."

Even though she'd just come from the gym, Claire's makeup was perfect and her long blond hair was pulled back into a neat ponytail. Her bright capris and purple tank top were perspiration free and her sneakers looked like they just came out of the box. Hope shook her head in amazement. When she finished working out, she was a sweaty mess while her sister looked like she stepped out of a magazine layout.

Bigelow settled down and retreated to his bed tucked in a corner of the family room. The kitchen was an open space that incorporated the cooking area, a dining space, and a family room. The large space was the heart of her home and where she did most of the work for her blog, so it made sense for Hope to have spent a huge chunk of her budget and time remodeling there first. What probably didn't make sense was buying an old, run-down house when she was recently divorced and starting a new business.

"What are you doing here?" Hope asked.

Normally she didn't arrive home to find Claire waiting for her. Especially now. Claire had been juggling her career as a real estate agent and running her campaign for mayor of Jefferson with raising her two kids, while her husband traveled often for business. Sitting around Hope's house waiting for her usually wasn't on Claire's to-do list.

Claire perked up. "Two things." She set the bottle down and walked around the island. "I was at the Workout Fix and you won't believe what I found out."

Hope went to the refrigerator and pulled out a pitcher of iced tea, then poured a glass. As a real estate agent in a small town, her sister had access to a lot of gossip, and spending time at the only fitness center in town meant she could find out anything about anybody.

After taking a refreshing sip Hope asked, "What did you find out?"

"Meg Griffin wants the position on the Planning and Zoning Commission that Lily Barnhart has . . . or had . . . whatever. Meg wants it."

"Can she do that? Lily hasn't officially resigned?"

In the past few years, the topic of development had become a hot button for town residents and Hope didn't envy Lily or the other members. From what she knew, serving on the P&Z Commission seemed to be wrought with headaches, primarily from unhappy homeowners.

"She's been missing for three weeks. The P&Z Commission needs to vote on very serious matters. The town can't wait for Lily to get her act together and come back home if she did take off. And, we can't wait to find . . ."

*We can't just wait to find her body.*

That was what they'd all been thinking. While everybody in town wanted to remain hopeful Lily would return safely, there was an unspeakable truth they all knew was a possibility. She was dead. She wasn't the type of person to run off. She was far too responsible to do something so reckless. She worked as an architect, served on the P&Z Commission, volunteered at the senior center and the library. No, Lily Barnhart wouldn't have walked away from her life.

"Hope, did you hear me?"

Hope snapped out of her thoughts. "What?"

"If Meg is successful in her bid, she'll be a nightmare on the board. She's more of a tree hugger than Lily was."

"Claire!"

"It's true. At least Lily had common sense on her side. She was open-minded about development, and I do have to admit she had some good arguments against some of the proposed developments. But Meg? And her Society to Protect Jefferson group? Ugh. She'll veto all development projects in town."

Hope shrugged. "If Meg wants to run, you can't stop her."

"True," Claire said. "However, I can find a candidate to oppose her."

*Oh, boy.*

"Who?" Hope dared to ask.

"Maretta."

"Are you serious?" Hope eyed the protein shake bottle. Was it spiked? Because Claire would have to be drunk to even consider Maretta Kingston as a potential candidate.

They'd both known the woman since childhood and, while some people loosened up as they got older, Maretta seemed to be more tightly wound. Rigid, righteous, and over-bearing summed her up nicely. Maretta was pro-development. After all, her husband owned a real estate agency in town, where Claire worked. Having Maretta on the P&Z Commission would definitely change the dynamics of the votes. "Isn't the fact her husband owns a real estate agency a conflict of interest?"

"Pish." Claire waved away the suggestion. "Don't worry about the details. I've got this all covered."

"You're running for mayor, which means you should be concerned about the details."

Claire shrugged. "I need your support. Well, Maretta needs your support. I think there should be some kind of get-together where Maretta can do a meet and greet with everyone now that she's officially a candidate."

Hope arched an eyebrow. "A meet and greet? Who hasn't she met and greeted in the sixty-plus years she's lived in Jefferson?" Or, rather, who hadn't she offended? Hope didn't want to emphasize the negative since her sister was excited about her plan.

"I would do it at my house, but I think it's better if someone else who isn't running for mayor host the event." Claire had a look Hope knew all too well.

"Oh, no, no, no." Hope shook her head. With her glass in hand, she walked over to the table and sat. She set the glass on a coaster and then unzipped her laptop bag. She had a blog post to write and she needed to check her e-mails. And maybe her sister would get the hint she was too busy to continue this conversation.

Claire swooped over to the table. "Come on. It'll be a piece of cake for you." She snapped her fingers. "A couple of hours, some beverages . . . ooh, we can do an English tea. You can serve scones. Everybody loves your scones. Especially those chocolate chip ones you bake with sugar sprinkled on top. So worth the extra time on the treadmill."

Hope hated when Claire appealed to the baker in her. Darn. But she would remain firm.

"You make it sound like it's no work at all. Invite people over. If you haven't noticed, I'm swamped. I have this photography class, I have my blog, I have Bigelow to train, and I have to finish putting up the shelving in the garage."

She wasn't sure when she'd be officially done working on her house, but she did know she was nowhere near that date. The construction crew had just finished building the garage, wrapping up two days earlier with the Sheetrock and paint. She needed to install the organizational system so everything had a place and her garage wouldn't end up a dumping ground.

"Oh, come on, who are you kidding? With your uber-ninja-like entertaining ability, you know it'll take you a couple of hours to pull the tea party together. You love stuff like this," Claire pointed out.

"True." Gosh, Hope was so easily manipulated. First by Drew and now by Claire. "But I don't love Maretta Kingston."

Claire rolled her eyes. "Nobody does. But you'll be doing this for Jefferson. For our town's future. This is bigger than Maretta. Trust me."

Before Hope could say something, the doorbell rang, sending Bigelow racing through the house to the front door. Hope leapt up and chased behind him at full speed. He had a bad habit of jumping on the door, leaving scratch marks. Since she'd spent hours stripping and painting the wood door, she needed to break him of the habit.

The dog training book she bought said she needed to create a calm environment for the training, and she needed to invite him to the closed door. Well, he wasn't waiting for an invitation. He was already at the door and was excited by the prospect of a visitor; he was barking loudly and dancing on all fours.

"Sit," she commanded.

A playful howl escaped Bigelow's lips. The medium-sized brown-and-white dog continued to dance as Hope approached. At least he wasn't jumping on the door.

Baby steps, she guessed.

"Sit," she commanded again, pointing with her finger.

The dog obliged. He settled into a perfect "sit" position as Hope reached for the doorknob. She pulled the door open and found her elderly neighbor, Peggy Olson, on her front porch.

Hope's smile faded when she saw the nervous look on Peggy's face. The petite woman wore a pair of white pants with a blue blouse and a matching cardigan. Her short, thin white hair was messy. Her brown eyes were wide with confusion, and she was wringing her hands together.

Hope immediately stepped out of her house onto the

front porch and placed a hand on Peggy's shoulder. "What's the matter, Peggy?"

"Oh, my . . . I can't believe . . . Please, come over." Peggy kept glancing toward the road. She lived a few houses away in a beautiful Victorian home her niece, Meg Griffin, had been maintaining while Peggy was recovering at a rehab facility. Hope had heard from another neighbor Peggy was home and she planned on visiting soon.

"Of course I will. Can you tell me what's happened?" Hope's mind raced with scenarios of what could have happened in Peggy's house. She tamped down the uneasiness that was settling in her gut. There was no need to jump to any conclusions. *Remain calm,* she told herself.

"I'm thinking we can have tea around eleven." Claire approached the doorway. She stopped when she saw Peggy. "Oh, hi. How are you today?"

Peggy's gaze darted to Claire. "Not good, dear. Please, Hope, come over. I don't know how I did it. I can't remember. Maybe I . . ." She turned and began walking down the porch steps.

"What's going on?" Claire asked.

Hope looked over her shoulder. "I have no idea. I'll be right back." She dashed down the steps after Peggy.

"Take your time. I'll check your schedule and pick a date for the tea," Claire called out as Hope caught up with Peggy, as the older woman stepped off the lawn and onto the road.

Peggy grabbed hold of Hope's arm as she walked. "Hurry, dear. There's so much smoke."

Hope did a double take. *Smoke?* She stopped. Peggy's house was on fire?

Hope entered the gracious Victorian house behind Peggy through a propped-open back door. The home was built in the mid-nineteenth century and was trimmed with elaborate gingerbread and painted a bright yellow. They walked through the butler's pantry to reach the kitchen. Hope winced at the excruciating beeping noise emanating from the smoke detector.

She dashed over to the stove, which was high-end thirty years ago. A six-quart yellow Le Creuset Dutch oven sat on a trivet next to the stove. She grabbed the potholder from the counter, lifted up the lid, and found a burnt heap of peppers and onions.

"Dear, please make it stop." Peggy pointed to the ceiling.

"Okay. I can do that." Hope returned the lid to the pot and looked around the kitchen. In its heyday it was top of the line and still hung on to its grandeur, even though the shiny newness had worn off. A hand-painted tile backsplash lined the granite countertop, while a butcher block center island with intricately carved legs stood solidly on the terra-cotta tile floor. She hurried over to the table and pulled out a chair. She moved the chair to under the smoke detector and climbed up.

"Be careful!" Peggy called out as she shuffled over to Hope and reached out a small, frail hand to steady Hope's body.

Hope glanced down and smiled. If she lost her balance, she'd fall and Peggy would get squished. The hand resting against Hope's leg was doing nothing to keep her from falling, but she appreciated the gesture. Finally, she was able to turn off the smoke detector and the high-pitched beeping stopped.

"Oh, thank you!" Peggy helped guide Hope off of the chair. "The noise was making me crazy."

"I can understand." Hope returned the chair to the table and walked back to the stove. "Would you like me to clean this pot out?"

Peggy nodded and then padded to the stove and looked at the pot. "I made a mess, didn't I?"

"Did you forget you were cooking something?"

"I must have. I woke up to the loud beeping and smoke."

"You fell asleep with something cooking on the stove? That can be dangerous."

"I really don't remember cooking. You see, Meg stopped by earlier with groceries and she bought me some of those prepared meals from the store that I just have to reheat in the microwave. So, I don't know why I would cook anything. What's in the pot?"

"Onions and peppers," Hope said.

Peggy frowned. "I always made that for Ricky. I don't cook that anymore."

Hope reached out and covered Peggy's hand with hers. Ricky was Peggy's late husband, and she'd doted on him. Now she was at an age when her mind could play tricks on her. She could've made the onions and peppers thinking Ricky was coming home from work.

Hope's heart ached for Peggy. Getting old wasn't easy. "Let me call Meg and have her come over."

"No!" Peggy grabbed hold of Hope's hand, tightly. "Please don't."

"Why not? She's your niece."

Peggy's eyes clouded with fear. "She wants me to go into a nursing home. I won't. It was bad enough being in that rehab place. I won't leave my home."

Hope bit her lower lip as she considered what to do. "Peggy, you fell asleep with something cooking on the stove. Maybe you shouldn't be alone."

Tears streamed down Peggy's face. She tried to wipe them away with her bony fingers, but there were too many. Hope extricated herself from Peggy's hold and went for some tissues. She returned and Peggy took the tissues.

Peggy dried her face as she settled at the table. "I want to stay in my home. Ricky died here. I want to also."

Hope sighed. She sympathized with her neighbor and

wanted to honor her request. She also knew she needed to be the reasonable adult in the situation and call Meg.

"I promise, I won't turn on the stove or oven," Peggy said.

Hope wrestled with what she should do and what she wanted to do. If Peggy were her aunt, she'd want to know she nearly burned down her house. But if she were Peggy, she'd want her wishes respected. Talk about being between a rock and a hard place.

"Okay. I'm going to hold you to your promise."

Peggy smiled. "Bless you. Bless you."

With the heavy pot in hand and full of doubt, Hope left the house. Had she made the right decision in promising not to call Meg? There was a chance Peggy overexerted herself and was tired. She'd been home for only a few days.

"Hello, Hope," a familiar voice called from a short distance away.

She was so deep in thought about Peggy, she hadn't seen her other neighbor Gilbert Madison walking toward her with his dog, Buddy. Twice a day Gilbert walked his golden retriever or was it the other way around? Hope wasn't sure. Gilbert maintained the routine for Buddy's health, but she suspected Gilbert enjoyed being out and about, chatting with the neighbors.

"Hi." Hope walked down the driveway and was greeted by Buddy. He and Bigelow had become fast friends and they often had playdates. Sometimes she envied the fact her dog had a more active social life than she did.

"Everything okay with Peggy?" Gilbert asked as Buddy sat next to him. The three-year-old dog was used to frequent stops during his walks because Gilbert liked to visit with his neighbors.

"I'm not sure." She shared with Gilbert what had happened and, even though Peggy promised not to cook, she was still worried.

Gilbert nodded. "She's just come home. She probably

overdid it. Mitzi saw her this morning out by the mailbox pulling up weeds. I'll ask Mitzi to check on her later." Gilbert tugged on Buddy's leash and they began walking away. "Have a good evening." He waved.

Feeling a little better knowing the Madisons would be looking after Peggy, Hope headed back to her house. She had a ton of work to do, so it looked like another long night ahead of her. She had a couple of blog posts to write and finish putting together the free e-book. The recipes were all done and photographed, so all she needed to do was the layout of the book.

Claire left after Hope returned from Peggy's house to pick up her kids from sports. Bigelow wasted no time in reminding Hope it was dinnertime. Beside his food bowl, he did his nightly "dinner dance." She quickly dished out his meal and, while he ate, she prepared a simple pasta dish for herself.

Once the dinner dishes were cleared, Hope prepared a cup of tea and settled at the kitchen table and started to work. She spent twenty minutes checking her social media followed by a quick scan of her e-mails. An old friend from her days in New York City sent a link to an article on a gossip website about her ex-husband. He'd liked the spotlight too much to give it up and wrangled his own reality TV show. Even though she had work to do, she clicked on the link. She had no business wasting time reading gossip.

Once the website was loaded and she found the story her friend linked to, she realized just how bad a decision it was.

"Has Tim Ward found his true love in Angelica Rios?"

Hope slumped in her chair. Her ex-husband had a new girlfriend. She closed the browser and opened up her publishing program to continue work on the e-book for her subscribers. She didn't have time to dwell on Tim or his new love, the ultra-lanky, boob-enhanced model Angelica.

She tapped feverishly on the keyboard. Only to stop typing mid-sentence. Against her better judgment, she opened her browser again and went back to the website and read the article that accompanied the photograph of the very happy couple in love.

"Tim Ward, ex-husband of food blogger and former *The Sweet Taste of Success* runner-up, Hope Early, has dated several women on the reality show *Life After the Big D*. It looks like this time Ward has finally found true love with international model Angelica Rios."

Hope huffed. Before she clicked off the website, she saw the links below the article under the title of "More from Celeb Watch."

Three links and the first one read: "Hope Early Assists with Murder Investigations."

Hope huffed again.

The second link read: "Hope Early's Sister Arrested for Murders."

Having her sister the person of interest for two murders a couple of months ago forced Hope into doing a little detective work of her own and nearly got her killed when she discovered the identity of the killer.

She closed the browser again. While the web articles would remain forever, she was glad there would be no more sleuthing in her future.

# Chapter Three

Hope took a sip from her travel mug. She'd brewed a whole pot of coffee to get her morning started. Getting out of bed was a struggle, but it wasn't because of soreness, which had become a common problem after purchasing an old house that needed a lot of work. Rather, it was plain old exhaustion.

The first day of her photography class left her mentally drained. She thought she had a good handle on snapping photos of her food, but she was wrong. There was so much to absorb from Cal's years of experience that her brain actually hurt. How would she remember everything he was teaching? If the class wasn't enough, she'd been dragged into Drew's drama, Claire's insane idea of hosting an English tea party for Maretta, worrying about Peggy's mental state, and to top it off, the cherry on the sundae was reading about Tim's new love, a leggy, boob-enhanced model. Yeah, last night was rough.

After she swallowed her drink of coffee, she chided herself for not making it stronger. She needed full-on diesel to get through the day. She was the first one to arrive at Cal's studio. Hope had a thing for being on time, which meant she always arrived early and waited a lot. She settled at the long table in the middle of the studio space and opened up her website. She needed to schedule some of her posts and a few quiet moments alone would allow her to finish the task quickly.

She worked with an editorial calendar, something bloggers usually had a hard time utilizing, but with her background in magazine publishing, using the calendar came naturally to her. When all of the posts were scheduled with their go-live date she let out a sigh of relief. Now she wasn't too far behind; she was making headway.

"Good morning, you're the first one here." Brenda Fowler, Cal's assistant, entered the studio carrying two overflowing reusable grocery bags.

"It's my nature to be early," Hope said.

"Maybe because it's your last name." Brenda smiled. She carried the grocery bags into the kitchen.

Hope laughed. Like she'd never heard that before, but she didn't want to be rude. "Interesting observation."

Brenda shrugged. "I didn't mean to interrupt your work." She unpacked the groceries and put them away.

Hope closed her website and walked over to the kitchen. Maybe Brenda could help get Drew an interview. When Hope was a magazine editor, she had her own gatekeeper and there were days she missed Cara. Brenda was Cal's assistant, which meant she was technically his gatekeeper. Maybe she wouldn't have to go directly to Cal and risk being thrown out of class.

"I'm very grateful the workshop wasn't cancelled. I'm learning so much. In fact, my brain hurt yesterday from all the information he gave us." Hope leaned on the counter that separated the studio from the kitchen.

Brenda nodded. "He likes to keep busy." She folded the grocery bags and set them in a drawer. Her long maxi skirt flowed easily with every move she made. Her light brown hair was pulled back into a messy ponytail and her skin was bare of any makeup.

"I can relate." Hope knew something about throwing yourself into work to forget what life was handing you. When she found out Tim had cheated on her, she went into her kitchen and didn't come out for days. She had over a dozen cakes and countless cookies to write about on her blog. Her kitchen, whether it was in her New York City condo or her farmhouse, was her sanctuary where she'd bake herself right.

"I suppose you can." Brenda exhaled a breath. "Unlike your fellow students, you know what it's like to be thrust into the spotlight when your life unravels."

"I only went through a messy divorce. Cal's wife is missing and there's speculation swirling around him."

Brenda straightened, her deep chocolate brown eyes narrowed. "It's a waste of time speculating. Cal had nothing to do with Lily's disappearance. He loved her. He would never harm her."

"Oh, I don't buy into that speculation. It's just what I'm seeing occur in the media."

"Well, then the media can stuff it!"

Hope pressed her lips together to stave off the smile ready to emerge. Brenda's G-rated outrage and protectiveness over Cal was endearing. This was going to be harder than she expected.

"Perhaps the media can help move the speculation off of Cal and back onto finding the truth."

Brenda gave Hope a pointed stare and challenged her. "How?"

Hope couldn't believe she was going say what was on the tip of her tongue. But Drew was her best friend and she'd do anything for him. Almost anything, within reason. Brenda's stare intensified so she needed to get on with it.

"An interview."

Brenda laughed. Not a funny ha-ha kind of laugh but a "you have to be crazy, girl" kind of laugh. "Absolutely not. Cal knows reporters will twist whatever he says. They do that!"

"All the more reason to do an interview with a responsible reporter. There are a few good, honest reporters out there."

"Good morning. Isn't it a lovely day?" Felicity bellowed as she entered the studio, with Louis trailing behind her.

"Too darn early. Take it down a notch already, Felicity." Louis slugged over to the table, where he dropped his camera and laptop bags. He pulled out a chair and plopped down. His clothes were rumpled, like they were yesterday. Hope wasn't sure if he changed or if he was just sloppy.

"I'm going to check on Cal. He should be about ready to start the class." Brenda darted out of the studio, leaving Hope with a firm "no" on the interview. She'd have to approach Cal.

"Louis has been crabby since we met in the lobby of the inn." Felicity looked around. "Where did Elena go off to?"

"Who cares?" Louis rested his head in his hands.

"Does he have a hangover?" Hope asked.

Felicity shrugged. "Maybe. He drank in his room last night."

"Did you all drive over together?" Hope headed back to her seat, with Felicity following.

"Yes. We figured it would be easier to carpool." Felicity wore a jersey knit wrap dress with a neckline that plunged a little low for daytime. Her hair was styled to fall in soft waves around her shoulders.

Louis leaned back and rubbed his face. "A freakin' rooster woke me up this morning. A rooster. Who has roosters anymore?"

"The Merrifields. His name is Sherlock." Hope pulled

out her notebook and opened it to her notes from yesterday. Jane Merrifield and her sister-in-law, Sally, managed Jefferson's only inn, and they liked to serve fresh eggs to their guests. Sherlock had been a staple on Main Street for years. Being a retired mystery author, Jane named her rooster after one of her favorite fictional detectives.

Felicity, who seated herself next to Hope again, leaned over and whispered, "I saw an article online last night about your ex."

*Of course she did.* Hope inhaled a deep breath. Most of Jefferson didn't know the celebrity website existed, and she could possibly go weeks without anyone knowing that her ex-husband was dating a supermodel. But bloggers knew what was out on the Internet. Felicity was no exception.

"I wish him well." Hope meant it. Well, at least she wanted to believe she was the bigger person.

Felicity chuckled. "I'm sure he's doing very well with that model."

"Sorry. I had to take a call." Elena rushed into the studio. She claimed a seat at the table and shrugged off her cardigan. She looked a little confused as she dug into her bag and muttered under her breath.

Hope sensed Elena had lost something.

"I was wondering what happened to you." Felicity pulled her camera out of its bag and cleaned the lens.

"You know, I was thinking last night it's rare for bloggers to get together in real life, so I thought you would all like to come over to my house for dinner one night. Nothing fancy, just good food and conversation," Hope suggested to her classmates.

"Sounds like fun. I'm dying to see your house," Felicity said.

"If you've got a grill, I'd be happy to cook something," Louis offered.

"Dinner sounds lovely," Elena chimed in.

They were all in. Great. They set a date and time. Hope began mentally preparing the menu while they waited for Cal to arrive. The door of the studio swung open and she expected to see Cal. Instead, Brenda marched in with a scarf in her hand. She approached Elena and extended her hand.

"I believe you dropped this by the back door of the house," Brenda said in a tight voice.

Elena looked sheepish as she snatched the scarf from Brenda and tucked it into her canvas tote bag. "Do you know how much longer we have to wait?"

Before Brenda answered, Cal strode into the studio and stopped when he reached the long table where the bloggers were seated. Unlike the day before, he looked tired. His dark eyes were hooded and the machismo he exuded had been taken down a notch. Maybe teaching the class was too much for him, with everything else going on in his life.

"We're going to begin with lighting today. I'll demonstrate first. It takes experimentation and practice to master good lighting." Cal moved over to one of the small tables and picked up his camera. "The setup I'm using is simple because when you're photographing in your kitchen, you'll be limited in what you can use."

"With him, lighting isn't what I'd want to master," Felicity said in a low, throaty voice, just loud enough for Hope to hear.

Hope shot her classmate a glance. Maybe getting together with other bloggers wasn't such a good idea. She refocused on Cal and the workshop flew by so quickly that by the time it was end of day, she was surprised.

Even though the class officially ended, Cal remained to answer questions. When the informal session finally broke up, Hope left the studio with the group. After setting her bags on the backseat of her SUV, she realized she'd left one of her lenses on the table in the studio. She headed back to the studio and saw Cal walking toward her with her lens in his hands.

"Great. You have it." She took the lens from Cal.

"How are you enjoying the class so far?"

"I have to admit, I'm a little overwhelmed, but it's amazing. I'm learning so much."

"It's hard to teach everything in a short period of time. With that said, I think everyone in the class had a good grasp on the fundamentals and implementing just a few of my suggestions will definitely improve everyone's photographs." Cal fell into step with Hope as she walked back to her vehicle. "I was a little nervous about teaching the class."

"You? The great Cal Barnhart? Nervous?" Hope reached her SUV and slid the lens into its pocket in her camera bag. She'd met Cal years ago while working for the magazine *Meals in Minutes*. He'd done some freelance work, but it wasn't until she had more time to talk to him at a food blogging conference she'd learned he lived in Jefferson. Small world. Despite her move back to town, she didn't have the opportunity catch up with him. His schedule had him traveling all over the country for photo shoots.

"Normally I'm not, but I worried I'd be too distracted by recent events to focus on the class like I should."

Hope nodded. "I only met Lily a few times in town since I've moved back." Working from home, Hope was holed up inside most of the day, either writing or developing recipes. The past couple of months she'd been training Bigelow and tackling one DIY project after another. She wouldn't be surprised if people thought she was a hermit.

Cal lowered his gaze and turned his face away from Hope for a moment, as if he were hiding. Her heart squeezed; he was sad, and he didn't want her to see that.

"Too bad you don't know her better." He turned back to Hope, his emotions in check. "She's a wonderful woman."

Hope nodded in agreement. "I'm sure she is." She wasn't sure what to say next. She knew what to say if Cal's wife had died or had filed for divorce. Actually, she had a lot to say on the latter.

"It's been a long time since we've seen each other. Would you like a cup of coffee so we can catch up?" Cal asked.

Coffee, her weakness, and catching up on their careers would be nice. "I'd like that." She followed Cal along the sleek honed bluestone paver path embedded in crushed stone. The austere walkway led to the glass front door of the modern house. They entered and Hope's breath caught when she entered the living room.

The floor-to-ceiling windows offered spectacular views of the gentle rolling hills of northwestern Connecticut, which were coming into their summer lushness. The furnishing style was minimal. The living area had two gray tufted sofas with stainless steel feet and an eye-catching dual layer coffee table that was two-toned, high gloss white lacquer and walnut wood. Definitely a work of art but void of any personal touches, not even a remote control. How did they use the massive television that hung on the stark white wall?

"Good, Brenda made a fresh cup of coffee." Cal showed her into the galley kitchen.

Obsessed with kitchens, Hope didn't pass up the opportunity for a closer look at where the Barnharts cooked their meals.

There were no upper cabinets due to the expansive window that ran the length of the countertop. The appliances were integrated into the kitchen design so all you saw were sleek white lacquered cabinets. The term for the Barnharts' kitchen was "a showcase kitchen." Decked out in the best cabinetry and appliances money could buy but there was no cooking going on. What a shame. The place that was supposed to be the center of the home was simply a showpiece.

"Let's sit." Cal handed Hope a full cup of coffee and led her to the dining table.

Hope eyed the interesting piece of furniture. The glass top was set on two stainless steel stacked V-shaped bases. Where did they shop? Cal had pulled out one of the buttoned tufted high-back chairs for her and she sat. Thank goodness, the chair was comfortable.

After pouring a drop of cream into her coffee, she took a sip. "You have a beautiful home." While the modern clean and crisp lines weren't her thing, she did appreciate the beauty of the minimalist design.

"Lily did all this." He took in a sweeping glance of the space. "I just wanted someplace peaceful to come home to."

"I'm very sorry about what has happened."

Cal nodded. "You read about this type of thing, but you never think one day it will be your wife. Then you have to deal with all of the questions from the police and those vultures from the newspapers." His voice was laced with contempt.

"I'm sure the police are doing the best they can and their questions are for the purpose of finding Lily." Hope suspected Detective Reid was the lead from the Jefferson Police Department on the case. She'd encountered him two months earlier when a local real estate agent was murdered and Claire was the person of interest in the investigation. Luckily, Hope did a little snooping on her own and eventually discovered the true identity of the killer.

"Forgive me if I don't share your opinion of the police here. This isn't exactly New York City, and my wife's life is in the hands of a small-town police department."

"I know Chief Cahill personally, and I can assure you he and his officers are highly trained and qualified." She'd known Ethan Cahill since they were teenagers and, since moving back to Jefferson, he'd been her rock to lean on. Over the past few months she'd noticed a change in her feelings toward him, and she wondered if he felt it too. She wanted to ask, to find out either way, but the fear of messing up a good friendship held back the question. So, she'd decided to take the wait-and-see approach.

Cal took a drink of his coffee and sat quietly for a few moments. The worry about his wife was etched into his face and when Hope looked close enough, she saw the fatigue in his dark eyes.

"You know, why don't we start catching up?" Hope prompted Cal out of his deep thoughts.

"Yes, let's. You can begin by telling me all about your blog." Cal smiled a little and he looked genuinely interested in Hope.

She wasted no time in telling him how she first began the blog and the time flew by so fast she didn't realize they'd been chatting for over an hour.

"I can't believe it's so late." Hope stood. She picked up her coffee cup and took it to the kitchen sink. "I lost track of time."

"So did I. I guess it's the company." Cal joined Hope at the sink. "Are you sure you have to go?"

Hope nodded. She had Bigelow to feed and she had work to do. "Sorry, I do. How about we do this again?"

"Sounds good to me. I'll walk you out."

As they approached the front door, Brenda appeared from the long hallway, startling Hope. She held a leather agenda close to her chest and glared at Hope for a long moment.

"There you are." Cal opened the front door. "I'm going to walk Hope out. I'll be right back."

"Bye," Hope said in a light voice, and stepped outside.

The sun was still bright and the late afternoon temperature still hovered around eighty degrees. Perfect gardening weather. Too bad she'd spent the whole day indoors.

"I enjoyed our talk. Thank you for distracting me for a little bit," Cal said in a serious tone. When they arrived at her vehicle, he stepped closer to Hope and wrapped his arms around her in a friendly embrace. His hug was gentle and surprising.

"You're welcome. I enjoyed myself too." Hope returned the hug and, over Cal's shoulder, she caught Brenda staring out the window. When Brenda realized Hope saw her, she quickly stepped back. "I better get going. See you tomorrow."

Hope slipped into the driver's seat and Cal shut the door. She turned on the ignition and waved as she pulled out of the driveway. As she navigated the gravel driveway that led to the road, she couldn't help thinking about how frightened he must be with not knowing what happened to Lily. While she defended him to Drew the day before, she had no knowledge of the relationship between Cal and Lily but, after talking with him for over an hour, she couldn't believe he would have hurt his wife. Then again, she had been mistaken about her ex-husband. Maybe she wasn't the best judge of character.

"In my research I found that Cal Barnhart is an avid hiker." Drew scooped a heaping spoonful of meatball hero casserole onto his plate.

Before Hope left for the workshop that morning, she'd collected eggs while she did her barn chores. Helga, the alpha hen, had been more disagreeable than normal, and Hope had the peck marks on her hand to prove it. She usually admired the hen's spunk, but the chick really needed to tone it down.

After the assault, she'd cracked a couple of the eggs for the meatball mixture and added in fresh herbs from her garden. After the meatballs were formed, she'd tossed them into a slow cooker and covered them with her homemade sauce and let them simmer all day. The meatballs and sauce were ready when she got home and into a deep casserole dish they went over a layer of garlic bread and then smothered with cheese.

"A lot of people are avid hikers, especially up here." Hope joined Drew at the table with a bowl of salad. She set the dish down and took a seat.

"But it's his wife who's missing." Drew served himself some salad. "He could have dumped her body in the woods."

"Drew! That's a terrible thing to suggest." Hope scooped out a portion of the casserole and set the dish in front of the third place setting.

"What's a terrible thing to say?" Ethan entered the kitchen. The sleeves of his faded denim shirt were rolled up, revealing muscular forearms. Even though his job as police chief was mainly administrative, he didn't let his job go to his gut. He worked out every day, in the gym, on trails with his bike, or in his pool in the warmer weather. So, assembling the shelving unit in Hope's garage was a piece of cake for him. He barely broke a sweat. While she wanted to do all the work, realistically she'd had to delegate some jobs like assembling large shelving units or painting the exterior of her farmhouse. Ethan had been helping out as much as he could since she bought the house. She wasn't sure he'd make it over tonight because of Lily's case. His department had been chasing leads to find her and nothing panned out, leaving him little free time.

"My theory is Barnhart killed his wife and dumped her in the woods." Drew dug into his dinner. As he chewed, he made yummy noises. "This is delish, Hope. Seriously. Oh, my, goodness. Is that garlic bread?"

Hope smiled. She loved feeding her friends and family. There was nothing more satisfying to her than to tie on an apron, cook, and then share her food with those she loved. That was partly why she started her blog. She'd been living in the city where life moved at warp speed and dinners were either served out of a container or on fancy plates in crowded restaurants. Where she came from, dinner was served at a big table by her mother and eaten with the whole family. The conversations were about life, sometimes silly, sometimes serious, not about deals or about weekend plans in the Hamptons.

She wasn't so naïve to think her blog would make everybody change their lifestyle, but if it gave someone pause to think about other options for meals with other people then she achieved her goal. And while she couldn't force people to make time for a sit-down dinner, she could do it herself.

"We've been searching the woods for Lily." Ethan smiled at his plate covered with thick slices of bread, fat meatballs, and gooey cheese. He looked like a satisfied man as he took a forkful and chewed.

"I'm sure your department is doing everything possible to find Lily." Hope wanted to steer the conversation away from Lily for two reasons. The first was because she wanted to avoid telling Drew she failed at her attempt to convince Cal to agree to an interview. Second, after her first foray into amateur sleuthing two months earlier, she wasn't eager to discuss another possible murder.

"Thanks." Ethan smiled.

His smile sent a zing of warmth through her, right down to her toes.

*Oh, boy.*

Ethan had gone from the rock in her life she leaned on to

a guy who sent zings of heat through her. At first she tried to ignore the subtle signs of their relationship shifting into unmarked territory. They'd been friends since high school and not once, in all those years, did she ever consider him anything more than that. Definitely not as a boyfriend. She had to chalk her rogue romantic feelings up to still being unsettled about her life shakeup. Before she entertained thoughts of being involved with another man, she needed to put her divorce behind her and find the financial stability she lost when she walked away from her career to appear on the reality show.

So, zings of any sort needed to stop.

"Your department's stonewalling isn't helping me." Drew served himself another portion of meatball casserole. "But I won't be deterred. I have a job to do."

Hope glanced at Ethan, who was scraping up the last bits of sauce from his plate. He let Drew get the last word on the topic of Lily Barnhart's disappearance. She was grateful because Drew could argue for hours about the freedom of the press and the public's right to know.

"However, Drew does have a point." Defending her friend prompted a frown from Ethan. She should've said something about the weather instead. She dipped her head and scooped up a forkful of meatballs and cheese.

Drew grinned. "Thank you."

"Yes, thank you, Hope." Ethan looked back to his plate and continued eating his dinner.

Now was a good time to change the subject. "Peggy Olson is back home from rehab. She's doing remarkably well in getting around." Hope refilled her wineglass. After the day she'd had, she'd earned a fair amount of alcohol consumption. The dinner conversation shifted to subjects that didn't include active police investigations but rather Hope's plan to hire a trainer for Bigelow. She wasn't having any success with the stack of training books she'd purchased. She'd be donating them to the library's annual book sale.

"Dinner was delicious." Ethan pushed his cleaned plate away and then wiped his mouth with a napkin. "I'm sorry, I have to get back to work."

Hope cleared his plate from the table and excused herself before she followed Ethan outside. She closed the mudroom door behind her and followed Ethan's path to his truck. The daylight was slowly fading and the air was cool. She treasured those nights because, within a few weeks, the humidity would take hold and linger well into early fall.

Ethan reached his truck and was heading around to the driver's side. He was almost six feet, and his stride was long and purposeful. He'd be climbing up into his truck in no time.

"Ethan! Wait up!" Hope dashed to the fully loaded pickup truck. Dark green, chrome grille, and a roof rack, the truck was all man. He drove it to the woods for camping, to the lumberyard for wood, and to the range for target practice. Though, the truck wasn't all testosterone and manly. It often chauffeured Ethan's two little girls. On any given day, a stuffed bunny or doll could be found in the cab of the truck. And Ethan was secure enough in his manhood that he didn't mind one bit.

"What's wrong?" Ethan pulled open his truck door.

"Something happened at Peggy's house. I'm worried about her."

Ethan's brows furrowed. "Is she okay?"

Hope shrugged. "I'm not sure." She filled him in on what happened the day before and the promise she'd made to Peggy. After coming home with the burnt pot, she kept replaying the events over in her mind. By the time she went to bed last night, she was certain she'd made a mistake.

"You have to tell Meg. There's a lot of other options

available to Peggy than just going to a nursing home." Ethan reached out and set his hand on Hope's shoulder. "I know you don't want to break your promise, but I don't see you have a choice."

"You're right. I have to tell Meg." Easier said than done. She and Meg Griffin had history and it wasn't pretty.

In first grade they were the best of friends, having lunch together every day in the cafeteria and sitting together on the school bus. By third grade their friendship was tested by a spelling bee and Hope first saw Meg's competitive side. After Meg lost to Hope for misspelling the word *bare*, she spelled *bear* instead, Meg took her Barbie lunchbox to another table in the cafeteria and sat with another girl on the bus. From then on their relationship was a confusing mess of emotions. They'd make up and then Hope would get something Meg wanted and the cycle of the aftermath of the spelling bee would replay. Looking back, they were what was now called frenemies. While they couldn't seem to outgrow their silly childhood rivalry, they did manage to be cordial to each other. "I'll call her first thing in the morning."

"I hope Peggy's okay. She's a sweet lady." Ethan climbed up into the driver's seat and, within a few minutes, he was pulling out of her driveway and his taillights faded away.

Not too long after Ethan left, Drew left to go back to his office. Since the *Gazette* hired Norrie Jennings, he'd been burning the midnight oil trying to keep up with the newspaper's rising star. Because she had just landed an interview with Lily Barnhart's secretary, Drew was desperate to get his own scoop.

With the dinner dishes cleared and a final check on her Facebook page and blog, Hope tied her laces and went out for a night run. The sun was almost set and the clear, dark sky seemed to wrap around Jefferson in a gentle, secure hug.

There were so many reasons why she disliked running at night, but her day was hectic and she couldn't squeeze in a workout. She'd already gained the new homeowner/ business owner/divorcee ten-plus pounds. So, if her work-out needed to be at night, so be it.

When she reached the top of her road, she turned left and ran along Carriage Lane. She fell into her zone, her pace steady and her mind clearing. At the half-mile mark her worries about her inadequate photography skills fell away.

At one mile, the knot in her stomach about Tim's new romance untangled. He'd managed to move on after their divorce, so maybe it was time for her to also.

Well into her second mile, her heartbeat peaking and sweat beads forming along her brow, she was at peace with her decision to contact Meg. It wasn't as if she and Peggy pinkie swore. Those were sacred. Peggy's safety was far more important than keeping a promise and if the old woman became angry with her, she'd have to deal with it. The rest of her run was energizing and cleansing to her mind.

Looping back to her road, she slowed her pace to lower her heart rate. Her arms pumped slower at her side and her stride was relaxed. She loved the cool-down phase of her workouts.

She passed Gilbert's gray Colonial house. Lights on in the living room. No doubt, he was watching some barn picking show. She guessed he lived vicariously through those shows because Mitzi wouldn't let a piece of junk into her immaculate home.

Hope turned her focus back to the road. Her house would be coming into sight any minute. But before she could see her home, her eyes widened in horror. She came to a dead stop.

Smoke.

Big puffs of black smoke billowed out of Peggy Olson's house into the night sky.

The house was on fire.

# Chapter Four

Instinct kicked in, and Hope bolted toward the Victorian house. She sprinted across the street on the diagonal, her sneakers slapping the pavement hard. She unzipped her waist pack and pulled out her cell phone. Clumsily, she punched in 9-1-1 as she closed in on Peggy's beloved home. The neighboring houses were a blur as she passed. Her gaze was fixed on the flames shooting out of the dwelling.

The closer she got, the more real the nightmare was becoming.

Peggy's house was burning.

She prayed to God Peggy made it outside safely.

"Nine-one-one. Where is your emergency?" the dispatcher asked.

"Thirty-three Fieldstone Road. The house is on fire!" Her heart pounded against her chest. The unimaginable flashed through her mind.

*Please, God, let Peggy be okay.*

Hope reached the curb. Why hadn't she called Meg earlier? Why did she make that stupid promise to Peggy? She jumped on the grass just as a police car sped down the road, sirens blaring and lights flashing, and came to a quick stop.

She disconnected the call and shoved the phone back into her waist pack.

She waved to the officer. "Hurry! We have to find Peggy!"

Flames burst out the first-floor windows. Wild and angry, they lit up the night. The smell of smoke choked Hope's lungs. *Poor Peggy*. She couldn't handle that much smoke, and her frail body didn't have the strength to escape through fire. Hope coughed, but she wouldn't be deterred. She wasn't frail. She'd find her friend. Just as she reached the brick path leading to the front porch, she was grabbed around the waist and yanked back.

"No!" The police officer's hold got tighter as Hope struggled to break free.

"Peggy! We have to find her!" Hope's arms flailed. Her feet kicked feverishly.

"Ma'am, it's not safe. The fire department is on its way," a calm male voice said as she was pulled back to the curb.

"It'll be too late!"

"It's too dangerous."

"It's too late." Hope stopped struggling as the hold on her eased. The adrenaline rush that had propelled her toward the burning house was dissipating as reality sank in.

The whole first floor of the house was consumed with flames. Tears stung her eyes, and she tried to wipe them away with the back of her hand. She turned to the officer. He looked familiar. It only took a moment to place him. He was one of the officers who responded to a break-in at her house a couple of months ago.

"Maybe she got out." She clung to any sliver of hope she could find. She craned her neck and looked back at the house. There was a chance Peggy escaped. It was possible. If she'd managed to get out of the house, she needed help. "We have to look for her. She could be hurt."

"We will, Miss Early." The police officer rested his hands

firmly on her shoulders, establishing eye contact. "You need to stay over there." He pointed across the street, where her neighbors had gathered. "We need this whole area cleared so we can do our jobs."

"But . . ."

"No buts." The officer guided Hope off the curb and sent her in the direction of her neighbors. They were huddled together and looked on in horror as their voices were muted to Hope as she joined them.

The officer jogged toward the speeding fire truck coming down the road. The truck came to a hard stop just as someone wrapped an arm around Hope's shoulders and squeezed tightly. Another neighbor patted her arm and there were murmurs, probably reassuring thoughts, but Hope couldn't hear what was being said. She wanted to embrace the comfort of her neighbors, but all she could think about was Peggy. Tears streamed down her face as the flames became more intense and dark smoke puffed out of the house. Her lips quivered and her jaw quaked.

What had she let happen?

The firefighters jumped off their truck and accessed their apparatus before running to the house. The Jefferson Volunteer Fire Department comprised town residents who gave selflessly to help their neighbors. They ran into burning buildings while people like Hope stood on the sidelines and watched.

Frozen in place, she scanned the scene unfolding in front of her. Chaotic but controlled. More police arrived, followed by an ambulance. Loud voices shouted instructions while more neighbors streamed out of their homes to look on in horror. Helplessness washed over Hope. She pulled away from her neighbors.

She'd caused this and she didn't deserve their compassion. After a few short steps, the weight of the situation collapsed on her. Her body folded over, caving to the grief and worry that consumed her. Her palms pressed against her thighs and she sobbed. A touch on her back startled her. Her body tensed until she heard his voice.

"Hope, are you okay?" Ethan asked.

Hope shook her head. She wasn't okay. She should have done something earlier. Checked on Peggy, instead of going for a run. Tell Meg about the burnt pot the day before. If only she could turn back time.

Ethan guided her upright and turned her around to face him. He pushed back a lock of her dark hair off her face and his fingers gently caressed her cheek as his hand fell away. "What were you thinking? Running to the house? You could have been hurt, or worse."

"I don't know. I had to find Peggy. Ethan, if she's . . ." Her voice cracked. "It's all my fault." Hope fell onto Ethan's chest and he caught her, wrapping his arms around her trembling body.

"This isn't your fault." His voice was low and his embrace gentle.

"Chief, this is awful. Just awful."

Hope lifted her head and glanced over her shoulder. A neighbor, Everett Cranston, stood there with his hands tucked into his pants pockets, shock etched on his face.

"Yes, it is, Everett." Ethan loosened his hold on Hope and she pulled herself away. "Hope, I have to work, so why don't you let Everett walk you home?"

She wiped her face with the sleeve of her hoodie. She shook her head in protest. "I'm not leaving until I know Peggy is okay."

"There's nothing you can do out here. And it's easier for us to do our jobs without civilians in the way."

She hated when he used logic. Of course the jobs of the firefighters and police officers would be easier without a

crowd to control and keep safe. Too emotionally exhausted
to argue, she nodded. She'd go home and wait.

"What about Meg? Somebody has to tell her." Hope
couldn't imagine that conversation. A knock on the door
late at night followed by the devastating news of the fire.

"We'll take care of the notification. Everett, do you mind
walking Hope back to her house?"

"Of course not, Chief." Everett extended a guiding hand
to Hope and led her away from Peggy's house. "I can't believe this is actually happening. It's such a beautiful house.
Peggy took such good care of it."

Hope kept glancing backward as she followed Everett
along the road. Less than an hour before the road was dark,
quiet, and tucked in for the night. Flashing emergency lights
and the sounds of rescuers and squawking radios filled the
night air and heavy hearts beat with sadness.

"Peggy loved her home." Hope's throat felt raw, probably
from the smoke she inhaled as she got closer to the burning
house. "She and Ricky purchased it just after they were
married." Everett guided Hope around a pothole.

Everett was one of the last neighbors she met after she
moved onto the street. And it was by accident. She had been
out running one Sunday afternoon. He was moving a
dresser into his house. The ornate piece of furniture caught
her eye and she stopped to inspect it and introduce herself.
He was oblivious to her brief stardom on reality television,
and he didn't know what a blog was. His world revolved
around antiques. He owned the Red House Antique Shop on
Main Street. The next morning she made a point to visit his
shop and, ever since, there'd always been something she
coveted there.

"She's lived here for so long. I remember coming here
to trick-or-treat as a kid. She always had the best candy,"
Hope said.

"Last Christmas she delivered a tin of cookies to me. No

one had ever done that before. Definitely not the neighbors where I lived in Fairfield. She told me she loved to bake," Everett said.

"She baked for everyone. She's a kind person." Reminiscing eased the heavy weight of guilt and sadness that overwhelmed Hope.

"It's good she shared what she loved." Everett paused and looked over his shoulder and tsk-tsked. "She must've fallen asleep while cooking again."

Hope followed Everett's gaze and her heart seized. *Stupid. Stupid. Stupid.* She should have done something more than promise to check on Peggy.

"I couldn't believe what I was seeing when I looked out my living room window. The smoke coming from Peggy's house. I practically hung up on Milo."

"Milo?"

Everett nodded. "We were well into an hour-long conversation about town business. To be honest, it's getting a bit tiresome. The mayor may work twenty-four/seven, but just because I'm on the P&Z Commission doesn't mean I do. Listen to me, complaining. I should be grateful, right?"

"Oh. My. Goodness." Leila Manchester rushed Hope and Everett. "I looked out my window and saw smoke and the fire trucks. Is Peggy okay?"

"We don't know yet," Everett answered.

Hope appreciated that Everett took the lead with the question because she couldn't engage in conversation with Leila or anyone at that moment. She continued walking. Her thoughts were too dark.

"Terrible. Just terrible." Leila fell into step with Hope and Everett. "I can't believe I was just sitting at my table talking to my sister on my webcam. I smelled something and then I looked out the window. Terrible. Just terrible."

They finally reached Hope's house.

"Thank you for seeing me home," she said to Everett.

"Excuse me!" a young woman called out as she approached Hope and her neighbors. "I'm Norrie Jennings from the *Gazette,* and I'd like to ask you some questions." She held a notepad in one hand and a pen in another. "You're Hope Early, right?"

Hope nodded. "I have no comment." She climbed the steps to her front porch. "Thanks for walking me home, Everett." She opened the door and stepped inside her house.

Bigelow, hyped up and barking, greeted her. The noise and excitement outside must have woken him. She squatted down and wrapped her arms around his neck and held on to him tightly and sobbed. He steadied himself and rested his head on her shoulder and let her cry.


Hope plunged her spoon into a container of chocolate chip ice cream she made a few days earlier and scooped out a generous portion of comfort. There were four containers stashed in the freezer for a blog series on what she considered the perfect summer food—ice cream. At the moment, the ice cream was perfect for swallowing her feelings. Eating ice cream out of its container alone after a traumatic event was a bad idea, and yet, she plunged the spoon back into the container for another serving.

"Whoa. How much have you eaten?" Drew eyed the quart of ice cream with concern.

Hope glanced up before sinking her spoon back into the ice cream. "Don't even think about it." Her voice left no doubt of her seriousness.

Drew looked shocked. "You'll thank me tomorrow." He grabbed the container and scooted over to the freezer drawer. With the lid back on, he set the ice cream into the freezer and closed the drawer.

"Hey! I wasn't done."

"Yes, you are." Drew walked over to the stove, lifted the whistling kettle off the burner, and filled two cups, then dropped a chamomile tea bag into each cup. "This is better for you than a quart of ice cream." He carried the cups over to the table and set one in front of Hope and then the other in front of him as he sat on a chair. "Bad night?"

Hope gave him an "are you serious?" look.

"I know you're a little cranky because I took your ice cream away."

"I'm cranky because Peggy died in that fire, and I'm responsible." Hope slumped.

Just before Drew showed up, Ethan came over to confirm Hope's fear—Peggy's body was found in her bedroom. He didn't provide any further details.

"What are you talking about?"

"The fire. Peggy shouldn't have been home alone. She was probably cooking something and fell asleep like she did the other day." Hope leaned forward and took a sip of her tea. She needed something stronger than tea with fewer calories than ice cream.

"You think something she left on the stove caused the fire?" Drew reached for his phone and tapped on the screen. "Exactly what happened and when?"

Hope's eyes narrowed and her lips pursed. He wanted to quote her for the story on the fire. "I'm devastated and you're looking for a quote?"

"No, no, no, it's not like that at all."

"Yes, it is." She gestured to the phone. "You can't use anything I've just said in your article. Do you understand?"

"Do you know Norrie's here on scene, too?" Drew pointed toward the front of the house. "She's talking to all the neighbors."

"Then why don't you talk to the neighbors she's not talking to?"

"Because I'm here with my friend who is upset about

losing a friend." Drew tapped on his phone's screen again and set it facedown on the table.

"Oh." Hope cast her eyes downward for a moment. Drew was being sweet and she didn't deserve it. "You should go back to work. Get your story." She took another drink of her tea.

"I'm not leaving you. When I arrived and spoke with Everett Cranston, he said you were upset. He said a police officer stopped you from running into Peggy's house. Did you do that?"

Hope nodded. "I wasn't thinking. I just wanted to find Peggy."

"Admirable. But stupid. You could've been killed."

"I know."

"Look, I don't think the fire was a result of Peggy falling asleep while cooking."

"Why not?" Hope took another drink of her tea.

"The police found an empty gasoline container tossed by the garage. The fire is now labeled as suspicious."

Hope's head swung up. "Suspicious as in arson?"

"Possibly. So, if you know of any reason why someone would set fire to Peggy's house, I beg of you to tell me so I can have an exclusive that will finally blow Miss Ace Reporter, Norrie, out of the water."

Hope lifted her cup and leaned back. As she finished her tea, she racked her brain, thinking of who on earth would intentionally set fire to Peggy's house. She didn't have an enemy in town. Everyone loved her. Arson didn't make sense. There had to be another reason for the gas container being by the garage. But if someone did set Peggy's home on fire, Hope was going to make certain the person was found and arrested and that justice was served.

# Chapter Five

Hope's breath caught at the devastation in front of her. Peggy's once-beautiful house was charred and damaged in so many areas. Upstairs, downstairs, even the porch wasn't spared. The delicate gingerbread trim was now scattered on the front lawn, along with shards of glass from the blown-out windows and jagged strips of wood siding. If Peggy had survived the fire, the sight of her beloved home would have killed her.

Yellow caution tape was strung around the front of the property. With all the debris, the lawn wasn't safe to walk on, and if Drew was right about the fire being suspicious, then the police would be conducting a full investigation.

Hope looked to her right and then to her left. She didn't see anybody. She lifted the yellow tape. Surely a quick look around wouldn't do any harm. She had on her barn boots and she'd be careful where she stepped. She had no idea what she was looking for. If there was any evidence of arson, the police would have removed it from the scene by now. All that was left was destruction.

Just as she was about to duck under the yellow tape, she heard, "Good morning, Miss Early."

She cringed. She knew that voice all too well. Where did he come from?

"For most people the yellow tape is a deterrent from trespassing."

Hope let go of the tape and turned around to face Detective Sam Reid. "I'm not most people."

"No, you're not. I was on my way to your house. Looks like you'll save me the trip."

She forced a smile. "Anything to help you."

He eyed her suspiciously. "Somehow I doubt that. What are you doing here?" He propped a hand on his hip, brushing his blazer back and revealing his holstered weapon.

"To be honest, I have no idea."

"Are you sure you're not playing amateur detective like you did a couple of months ago?" The detective was never going to drop that she'd taken an active interest in his last murder investigation. But her interest had helped clear Claire, so Hope had no regrets.

"I'm just trying to make sense of this tragedy. I can't believe Peggy died in the fire."

"I've heard Mrs. Olson was a nice lady. For what it's worth, she died from smoke inhalation. The firefighters recovered her before the fire had spread to her bedroom."

The news Peggy wasn't consumed by the fire overwhelmed Hope, and she crumpled a little, which propelled Reid toward her. He grabbed hold of her.

"Thank goodness . . . I'd been imagining . . . Never mind." She straightened herself and found solid footing. "I'm okay."

"You're sure?" Was that a hint of concern Hope heard in his voice?

She nodded and pulled away from the detective. She regained her composure. "What did you want to see me about? I gave a statement last night."

"I have a few follow-up questions. How well did you

know Mrs. Olson?" He pulled a notepad and pen from his blazer's breast pocket.

"I've known her all my life but not well. Not until I bought my house and we became neighbors." Hope looked at the charred house and regret hit her like the first blast of heat she felt from the fire the night before. "But we weren't close."

Reid jotted down some notes. "Do you know if she had company recently?"

Hope dragged her attention from the house and focused back on Reid. She shrugged. "She's been in rehab for a while and I've been busy with my house and work. Besides, I really don't pay much attention to the comings and goings at my neighbors' homes."

The houses weren't close. Each house was on a minimum of two acres. She loved the privacy the road provided, yet she wasn't completely isolated and was within walking distance to town. Peggy's house was set on three acres, and, with a couple of homes between them, Hope wouldn't have easily seen anyone coming and going unless she was that *nosy* neighbor every street had.

"When was the last time you were in her house?"

"Two days ago."

"Was she alone?"

"Yes."

"Did she mention anybody else being in the house at the time? Perhaps staying with her?"

"No." If there had been someone there, why didn't he or she turn off the smoke alarm the other day?

"How are you so certain?"

"Well, I'm not. I didn't search her house. Why are you asking?"

He looked at Hope point blank. "We found a second, badly burned body in the kitchen. Preliminary reports tell us it was a female."

Hope gasped. Her hand covered her mouth as she processed what she'd just been told. A second victim? A woman? *Oh, no!* "Meg?" She was the only person Hope knew who visited Peggy.

Reid held out his hand to stop Hope's racing thoughts. "Mrs. Griffin is alive. I spoke with her earlier."

Hope exhaled a relieved breath. "Thank goodness. We're not the best of friends. Not since grade . . ." She realized she was rambling and stopped short. Her rocky relationship with Meg wasn't important. There was a second fire victim. Who was she? Why was she at Peggy's house? Could she have set the fire? Maybe something went wrong and she got trapped inside.

"Do you think she's the one who tossed the gas container by the garage?"

"How do you know about that?" Reid's dark eyes narrowed and he frowned.

She knew that look all too well. "I heard about it last night and the fire chief labeled the fire as suspicious."

"Thank you for answering my questions." He flipped his notepad closed. "I understand you tried to get to Mrs. Olson last night. For what it's worth, I'm glad you weren't injured or worse." He turned and began to walk away but stopped. He looked over his shoulder. "One more thing, Miss Early."

Hope met his gaze.

"This is an official police investigation, and I expect you to stay out of it. Am I clear?"

"Yes, you are very clear."

He nodded and then continued to his sedan parked along the curb. Yes, he was never going to let that last incident go.

Hope looked back at the house and to the garage, which was detached and showed signs of neglect, unlike the house. If the other woman set the fire, she would have had to douse the house with the gasoline, toss the can toward the garage, and then go back inside, where she eventually died. Why would she do that? Hope tried to put herself in the woman's shoes. If she set a house on fire, she would hightail it out of there without looking back.

She stepped away from the yellow caution tape and off the curb. Could Peggy have had someone visiting for the evening? Or, maybe Peggy had a friend staying with her. Whoever it was, there was a chance she could have been the target of the arsonist. Could Peggy be dead now because she was in the wrong place at the wrong time? As Hope looked at the fire-damaged house, a shiver coursed through her body. Two women were murdered the night before. Just a couple of houses from her.

Hope used the short walk back to her house to review her to-do list. Mornings were her busiest time of the day. She'd fed the chickens and cleaned their coop. Next she'd fed Bigelow and walked him. Their twenty-minute walk did double duty—Bigelow expended energy and she checked social media on her phone. Normally after they returned home, she'd start work, but that day she had the photography workshop. Later in the day, she wanted to pay a condolence call to Meg. Tears welled up, but she pushed the emotion down by focusing on her to-do list.

At some point she needed to select which recipes she'd feature for the fall season on her blog. Even though it was the very beginning of summer, she planned several months ahead for the content on her blog, just like she did when she was a magazine editor. At the magazine she would be working on Thanksgiving and Christmas features now because the magazine was always six months ahead. As the publisher of a blog, she could comfortably work three months ahead, which gave her more flexibility.

Her head spun with all the things she needed to do until she saw Claire's Mercedes parked in the driveway. Claire usually spent her mornings at the real estate office prepping for house hunting with clients or at the gym, looking for new listings. Recently, she'd been cramming campaign work for her mayoral bid into the first part of her day. So, what was she doing at Hope's? The fire. Her sister was checking on her. She stepped up onto the curb and un-hitched the latch on her front gate.

Claire came into view as she stepped out of the barn. Clearly, her sister wasn't dressed to be in a barn. Even though Hope kept her barn tidy, it wasn't the place for high-heeled pumps and silk blouses.

"There you are!" Claire made her way across the grass, which was damp from the morning dew. Her poor over-priced designer shoes.

They met on the flagstone patio in the back of the house. "What are you doing here so early?"

"I heard about the fire. Did Peggy fall asleep again while cooking?"

"No, we don't think so."

"Then what happened?" Claire shifted so the bright morning sun wasn't shining directly in her eyes.

"Drew told me last night an empty gasoline container was found out by the garage. And I just saw Detective Reid at Peggy's house." Hope still couldn't believe he caught her about to duck under the crime scene tape and trespass onto a crime scene. Who would have thought he started work so early in the morning? Lesson learned. Snooping was better late at night.

"What did Barney Fife have to say?"

Hope cringed at Claire's unflattering nickname for Reid. But she couldn't blame her sister. While she wasn't present when Reid arrested Claire for the murders at the end of winter, she was certain the event wasn't pleasant for her sister. So, she kept her mouth shut about the nickname. At least for now.

"There was a second woman in the house last night. She perished in the fire."

Claire drew in a shocked breath. "Who was it?"

"From what he said, I don't think they've identified the body yet." Chills skittered along her spine. "I guess it's possible Meg hired a caregiver for her aunt."

Claire arched an eyebrow, which told Hope her sister was due for a Botox injection. "You know she wouldn't have done that. She'd put her aunt into a nursing home and sell the house. I hear Jerry's business isn't doing too well. In fact, they turned in their lease for their car sooner than necessary in order to downgrade to a less expensive model."

The amount of gossip her sister was privy to amazed Hope. Maybe if she didn't spend most of her time in the house she'd know what was going on in town too.

"If the woman wasn't a caregiver, then who was she? And why was there a gas container by the garage?"

"The gasoline could have been used for yardwork. A weed whacker or chainsaw. When you were over there the other day, did you see any signs of work outside?"

"No."

"I hope you aren't entertaining thoughts of investigating. Remember what happened last time," Claire warned, pointing her finger at Hope. "The last time you did, you found yourself with a gun pointed at you. That was too close of a call."

Hope let out a sigh. She didn't need a lecture from her sister about the dangers of actively tracking down a murderer when you're a full-time blogger because she knew firsthand. "Why are you here?"

Claire lifted her chin and gave a small nod, signaling she'd let the topic go for now. "Maretta's tea." She reached into her purse and pulled out a sheet of paper. "Here's the list of people I invited to the event."

Hope scanned the long list of names. What was her sister thinking? "I thought this was supposed to be a small, intimate group."

Claire laughed. "A small, intimate group won't get Maretta on the P&Z Commission. We're up against Meg and, given what happened last night, she'll use the sympathy vote to get the advantage. No, we need to go big. Thanks so much for doing this. It's going to be great." Claire adjusted the strap of her purse on her shoulder. "I'm showing Matt Roydon some houses this morning." She flashed a big smile and her eyes twinkled.

Hope was all too familiar with that twinkle. Flashbacks to her early days in the city when her sister set her up on a blind date all the way across town. She'd ventured out of her cozy apartment and trudged through a raging storm to meet an accountant for dinner. Hope later informed Claire being drenched in the rain was the highlight of the evening. So, seeing the twinkle in Claire's eyes had Hope on the verge of dropping to her knees to beg her not to play matchmaker again. Even though Matt wasn't anything like the boring accountant, who had mommy issues, she didn't want to be set up.

"I'm sure he'll love all of the houses you show him."

"And I'm sure he'd like a little help decorating when he finally does make a purchase. You're so good at decorating." Claire shifted and began walking in the direction of her car. "I think we should all have dinner since he's in town looking for his weekend house."

"I am a big girl and I can handle my own love life."

Claire stopped walking and turned to face Hope. "Which is pretty nonexistent at the moment. Matt is handsome, single, and successful. And he's going to have a great house very soon."

"I'll think about it," Hope relented.

"That was easy." Claire sounded surprised. "I need to go. Talk later." She turned and continued to her car.

Hope headed into her house through the French door on the patio, while Claire drove off. If she continued to resist

Claire's matchmaking attempts, then she'd be pestered constantly until she caved. Hope's agreeing to think about it would lead Claire to back off, which would give Hope time to find out who the mystery woman in Peggy's house was and why she was there. She closed the door and stared out. Off into the distance, the rolling hills of her corner of the world seemed to reach the sky. Sadly, all of the beauty around her couldn't erase the ugliness of the night before. Because of that, the next person Hope wanted to find was the person responsible for killing two women down the street.

# Chapter Six

"I can't believe you didn't call me last night." Jane Merrifield wagged a finger at Hope. "I had to hear it from a guest who went out this morning and overheard people talking about it at the Coffee Clique."

"I'm sorry. It was late and I didn't want to wake you." Hope expected the scolding so she was prepared with a plate of Lemon Bars when she entered the Merrifield Inn. After Claire left, Hope received a text message from Cal's assistant informing her the workshop was postponed until the afternoon. That left time for Hope to do some baking for her impromptu visit with Jane.

"There'll be plenty of time to sleep when we're dead. You know Sally and I are night owls." Jane leaned forward on the reception desk, which was polished to a high-gloss shine. Guests had registered there for over a hundred years. Built in the late 1700s by merchant Edmund Merrifield as a private residence, the house was turned into an inn by a descendent a century later. It was still in the family, and Jane, along with her sister-in-law, Sally, came in each day for a few hours to work. "Why don't I have Carly take over the desk and we can have a pot of tea and you can tell me everything that happened?"

Before Hope could decline the invitation, Jane stood and stepped away from the desk. Who was she kidding? Hope couldn't say no to Jane. The woman was practically an institution in town. The spry seventy-something married into one of the founding families of Jefferson and selflessly volunteered for any good cause. Before her marriage, she wrote five mystery books. Though she hung up her writing shingle, she didn't lose her curiosity or propensity for looking for the mystery in anything and everything.

"Tea would be lovely," Hope said. "I've baked Lemon Bars. I know how much you enjoy them."

The twinkle in Jane's pale blue eyes told Hope she'd been forgiven for her lapse in judgment the night before.

"Now, start from the beginning so I have a clear understanding of all of the events." Jane began to lead Hope away from the desk and into the living room.

"I hate to disappoint you, but there isn't much to tell."

"Peggy and a mysterious woman died in a house fire that's labeled suspicious? My dear, that's quite a bit to tell." The telephone rang and Jane frowned. "Don't go anywhere." Jane shuffled back to the desk and lifted the phone's receiver. The inn still used a clunky multi-line unit that wasn't hands-free. "Thank you for calling the Merrifield Inn. How may I help you?"

Hope heard footsteps on the stairs as Felicity's voice drifted in the air and she looked over her shoulder.

"They have my rate card. There's no negotiation." Felicity descended the staircase, one hand on the railing and the other holding a cell phone to her ear.

Hope wasn't trying to eavesdrop, but Felicity was talking so loudly she couldn't help overhear one half of the conversation.

Felicity tossed her head back and laughed. "Good one. What did he say? Really?" She laughed again.

From what Hope heard, it sounded as if Felicity was

working on getting a sponsorship with a brand. Every food blogger craved such a deal. Those arrangements ranged from writing posts to recipe development to representing a company at events. Gone were the days when bloggers earned money solely from small ads on their websites. Now bloggers had to hustle for income. Hope was logging more working hours as a full-time blogger, but she loved the job.

"She's always attached to her phone," Jane whispered to Hope, who walked back to the desk, as she set the receiver back down.

Felicity caught Hope's eye and smiled smugly, while continuing her conversation. "See what you can do. I want to work with them, but I won't come down, considering all of the followers I have on Instagram," Felicity said.

"You're on Instagram, aren't you, Hope?" Jane asked.

Hope nodded. There wasn't a blogger she knew who didn't have an Instagram account. That social media platform gave bloggers a place to gain new followers, to create engagement with their community, and to post the best food porn photographs that left mouths watering. Hope loved her Instagram page and often spent too much time there.

Felicity ended her call as she came off the last step and joined Hope and Jane at the desk. Her thick auburn hair was swept back into an updo, with tendrils framing her high cheekbones. Her lined eyes sported false lashes, because nobody was born with those kind of lashes, and a gloss added shine to her deep burgundy-colored lips. She wore a navy blue shirt tucked into a pair of white capri pants and nude ballet flats. "I didn't expect to see you here," she said to Hope.

"Hope visits often. She's a dear friend." Jane sat again. "Miss Campbell was out on a run this morning. She said it was very different from her usual run."

Felicity's head bobbed up and down. "Totally. It was nothing like running in Brooklyn. There wasn't anybody out. I finally found people in the diner. Which, by the way, is so quaint."

The tone of Felicity's voice left Hope unsure as to whether the diner had just received a backhanded compliment. Many city people didn't appreciate the charm of living in a small town. And since the perky Brooklynite standing next to her wasn't visiting Jefferson to sightsee, she probably didn't see any charm in a town with a historic Main Street, steepled churches, or horse farms dotted along the winding roads that connected Jefferson together.

"What's up with the class delay? Do you have any idea why we're not starting until later today?" Felicity asked Hope.

"No." Hope had replied to Brenda's text and asked why the class was delayed, but Cal's assistant hadn't answered.

Felicity shrugged. "Oh, I just thought since you and Cal are friendly, he might have told you what was up."

"Your friends are out on the patio finishing their breakfast." Jane pointed to the set of French doors at the end of the dining room. "Perhaps you'd like to join them."

"Guess I can grab another cup of coffee. If you have time, maybe you can join us too, Hope."

"Thanks. I'll be right out."

"Great. I can tell you all about my new agent. She's a dream and she's landing me some sweet projects." Felicity flashed a smile, then walked away from the front desk and through the dining room. When she reached the French doors, she pulled one open and stepped outside, closing the door behind her.

"She's up to something," Jane said.

Hope's brow furrowed. "What are you talking about?"

"My instinct tells me she's trouble. Be sure you watch yourself around her, Hope. What was she talking about an agent? Bloggers have agents? Do you have one?"

"Yes. I signed with her a couple of months ago." When Hope began her blog in her Upper West Side condo, she never thought about an agent. Back then agents were for authors and actors. Bloggers? They didn't need representation. They reached out to companies on their own or vice versa. Fast-forward a few years and bloggers became influencers and in demand by big companies, who paid big bucks. Having reached a respectable following across several social media platforms, Hope had decided it was time to find out what an agent could do for her.

"Fascinating." Jane held Hope's gaze for a moment. "Before I forget, Sally and I will be attending the tea for Maretta. It's very nice of you to host the event. You know, she can be a bit prickly, but she does have the best interest of Jefferson in her heart."

Prickly? Seriously? Maretta was practically an entire saguaro cactus. Not too long ago, when Hope attended a funeral reception at Maretta's house, Maretta threw her out. Then Maretta publicly accused Claire of murder in the General Store. And as a housewarming gift, she gave Hope a broom. A broom.

"I'm glad you'll both be there. I'm going to join Felicity and the others for a cup of coffee. I'll come back and fill you in on what I know about the fire."

"All right, dear. It's a beautiful day and it should be enjoyed."

Hope nodded and walked toward the patio door. Jane was right. It was a beautiful day and since she had the morning to herself, she'd make sure it didn't go to waste. A cup of coffee, a chat with fellow bloggers, which was a rare treat in her hometown, and maybe some antiquing.

"Hope, dear . . ."

Hope looked over her shoulder.

"Be sure to keep me updated on anything you learn about the mysterious woman they found. It's quite . . . fascinating."

Hope grinned. The retired mystery author was always

looking for intrigue, and Hope often wondered why Jane hadn't gone back to writing after her children went off to college and began their own lives. One day she'd ask Jane, perhaps over a cup of tea and one of Jane's favorite blueberry muffins. Until then, Hope had work to do and a bit of her own curiosity to satisfy.

She made her way to her friends on the patio. Louis noticed her right away and waved her over to the table he shared with Felicity and Elena. Felicity had settled in with a cup of coffee and her cell phone, while Elena was reading on her tablet.

"Finally. Someone to talk to." Louis stood and pulled out a chair for Hope. He looked less rumpled and more relaxed. Maybe the fresh air in Jefferson was agreeing with him. "You know bloggers, always on their devices posting or checking stats."

"Necessary evils. Do you mind if I pour myself a cup of coffee?"

"No, not at all. Help yourself. I heard what happened at your neighbor's house last night. Felicity said everyone at the diner was talking about it. Do you think there's a connection between the fire and the postponing of the class? Did Cal know the homeowner who was killed? Do you think the class will be cancelled?" Louis's rapid succession of questions finally ended when he bit into a buttered bran muffin.

Felicity and Elena both looked up at the same time and annoyance flashed on their faces.

"Seriously? Chill, Louis," Felicity snapped.

"Why are you being so morbid, talking about that tragedy over breakfast?" Elena asked.

"I'm not being morbid. Aren't you a little curious?" Louis spoke around a mouthful of muffin.

"I don't think Cal knew Peggy." But what about the mysterious dead woman? Hope poured a drop of cream into her coffee and stirred. There was a missing woman in town. Lily Barnhart. Could she be the unidentified victim in Peggy's house? No. That was crazy. What would Lily have been doing at Peggy's? She doubted the women knew each other. But, what if they did?

She had to find Ethan. There were perks of being friends with the police chief, like being able to have access to him, even in the middle of a high-profile case.

"I'm sorry. I have to be somewhere." Hope stood and rushed back into the inn. Luckily, Jane was on the phone and Hope didn't have to explain her abrupt exit.

She hurried along Main Street, heading south to the police department. The possibility the unidentified woman in Peggy's house was Lily Barnhart was a reach. Most likely the dead woman was an old friend of Peggy's or a care-giver. Those two options made more sense. Though, it was possible Peggy and Lily were friends. Hope didn't know everything about Peggy's life and barely knew anything about Lily's life. Which meant anything was possible.

She arrived at the police department, a one-story brick building set back from the road. A long concrete path led to the front door, while a wide driveway led around to the back of the building to a parking lot. Hope made her way along the path, passing a teak bench surrounded with bright flowers. A birdfeeder hung from the tree beside the sitting area and a loud chorus of chirps welcomed her to the tran-quil spot for visitors. Well, at least those visitors not wearing handcuffs.

Hope pushed open the front door of the building and stepped into the main reception area. Behind a protective glass wall, the dispatcher sat at an impressive electronics board. Hope tried to look over the dispatcher's head into the open work area, where the officers had their desks and where Ethan's office was. She didn't see him.

Freddy moved the microphone in front of his face and smiled. "Hi, Hope. What brings you here?"

"I'm looking for Ethan. Is he around?"

Freddy shook his bald head. "Sorry. He's out. Want to leave a message?"

A message? How would that go? *Ethan, I think the dead woman in Peggy's house is Lily Barnhart.* No, Hope didn't want to leave a message—written or voice mail. Her theory was better shared in person.

"I'll be happy to take the message for you, Miss Early." The familiar voice from behind made her sigh with frustration.

Her lips formed a thin, tight line. Detective Reid. Was he *everywhere*?

She turned around. "Thanks. I'll just leave a voice mail for him." She'd only tell Ethan she needed to see him and ask to meet up with him. Reid didn't need to know her completely speculative theory about what happened at Peggy's house.

"I'm sure whatever brought you here is important, so I'm happy to assist. Unless it's personal."

"I wouldn't come to see Ethan . . . er . . . Chief Cahill for personal business while he's on duty." Why was she explaining herself to him? She came to see Ethan, he wasn't there, nothing more to say. Especially to Reid. Except, Cal's missing wife could be the mystery woman from Peggy's house. "I had a thought about the fire at Peggy's house." Why was she still talking?

Reid crossed his arms over his chest and gave her a pointed look. "I'm listening."

She paused for a moment. Was Reid actually taking her seriously? There was a first time for everything. "The other woman who died in the fire could have been Lily Barnhart."

Reid's demeanor didn't change one iota. He showed no

reaction, positive or negative, to her theory. "Why do you think that?"

"Lily's been missing for several weeks and an unidentified woman was discovered in Peggy's house. Plus, Cal has postponed his workshop this morning."

"What makes you think we haven't identified the body?"

"I . . . I just thought . . ."

"And if you're correct, it would seem more reasonable Mr. Barnhart would have cancelled the workshop rather than postponed it. Thank you for stopping by. Have a nice day, Miss Early."

She hated to admit it, and would be loath to say it out loud, but Reid did have a point. If Lily was the woman who died in the fire, then Cal wouldn't be holding class in the afternoon. So much for her sleuthing skills, which were pretty much nonexistent.

"Then I won't waste any more of your time." Hope began to walk past the detective.

"One more thing, Miss Early."

*Ugh.*

"Remember, this is a police matter and civilian interference is not needed or welcomed."

*Right.*

"Good-bye, Detective." She pulled open the door and walked out of the police department. Everything Reid said made sense, so why did every fiber of her body tell her that her instinct was right?

# Chapter Seven

Hope balanced the six-quart Dutch oven in her hands as she walked along the gravel path to Meg Griffin's front door. Before she reached the front step, the door swung open and Meg appeared. Her normally flawless face was blotchy and haggard, while her brown eyes were teary and guarded.

"I'm so sorry, Meg." Hope's words were automatic and sincere. Whatever differences they'd had weren't important. She hoped Meg felt the same way.

"Thank you. Please come in." Meg stepped back and allowed Hope to enter the foyer, which was open on both sides to a living room and dining room and a staircase straight ahead. Sunlight streamed in from the open kitchen and family room at the back of the house.

"I made a batch of chicken orzo soup." When Hope left the police department she had thrown herself into a cooking project to take her mind off the run-in and rejection from Detective Reid and the fact Ethan still hadn't called her back. She debated sending him a text message but decided to be patient.

Meg took the pot and led Hope to the kitchen. "You're always so thoughtful."

Hope paused mid-step when she realized she hadn't heard a sarcastic tone in Meg's voice. She'd entered into unchartered territory and didn't know quite how to handle herself. Pleasantly surprised, she hurried to catch up with Meg. Perhaps there was a chance the tragedy could bring them closer together. Maybe they could be friends again.

"I can't believe she's gone. I mean . . . I knew this day would come. When she got sick and was rushed to the emergency room, the reality she wouldn't be around forever hit hard." Meg set the pot on the peninsula. "So, I began to mentally prepare for her passing. Isn't that a horrible thing to say?"

Hope arrived at the other side of the peninsula. She reached out and covered Meg's hand with hers. "No, it isn't. This is a part of life, and we shouldn't avoid thinking about it or preparing for it. What happened isn't your fault."

"You know, I was named after her. She was also my godmother."

For a brief moment, Hope stared at Meg. Gone was the competitive woman she'd known for far too long. In her place, Hope saw a sad little girl. Claire's words earlier about Meg's motives for wanting to keep Peggy in a nursing home were harsh. She wasn't staring at a person who was counting her inheritance. It was clear how much Meg loved her aunt.

Meg pulled her hand back. "How about some coffee? I have a fresh pot." She busied herself with preparing two cups before Hope could answer. "Sally Merrifield came by earlier with a loaf of zucchini bread. Would you like a slice?"

The thought of Sally's famous zucchini bread had Hope's mouth watering. She would have loved to indulge in a thick slice, but she was trying to watch her calories, and there wasn't any time for a run later. She politely declined the bread but gratefully accepted the steaming cup of coffee. Restless nights made staying awake during the day challenging. Hope sat on a stool and looked around the kitchen.

It had been years since she'd been inside Meg's house. She actually couldn't recall the last time she was there.

"When my dad died," Meg said as if reading Hope's mind. "That was the last time you were here. Five years ago."

"That's a long time."

"You're right. What happened to us? We were friends. We had fun together."

"We did."

"Now we barely speak a civil word to each other." Meg dipped her head and took a sip of her coffee.

Hope drank her coffee. She wasn't there to rehash their history. For that, they'd need something a hell of a lot stronger than coffee. She was there to support and offer her condolences to a person she'd known since grade school. "It would be nice for that to change."

Meg's lips curved into a small smile. "Yes, it would."

For the next twenty minutes they talked about Peggy. Meg shared some family photographs and stories about her rebel aunt, many of which Hope hadn't heard before. Such as the period in Peggy's life when she was a hippie. With a van full of friends, she went to Woodstock against her parents' wishes. Then off she went with Ricky and eloped. Meg said her family was furious, not only because of the elopement but also at the newlyweds' living in a motor home for three years. Hope shook her head in disbelief. Peggy was a wild child back in the day.

"I probably should get going." Hope didn't want to overstay her welcome. It looked like their relationship had taken a positive turn.

"First, let me get a bowl for the soup so you can take your pot. It'll just take a moment to rinse out." Meg went to where she'd set the pot on the counter.

"Oh, it's not mine." Hope stood and carried her mug over to the sink. "It was your aunt's pot."

Meg's forehead crinkled with confusion. "Why do you have it?"

"I took it from her a couple of days ago to clean."

"Why?"

"There was a little incident. She burnt some peppers and onions, so I told her I would clean it for her. It's not that hard, but the process is a little time-consuming. You see, you fill the pot with warm water and mild detergent and let it sit overnight. Then in the—"

"Wait, she was cooking and burned her food? Peppers and onions? That was Uncle Ricky's favorite dish."

Hope nodded. "That's what she said."

"Why didn't you call and tell me? Oh, my God. She must have been cooking last night. I told her not to cook. I provided her meals to heat up in the microwave. This is exactly why I wanted her either to have a live-in aide or relocate to a senior facility. You should have told me!"

"She made me promise not to tell. She told me she wouldn't cook anymore."

Meg's face darkened as she crossed her arms over her chest. "Promise? What are you? Ten? You should have known better!"

"She said she was going to use the meals you gave her. She was just going to use the microwave. Besides, the police—"

"She probably forgot she told you that. I don't believe this. Her death could have been prevented." Meg unfolded her arms and stabbed a finger at Hope. "You were right before, this wasn't my fault. It's your fault!"

Meg's words hit Hope hard, like she'd been slapped in the face. "I don't think it's fair of you to say that."

"Fair? My aunt is dead. That's not fair. You need to leave. Now."

Hope opened her mouth to defend herself, but Meg raised a palm, stopping Hope. In one sweeping motion,

Meg lowered her hand, grabbed Hope's purse, and shoved it at Hope. "Let me show you out." She spun around and marched out of the kitchen.

Hope followed. She tried to figure out a way to tell Meg the fire was most likely not started by her aunt's cooking but by an arsonist. Why hadn't the police told her last night? Her cell phone chimed Drew's ringtone. Meg threw an irritated look over her shoulder as Hope pulled the phone out of her purse and swiped it on.

"Now's not a good time."

Based on the intensity of Meg's glowering that was an understatement.

"They've identified the second body in Peggy's house," Drew said. In the background Hope heard a horn honking and the rumble of a truck.

Hope stopped walking. Meg must have heard Hope's footsteps stop on her cherrywood floor because she turned and propped a hand on her hip.

"Who was it?" Hope asked.

"Surely you can take that call outside." Meg continued to the front door.

"Lily Barnhart! I'm on my way to Cal's house. Gotta go." The line went silent.

Hope pulled the phone from her ear and stared at it for a moment as she processed the news. Turned out she was right. Her instinct was correct. But instead of feeling triumphant, she was sad. Two women were dead. There was nothing to be happy about.

"Good-bye, Hope." Meg pulled open the door and stood aside for Hope to exit.

"The woman in your aunt's house was Lily Barnhart." Hope swiped her phone off and slid it back into her purse.

"What? Why was she in my aunt's house?"

"Did they know each other?"

Meg shook her head. "I have no idea. And even if I did,

it's none of your business. I have things to do today. Like plan my aunt's funeral."

"Of course." So much for not overstaying her welcome. Hope stepped out onto the front step and turned to face Meg. "I am very sorry for your loss."

Meg closed the door hard, without as much as a good-bye. Hope sighed. The condolence call didn't go as she expected. After adjusting her purse strap on her shoulder, she descended the front steps.

"Hope Early?"

Hope looked over her shoulder and saw a woman rushing from a trendy compact car parked next to her sensible SUV. The woman looked familiar and then it clicked as she got closer. Norrie Jennings, Drew's competitive coworker. Wearing a floral dress with ballet flats and a crossbody bag, the young woman looked like she was dressed for a summer luncheon, not chasing down a story for the newspaper.

"Yes." Hope pulled out her key fob from her purse. There were several voice mails on her phone from reporters who wanted a quote from her about the fatal house fire. She didn't call them back because there wasn't an ounce of desire in her to do so.

Norrie extended her hand to Hope and pumped a firm handshake. She was petite with short hair the color of ginger and had big green, inquisitive eyes. She didn't appear to be the hard-nosed, career-driven, overachieving reporter Drew made her out to be. "It's nice to finally meet you. I'm Norrie Jennings. I've heard so much about you. You're quite a celebrity in town."

"Not really." Hope waved away Norrie's big fuss. "I was just on a baking competition show a couple of years ago."

"And you're friends with Mrs. Griffin?"

"I have no comment." Hope walked past Norrie toward her car. Since her reality show days, she'd gotten used to the "no comment" comment. She only wished her ex-husband had embraced the term at some point.

"Oh, I'm not looking for a comment. I was just curious. I'm new in town, so I'm trying to get the lay of the land, you know?" Norrie flashed a bright smile that appeared to be sincere, but Hope had a feeling the young reporter wasn't as wet behind the ears as she claimed to be. She'd already landed interviews with those close to Lily Barnhart.

"Meg and I have known each other since we were children. I came here today to pay her a condolence call." Hope figured that much Norrie would be able to figure out on her own, so there was no harm in sharing the information.

Norrie's glance darted to the door and then back to Hope. "She slammed the door pretty hard."

Hope had to give Norrie credit. She was observant. "She's obviously upset." Once Meg calmed down and the police confirmed the cause of the fire was arson, she'd probably forgive Hope. Maybe. Hopefully.

"Right. So, it has nothing to do with what happened in the spring and the murder investigation you became involved with?"

Hope squared her shoulders. She wished she had a door to slam in Norrie's face. During the murder investigation, Hope did ask a lot of questions and present her theories to the police. Like the old saying goes, you have to crack a few eggs to make an omelet. Not everyone was happy with Hope's sleuthing, including Meg.

"Good-bye, Miss Jennings." She continued past Norrie to her vehicle and pulled open the driver's-side door. She slid in behind the steering wheel and started the engine.

Drew definitely had his hands full with that one.

On Hope's drive home, she received a group text message from Brenda that the workshop had been cancelled for the day and she would be in touch regarding the remainder of the class. Disappointed, yes, but Hope understood. Cal had just learned his wife was dead. She hadn't even thought about the workshop after Drew's call. Her mind was churning about how Lily ended up in Peggy's house. What was their connection? How did they know each other? Why was Lily there?

Hope reached a stop sign and waited for two other cars to decide who went first. While she waited, she drummed her fingers on the steering wheel. It could be a while.

Finally, the car to Hope's right drove through the intersection, followed by the other car. It was her turn next. As she proceeded through the intersection, she realized somebody had to know if and how Peggy knew Lily.

Hope drove along a stretch of narrow road butted up against a thick wall of rock on one side and a questionable safety rail on the other. The winding road challenged even the most experienced driver in bad weather and, on beautiful days, it was easy to become distracted because of the burst of colorful wildflowers provided along the railing. Falling into a lull as her car glided along the sloping road, she caught herself just before she came to a sharp curve. She should have known better. She shifted in her seat, eased off the accelerator, and turned her thoughts back to Peggy and Lily.

How could she find out if the two women knew each other? The first place to look for friendships would be on social media, but Hope doubted Peggy was on the Internet in any capacity. A quick look at Lily's social media might reveal any common interests the two women shared, like community volunteering or church. She'd have Drew look into the applications before the Planning and Zoning Commission on the off chance Peggy had filed for some type of permit beyond the scope of the Building Department. She'd like to talk to Peggy's friends but, besides the residents on her street, she didn't know Peggy's friends. There was a place where Hope could start and she was halfway there. Peggy had spent several weeks in the rehab center and surely she'd made a friend or two there.

She glanced over to the passenger seat. The container of oatmeal raisin cookies she was going to photograph in class would now be put to another use. Who didn't love cookies?

# Chapter Eight

Hope reached over the center console and grabbed the container of cookies. After stepping out of her vehicle, she had a brief moment of doubt about visiting the Nutmeg Rehabilitation and Physical Therapy Center. Would she be allowed in? If so, would she be able to speak with Peggy's former roommate, assuming she had a roommate during her stay there? If she did share her room, the roommate could have been released.

Maybe she should have thought the plan through a little more. But since she was there, she might as well continue on.

A deep inhale of resolve propelled Hope forward, and she crossed the visitor section of the parking lot and reached the sidewalk that wrapped around the two-story building. She smiled as she passed residents out enjoying the warm day. Just as she reached the main entrance, the glass door slid open and Jane emerged from the lobby.

"What are you doing here?" Hope asked.

"I suspect I'm here for the same reason you are." Jane clasped her hands together. She wore a green floral dress and her structured beige purse dangled from her arm. Her white hair was styled in a layered bob with wispy bangs that brushed over her bright blue eyes, and she'd applied a touch of her signature pink lipstick. She must have had all the old men's eyeballs popping out of their sockets.

"To speak with Peggy's former roommate?"

"She's a lovely lady, though her memory isn't very good. I suppose being in a place like this can drain a person mentally and emotionally. Trust me, it's much nicer out here than it is inside."

"You heard about Lily Barnhart?"

"Dear, by now everyone has. As soon as I heard, I asked Sally to give me a ride over here. You know, one of my closest friends is here. She had a terrible bout with pneumonia and ended up falling."

"I'm sorry."

Jane patted Hope's arm and smiled. "Now, why don't I tell you what Lorraine told me? She's taking a nap now." She leaned forward as she noticed the container in Hope's hands. "Are those cookies?"

Hope nodded. "Oatmeal raisin. One of your favorites."

The truth was Jane had many favorites when it came to baked goods. She handed the container to Jane and they walked along the sidewalk to the pond area. People weren't the only ones out enjoying the weather. Hope caught glimpses of ducks diving into the water, their feathery bottoms popping up. At the far end of the pond there was a mama duck leading her ducklings on a swim. From the thick forest of trees that surrounded the grounds, bird songs filled the air. The tranquility was intoxicating. Hope could stay there for hours.

They reached a table and sat. Wasting no time, Jane opened the container and took out a cookie. She took a bite and savored the cookie. "Delicious as always."

"Thank you. Now tell me, what made you come here?" Hope reclined back and lifted her sunglasses up, pushing back her hair from her forehead.

"When I heard the unidentified woman was Lily, I was

puzzled because, to my knowledge, she and Peggy weren't friends. I saw Peggy often because she visited the inn when she went to the library. That was the only time she really got out on her own. She needed to rest up before walking back home, so she came into the inn. We had tea and chatted. There was one afternoon when Lily came into the inn. Let me think."

While Jane searched her memory, Hope looked around and saw many elderly people, most in wheelchairs, staring off to the distance. She had a hard time imagining Peggy there. She'd been so full of life before her illness. Living at the rehab center, even for a short period of time, must have been difficult for her. Now Hope understood why Peggy was so worried about being put into a nursing home permanently.

"I remember. It was a luncheon for the July Fourth parade organizers. I was in the living room with Peggy when Lily came in and asked me something. Oh, darn, I can't recall."

Hope helped herself to a cookie. "I don't think the question is important."

"You're right, dear. Anyway, it didn't appear that Peggy and Lily were acquainted. In fact, I introduced them."

"How long ago was that?"

"Months ago. Before Peggy was taken to the hospital."

"What did Peggy's roommate tell you?"

"The only people that visited were Meg, Jerry, and their kids. Mitzi and Gilbert stopped by a couple of times."

Hope swallowed a bite of cookie. "So, we've hit a dead end."

"Looks like it," Jane said glumly.

Hope stared off toward the pond. "It's possible Peggy had a connection to the P&Z Commission. I'm going to ask Drew to check the recent applications."

"Good thinking. I hadn't thought about that. We need to

find out exactly what the commission was voting on and maybe that will lead us to the killer."

"Jane, I'm not looking to confront a killer ever again. Done that and got the T-shirt." Coming face-to-face with a murderer was nothing like what Hope had read in the mystery novels she loved, and she doubted they were anything like Jane imagined when she wrote her books.

"T-shirt?" Jane asked.

"Never mind. I should talk to Ethan about this so he and his officers can investigate."

"How is Detective Reid doing?"

"Busy." He was busy being everywhere Hope was, so she was a little surprised not to find him at the rehab center. Not wanting to push her luck, she decided it was time to go. The last thing she wanted was another run-in with the detective and having to explain why she was there.

Jane returned the lid to the cookie container. "Be a dear and drive me back to the inn. Sally is running errands, and I don't want to wait around here. It's a little depressing."

"Of course." Hope stood and waited for Jane to gather her purse and the container. Out of the corner of her eye, she saw trouble approaching. She was so close to making a clean getaway. *So close.*

"Miss Early, what a surprise." The sarcasm in Detective Reid's voice wasn't missed by Hope. "What are you doing here?" His gaze was trained on her while he waited for an answer.

"Ummm . . ." Hope began to answer, but fumbled. How was she going to explain being at the rehab center where Peggy had been a patient and not have him think she was investigating his murder case . . . again?

Jane stepped closer to Hope. "I have a friend who's staying here. She had a terrible fall a couple of weeks ago. You may not know this, Detective, but I don't drive. Luckily, Hope does."

Hope slid a glance to Jane. She was impressed. The older woman provided a very truthful answer to Reid's question. Technically, though, it was misleading. But she wasn't going to fret over semantics.

"What are you doing here, Detective?" Hope tried to read his expression, but he had his cop face on and that meant no information about the case would be forthcoming. "If I didn't know any better, I'd think you're following me."

Jane patted Hope's arm. "Dear, I'm sure this is just a co-incidence. The detective has his hands full with his case, which you're not a part of."

"Coincidence?" Reid sounded doubtful. "Is that what this is, Miss Early?"

"It appears so. Well, we won't keep you from your official business. Come on, Jane." Hope guided Jane around Reid and together they skedaddled to the parking lot. Making herself scarce around Reid would need to be a top priority. He'd threatened to arrest her for interfering in a police investigation last time there was a murder, and she didn't doubt he'd make good on his threat if he discovered she was poking around his newest case.

Hope pushed open the mudroom door and was welcomed home by Bigelow. After a round of pets and kisses, she stepped aside to let him go out to do his business. Despite all his bad manners, he was good about not straying off the property. She wanted to think he was grateful he had a loving home he never wanted to leave but, just to make sure, she kept an eye on him. Within a few minutes, he trotted back inside and over to his water bowl.

When he finally settled on his bed, Hope prepared the coffeemaker. She was in desperate need of caffeine. After pressing the brew button, she went through the house and opened the windows.

The day was still mild, with no humidity, so the air conditioning could remain off. Within a few weeks, she'd be cranking the unit to full blast. The coffeemaker beeped, signaling her caffeine fix was ready. Before she poured a cup, she pulled out an elastic band from her purse, gathered her hair up into a ponytail, and slipped off her shoes. After a long drink she was recharged and ready to begin her photo shoot.

On the drive home from the rehab center, she'd run through the shoot setup. It would serve both as a feature for her blog and as a practice assignment for her class, which she wasn't sure she'd be attending any further. Cal had just learned his wife was dead. He'd suffered through weeks in limbo, not knowing where Lily was or what had happened, and now he had a funeral to plan. She couldn't imagine him continuing with the workshop.

She set her coffee cup down, grabbed a tray out of a lower cabinet, and began gathering all the props for her shoot setup. Nothing said comfort like a pile of French fries, and she was inspired on a recent visit to a retro diner to make her own fries.

She plated the fries she'd set aside to photograph. The rest were taste-tested, a perk of her job she enjoyed very much. Next she grabbed a glass canning jar, parchment paper, a condiment bowl filled with ketchup, and a red-checkered towel. She'd been playing around with ideas for the layout since the beginning of the workshop.

With the filled tray, she walked into her office, which was just off the kitchen. The room was still a work in progress. One wall was covered with floor-to-ceiling bookcases while the other wall was covered with shelves of props and supplies. A work surface served dual purposes as her desk and craft station, while a table was tucked under a large window. She used the table to photograph her food and DIY projects.

She set the tray on the desk and began setting her scene on the top of a foam board on the table so she could move it around easily. A half turn there, a quarter turn in a different direction, using the foam board prevented her from accidentally knocking something out of frame.

She lined the canning jar with parchment paper and filled it with the French fries. She gathered the kitchen towel on the board and placed the canning jar on top of it. Next, she set the small condiment bowl into a fold of the towel and then grabbed for her camera. She snapped some photographs. She lowered the camera and adjusted the aperture, which was a part of the holy trinity of food photography—the other two were shutter speed and ISO. Understanding aperture was a little confusing at first for Hope but, after a lot of practice, she began to embrace the concept and found her photographs looked much better.

With the camera settings adjusted, she began snapping away again, rearranging as necessary and moving around her table to get shots at different angles. She was lost in the zone of food photography until Bigelow's deep bark broke the silence. Then she heard the doorbell. She set her camera down, snatched a French fry from the jar, and nibbled on it as she padded out of her office to the foyer.

Her eyes widened as Bigelow raced toward the front door, his strong and destructive toenails tapping on the hardwood floor. No! No! No!

She picked up her pace and intercepted the dog before he reached the door. "Sit!" she commanded.

The dog lowered his bottom to the floor and tilted his head sideways. His expression was wide with confusion. He simply didn't understand Hope's problem with the door.

The doorbell rang again and Bigelow made a move to rise to all fours.

"No! Stay." She reached for the doorknob, all the while keeping an eye on her dog. She twisted the knob and opened the door.

"Hello, Hope."

Hope's gaze shifted from her dog to the tall man filling her doorway.

What on earth was Cal doing on her front porch?

# Chapter Nine

"What are you doing here?" Hope was suddenly aware her hair was pulled back in a messy ponytail and her feet were bare. "I wasn't expecting you."

"I apologize for just dropping by. . . . I was driving and I just had to see . . ." Cal's head dipped.

"There's no need to apologize. Please, come in." Hope opened the door wider for Cal to enter. "I was just taking some photos. It was time for a break anyway."

Bigelow barked.

Hope guessed he wanted to be introduced. "This is Bigelow and his hobby is trouble."

Bigelow's tail wagged excitedly as he sniffed the visitor. "Don't mind him."

She started to shoo the dog away but Cal patted Bigelow's head. "He's a friendly little guy."

"Trust me, he knows how to use that to his advantage. Come on." Hope led her unexpected guest to the kitchen, with Bigelow trailing behind them.

"You have a lovely home." His voice sounded monotone, as if he were on autopilot. Considering the circumstances, she wouldn't blame him if he were. She glanced over her shoulder to see if he was even looking around as he walked to the kitchen. He wasn't.

"It's a work in progress." Hope walked around the island, while Cal stopped and shoved his hands into his pants pockets. The sleeves of his black shirt were rolled up, revealing an expensive watch. His eyes were hooded with despair and his shoulders slumped from what she guessed was the weight of grief.

What on earth was she going to say to him? "I am so sorry about Lily."

Cal nodded. "So am I."

"Coffee?" She moved over to the coffeemaker and pulled out the carafe.

"Yes, please. I don't know what possessed me to drive over here. I guess I needed to see where it happened."

"Maybe it's too soon." Hope filled two mugs to the brim with coffee and set one on the island in front of Cal. His presence filled the normally cheerful space with a heavy dose of sadness. She couldn't fathom what he was feeling. Heavens, she never wanted to find out.

He stepped forward and lifted the mug. "Perhaps. After Detective Reid made the notification, I think that's what they call it, I sat there on the sofa. Everywhere I looked I saw Lily. I heard her voice." He pulled a hand from his pocket and dragged his fingers through his dark hair. "It felt empty and lonely. I had to get out. I drove aimlessly and then ended up on your street, at that house . . . or what's left of it." He lifted the mug and took a drink.

"Are you hungry? I can warm something up."

Cal shook his head.

"It's no trouble. The best part of being a food blogger is there's always food in the fridge."

"Coffee is fine. Thanks."

With her mug in hand, Hope walked along the island and stopped when she reached Cal. "I'm glad you came here. It's probably not a good idea to be driving in the state you're in now. It must have been a shock to see the house. I know it was for me this morning. I couldn't believe the devastation." She dragged in a breath. The image of what was left of the Victorian house flashed in her mind and she blinked hard.

"I'm sorry. I didn't even ask how you're doing. I heard you called nine-one-one last night about the fire. Did you know the homeowner? Were you friends?"

Hope leaned her hip against the island. "We were. She was a nice lady. Everybody loved her. Did either of you know Peggy Olson?"

"I didn't." His brows furrowed, causing a deep line between his eyes. "Maybe Lily did. Since she was on the P&Z Commission, Lily knew far more people in town than I did."

Further confirmation to Hope's theory that Lily wasn't hiding out in Peggy's home for those weeks she'd been missing. Which seemed to make sense; after all, why hide out in your own town? It seemed more likely Lily was abducted or lured to Peggy's house and kept there . . . either alive or dead until the fire.

"Tell me about the photo you were taking."

Cal's question brought Hope's attention back to the present. "What? Oh . . . I was photographing French fries for the blog and for practice."

"I've seen your photos on your blog. You're good."

Hope's cheeks warmed. Goodness, she hoped she wasn't blushing. "For a blog, maybe, but I've been asked to contribute to a cookbook being put together by *The Sweet Taste of Success*. I have to develop a couple of recipes and photograph them. So, I need photographs that will knock the socks off my editor. That is, if I decide to participate."

"Why wouldn't you?"

Hope took another drink of her coffee. "There would be a fair amount of promotion involved with the other contributors, and I'm not sure I want to go back to that. I've worked hard to move on from the show."

Cal set his mug on the countertop, brushing Hope's arm with his body. His gaze lingered on her for a long moment before he returned both hands to his pants pockets. "There was a piece of advice my mentor gave me when I was just starting out, and it was to never forget where you came from. Before I made it big, so to speak, in food photography, my first job was photographing Santa at the mall."

"Really?" Hope cleared her throat. The teeny-tiny moment of Cal crossing into her personal space unsettled her. Which was ridiculous. The man was in mourning, not looking to pick up the first food blogger he saw. She really needed to work on interpreting signals because she was clearly rusty.

"Not a day goes by I don't think I'm one photograph away from being Santa's photographer again. I guess it keeps me humble."

"Point taken."

"It feels good talking to you right now." The corners of his lips curved into a small smile. "I have an idea. Show me your setup."

"Are you sure?"

"Yeah, I could use the distraction."

"Okay. Come on." Hope set her mug down and led Cal to the office.

He went right to her setup and studied it for a moment before picking up her camera. He scrolled through the shots she'd taken and, with his eagle eye, he reviewed each one.

She twirled a ring on her right hand as she stood, waiting for him to say something. Why was he so quiet?

"Good job. I can see you've been paying attention in class."

She blew out a relieved breath. "It helps to have a good teacher."

Cal turned to Hope and handed her the camera. "Let's see what else you've got."

Accepting the challenge, Hope took the camera. Her

palms were a little sweaty. Having someone with all the experience Cal had watching over her was more than just a little intimidating. It was freaking nerve-racking. What if he critiqued her posture, the angle she selected, the shutter speed, or a million other things she was doing wrong? *Stop!* She silenced the negative voice practically screaming inside her head. Cal was just looking for a distraction. He wasn't going to grade her.

"I've tried for years to get Lily interested in photography, but she was content with her cell phone to take pictures." Cal moved, positioning himself behind Hope.

"Sounds a lot like me only a few years ago." Hope snapped a flurry of photographs before leaning forward and spinning the foam board to get another angle on the French fries display.

Cal also adjusted his placement to stay close to Hope. "As much as it pains me as a professional photographer, I have to admit Lily took some wonderful photos with her phone."

"I'd only met her a few times. She was very nice."

"Yes, she was. That's why all of this doesn't make sense. She would have never taken off on her own just to end up a few miles from home."

Hope stopped taking photographs and lowered the camera. Nothing about the fire or the deaths made sense. "Do you mind me asking if there was anything unusual the morning she disappeared? Was she stressed? Nervous?"

Cal shook his head. "No more than usual. There was pressure from both her job as an architect and from her work for the town. I've gone over that day a million times. There wasn't anything different. When she said good-bye to me at the front door, she seemed like herself." He leaned forward to make a small adjustment to the angle to the canning jar of French fries, brushing Hope's side with his arms and pressing his body against her back.

Hope lifted the camera and leaned forward to continue photographing her setup and to put some space between her and Cal, just as she heard heavy footsteps approaching the office.

"Hope?" Ethan's voice pulled Hope from her camera and Cal's closeness.

She looked over her shoulder and found Ethan had stopped at the doorway and stood with a deep scowl on his face, and his dark eyes were laser-focused on Cal. She disengaged herself from Cal, putting a wide gap between them, and set her camera on the table.

"Ethan . . . I . . . I wasn't expecting you." Her heartbeat quickened and she swore the temperature in the room surged thirty degrees. Why did she suddenly feel guilty?

"I apologize for interrupting." Ethan's gaze was still on Cal.

"No, you're not interrupting. Cal just stopped by after seeing Peggy's house."

"I should go. I have plans to make for Lily's funeral." Cal reached out and touched Hope's arm. "Thank you for the company. I can show myself out."

"Anytime." Hope's heart stopped racing a mile a minute because it was now threatening to break at the sight of Cal's grief-stricken face.

"Mr. Barnhart, please accept my condolences and be assured we will do everything possible to find the person responsible," Ethan said to Cal as he headed toward the door.

"I appreciate that, Chief." Cal continued out of the room and then disappeared.

Bigelow came rushing in and playfully jumped on Ethan, who rubbed the dog's head. "I bought him a treat and it looks like he devoured it."

"Did he sit for the treat? I am training him." Hope picked up her camera and placed the lens cover on it.

"Are you listening? You're supposed to be behaving yourself. Sit!" Ethan commanded but Bigelow jumped up again.

Hope rolled her eyes. "The book isn't working."

"When Heather and I brought Molly home from the hospital, we had all of those books on how to take care of an infant. The only problem was that Molly hadn't read those books."

Hope laughed. Maybe Ethan had a point and she should chuck the books and go with her instinct on training Bigelow. He wasn't a bad dog, just a very energetic one.

"Both of your girls are doing well, so maybe I should give your advice a chance." She set her camera on her desk. She was done for the day so she snatched a cold French fry and bit into it. She hadn't realized how hungry she was.

"What was Mr. Barnhart doing here?"

"I told you. The least I could do was invite him in and offer him coffee and then he offered to help me with my photography. I'm in his class. Or, was in his class."

"His wife was just found dead after being missing for weeks and he wanted to give you pointers on your photos?"

"He said it would be a distraction for him."

"I bet."

"Why are you being so cynical?"

Ethan crossed his arms and assumed his official police officer stance—shoulders squared, legs spread hip width apart, and feet firmly planted. She'd been seeing a lot of that lately.

"Mr. Barnhart is involved in an active investigation."

"I know. His wife was found dead last night. I was there. Remember?" Hope gathered all of her props back onto the tray. "Was Lily dead prior to the fire?"

A neutral expression covered Ethan's face. "You know I can't comment."

"Can't or won't?" she challenged.

"You've been hanging around Drew too much."

Hope moved over to her laptop and connected her camera to the computer to download the hundreds of photographs she'd taken. "I've been thinking. First, is there a connection between Peggy and the P&Z Commission?"

Ethan stared at her blankly.

She ignored his no comment. "You know, her death doesn't have to be connected to her work for the town. Maybe something happened at her job. Maybe an angry client or coworker."

Ethan's stare didn't change one iota so Hope continued sharing her theories.

"Lily could've been murdered right after she went missing and then her body hidden in Peggy's house while she was in rehab. Jane and I were wondering if anyone other than family visited Peggy at rehab, perhaps to get an idea of how much longer she'd be there. How much time the killer had before he or she had to move Lily's body. But her roommate said only family and close friends visited."

"Her roommate? You went to the rehab facility? You and Jane?"

*Uh-oh.* Damage control. Fast. "It was nothing." Stellar damage control. "I mean, Jane barely spoke to the roommate."

Ethan took two steps forward, placing himself directly in front of Hope, and he raised his index finger in a "stop" gesture. "Hope, don't. We're looking at everything. You and Jane don't need to investigate. Don't forget, the last time you inserted yourself into a murder investigation you almost got yourself killed."

"I know and that's why I'm sharing this with you now." She reached out and wrapped her fingers around Ethan's index finger and smiled. "I'm not investigating. I'm just thinking out loud."

He shook his head and Hope knew that shake all too well. He was thinking she was incorrigible. "You looked pretty cozy with Barnhart."

Hope cocked her head sideways as she let go of Ethan's index finger and rested both hands on her hips. "Are you serious? He was helping me with my photography. He's a good man. I just know he didn't have anything to do with his wife's death."

"Please, just be careful. I probably should go. I have another long night at the station." Ethan turned to walk out of the office.

"Wait! Why did you come over?"

Ethan paused and looked over his shoulder. "I just wanted to check on you and make sure there were no ill effects from getting too close to the fire last night. Talk to you later." He continued out of the office.

After she heard the back door close, she looked at her computer. The photographs were downloading. Her mind wandered back to the fire and to what Drew said about the discarded gas container found behind the garage.

Who set the fire? It seemed unlikely Lily did because Hope was convinced Lily wasn't a willing guest in Peggy's house.

While she waited for the download to finish, she lifted the tray and carried it out to the kitchen, with Bigelow trailing her. She set the tray on the island while Bigelow trotted to his favorite spot in the family room. As he circled around several times before curling up on his bed, Hope stared.

There had to be a third person at Peggy's house last night. The person who doused the house with gasoline and then set fire to the house. Was the intention to let the fire consume both victims, rendering the identification of Lily even harder if not impossible? Could the fire have gotten that hot? If Hope hadn't been out for a run then there was a chance that might have happened. Just as Bigelow's eyes shut for his umpteenth nap of the day, the realization hit her hard like a truck—had she just missed the arsonist escaping?

# Chapter Ten

"Lead me to your grill." Louis entered Hope's house with a shopping bag from a local grocery store. "We're gonna eat good tonight."

Louis's enthusiasm was a welcome change from all of the sadness the past couple days. After Ethan left, Hope's thoughts had been ping-ponging back and forth from how Lily ended up in Peggy's house to how she may have just missed the arsonist when she arrived back on her street from her run. The second thought still sent chills through her. As frightening as the encounter might have been, she sure would have liked to have seen the person responsible for the fatal fire. From the way Louis bounded into her home, swinging his grocery bag, she was looking forward to a few hours of distraction so she wouldn't be dwelling on the what-if scenario.

"It's all ready for you." She caught up with Louis as he entered the kitchen and then led him to the patio, where her most recent indulgence was located. A state-of-the-art stainless steel grill that cost way too much money but was a dream to cook on.

Louis blew out a whistle. "Man, oh man, this baby rocks." He high-fived her. "Good job, Hope!" He lifted the lid and blew out another whistle. "Holy cow! You can feed an army with this thing. I may never be able to go back to my rinky-dink grill after cooking on this beauty. Warming drawer, too? You're killing me."

"Speaking of cooking, what are you planning on making? Ribs? Burgers?"

"I splurged and now that I'm cooking on this bad boy, I'm glad I did." He extended the shopping bag to Hope. "Beef tenderloin."

It was Hope's turn to whistle. "Wow, fancy. I'll go unwrap the tenderloins and season them." She started to turn, then paused. "Do you know where Felicity and Elena are?"

Louis shrugged. "They should be here by now."

Bigelow barked, signaling there was someone at the door. "Guess they're here now." Hope hurried through the kitchen, dropping the bag on the island, and welcomed Felicity into her home.

"Your house is so charming." Felicity followed Hope into the kitchen. "Wow, what a great kitchen. It makes mine look so teeny-tiny."

"I've had my share of small kitchens when I lived in the city."

"Right. Before you *had* to move back home." Felicity swung around and flashed a smile. "Louis said he'd be grilling beef so I picked up this bottle of wine."

Hope took the bottle of Cabernet and gritted through Felicity's passive-aggressive behavior. "Very nice choice. Thank you."

Felicity's head bobbed up and down. "I do know my wine. In fact, my agent is working on a deal with a winery out on Long Island. You have a deal, don't you?" She paused a nanosecond, as if she was trying to remember Hope's sponsorship deal. Felicity wouldn't have mentioned it if she didn't recall every little detail. "With a house paint company. Yeah . . . paint." She flashed a grimace before she shrugged off her wrap and draped it on a chair, along with her purse. "You'll have to give me a tour of your house."

Hope set the bottle of wine on the island. Over the winter she'd signed a deal with a paint company to write sponsored posts. It was a perfect partnership since Hope was painting every room in her house. Though it wasn't as glamorous as having a partnership with a winery like Felicity, it did help pay the bills and her readers responded positively.

"I'll be happy to." She wasn't going to let Felicity's snide comments get to her. Rather, she was going to rise above them and be the gracious hostess her mother taught her to be. Though, a few glasses of wine might help with the being gracious part.

"It's awful about Cal's wife. I can't believe it's real. You know?"

"I think it's still settling in for all of us." Hope pulled the tenderloins out of the bag, then unwrapped them. She placed them on a platter.

"I can't imagine being in a fire. Trapped. I'm getting chills just thinking about it. You saw the fire. Do you know how it started?" Felicity settled on a stool at the island.

"Are you sure you're not a reporter? You ask an awful lot of questions." Louis entered from the patio and made a bee-line for the tenderloins.

Felicity tossed back her head, her hair bounced, and she laughed. "I'm naturally curious. I can't believe the rest of the workshop has been cancelled."

"I'm disappointed, too, but I don't think there was any other option." During the grim phone call from Brenda she made it clear there wasn't a possibility for rescheduling and a full refund would be processed for each of them. While Hope was grateful to have all the money back, she felt a little funny accepting it because they did attend two full days of the workshop. But she wasn't going to argue with Brenda or Cal over the matter.

"I've trekked all the way up from Brooklyn for this workshop, and I spent money on a room at the inn, which isn't being refunded," Felicity said. "Wine opener?"

Hope nodded, pulled open a drawer to retrieve a wine opener, and handed it to Felicity.

"Same here, sister, well, not from Brooklyn. I'll just take those out to the grill. Where is Elena?"

Felicity opened the bottle of wine and let it breathe for a few minutes. "She said she had a call to make and she'd be here soon."

"She better hurry up. These babies aren't waiting for anybody." Louis walked out to the patio with the tenderloins.

Felicity tossed a look over her shoulder. "He needs to cool his jets. The tenderloins aren't going to cook in a couple of minutes. We have time."

When food bloggers got together for a meal, they were all experts. As the hostess, Hope was the referee. "I'm sure she'll be here by the time Louis is done cooking. I made a tossed salad and green beans with goat cheese." Hope pulled open the refrigerator door, took out a large salad bowl, and reached back in for a jar of homemade balsamic vinaigrette.

"Great. Low carbs. I tested cake recipes all last week. I'm dying for protein. Bless you." Felicity carried the wine to the table and then asked what she could do to help. Hope wasted no time in putting her to work and, by the time Felicity finished setting the table, Louis was bringing in the beef tenderloins perfectly cooked and charred just enough. Hope tented the meat with aluminum foil so it would finish cooking. Meanwhile, she set out the salad and green beans on the table. But Elena still hadn't arrived. Felicity left another voice mail for the missing blogger as they sat down to eat dinner.

"Wait!" Felicity yelled.

Startled, Hope and Louis snapped their heads up. "What?" they asked in unison.

With her cell phone out, she smiled. "Photos." She stood and clicked away on her phone.

"Ugh, I totally spaced." Louis shifted and pulled out his cell phone from his jeans back pocket. "Gotta take a photo of this."

Not to be left out, Hope stood and went for her cell phone. Together, the three of them snapped photos of their food and one another and then posted them across social media. The one truth about food bloggers was that no meal should go undocumented. Especially since they were in a private kitchen and there weren't any other diners around who would find the activity annoying.

After the photographs were shared, the three of them ate their meal over conversation that revolved around what else? Blogging. It was impossible for bloggers not to talk shop when they were together. Most of the time they worked in isolation, so when they were lucky enough to be in the company of other bloggers, they couldn't talk enough.

Through dinner they discussed recipes, how to come up with post ideas, newsletters, and promotion. The conversation flowed easily and, by the time Hope served coffee with dessert, they all agreed they should do some type of event while they were all together in Jefferson. Hope suggested a panel discussion at the library.

She was confident Beth Green, the head librarian, would be able to pull it off with short notice. Louis beamed with excitement and said he would discuss how bloggers work with brands. Felicity immediately jumped on discussing recipe development and Hope offered to talk about search engine optimization or SEO for short. She loved the topic and could go on endlessly about SEO, but it could be a dry subject for most people. Dull or not, it was an important part of their business, and she'd make the presentation as interesting as possible.

By the time they'd cleared the dishes, all three of them were officially worried about Elena. She hadn't called or texted again. She'd left the inn early in the morning and returned several hours later, Felicity said. At the time, there wasn't any indication Elena would be a no-show at dinner.

"Are you sure Elena doesn't know anybody in the area?" Hope asked as she closed the dishwasher door.

Felicity casually shrugged. "She didn't say she knew anyone up here. But who knows."

"Maybe she's just a flake." Louis had settled on a chair in the family room and was bent forward rubbing Bigelow's belly. "He's a great dog."

Hope eyed her canine companion. He was a great dog when he was getting a belly rub or eating or sleeping. "He's a work in progress."

"Something's up with Elena. She got weird after the first day of class." Felicity glanced at her phone. "Look at the time. We probably should get going. Ready, Louis?" She grabbed her wrap and purse off the chair at the table.

"Gotta go, dude," Louis said to Bigelow and Bigelow's head swung up. "Sorry."

Hope and Bigelow walked their guests to the front door. "Thank you for coming this evening."

"It was nice. Very . . . cozy. Quaint. Next time you must come to Brooklyn. The energy and food scene is amazing." Felicity air kissed Hope before she turned and walked out onto the front porch.

"You're always welcome in Hoboken. Thanks, Hope. Good times." Louis followed Felicity down the porch steps.

Hope closed the door and found Bigelow staring at her. "Next time you must come to Brooklyn. The energy and food scene is amazing," she said in a mocking tone. "What's wrong with Jefferson?"

Bigelow's head tilted sideways.

"I know. It's not the city. But it's pretty amazing here. Except for the murders," she conceded as she locked her door. "Let's finish cleaning up."

She walked back into the kitchen with Bigelow behind her. At the table she pushed the chairs under the table and adjusted the centerpiece. The telephone rang and she hurried over to the end table in the family room, with Bigelow following her. The caller ID came up as Corey Lucas, her former producer on *The Sweet Taste of Success*. She grabbed the handset and clicked the phone on. "Hello."

"Hey, I'm on my way to the Met, but I wanted to touch base with you about the cookbook. Are you in? If you are, we need to schedule a meeting."

Hope glanced at her watch. Corey was on his way to a performance at the Metropolitan Opera House while she was tidying up for the night. Maybe the energy in Jefferson didn't quite come close to that of New York City. "Good evening, Corey. I'm fine. Thank you for asking. How are you?"

Corey exhaled a deep breath. "Busy. Late. Ugh, this cab won't move. Midtown traffic is a nightmare."

"I need a little bit more time to decide."

"Time? Honey, we don't have time. I'm not thrilled being pulled back into *The Sweet Taste,* but we're all stakeholders in this. Are you in or are you out?"

Hope wasn't the only person who moved on after the reality show. Corey left *The Sweet Taste of Success* to work on a reality show about bad first dates while she came back to Jefferson. The show tanked her career in publishing but, for Corey, it helped him score a bigger job. Proof there were no guarantees in life but more than not, she was glad she took the risk to step out of her comfort zone and appear on the reality show.

She drifted over to the French doors and looked out to her expansive backyard. When she originally saw the property, her first thought was there was so much potential. The second thought was that potential cost so much money. Building the garage put a significant dent in her savings account, and there was still a long list of things that needed to get done and they all required money. And the cookbook meant money.

"I'm in. I'll do it."

"Great! Now I won't have to sue you. *Hey*, the light is green and it means 'go'! Sorry, Hope. If it's not traffic, it's the cabbies."

"Sue me? What are you talking about?"

"It's in your contract. I don't recall the exact wording, but you agreed to do a cookbook if the show decided to publish one—*hey!* Seriously? Do you even have a driver's license?"

"I did?" Hope racked her brain to recall the contract she signed so long ago. Why didn't she remember the clause? Oh, boy. What other clauses were in the contract she didn't remember? She'd have to review the contract ASAP.

"You could sound a little more enthusiastic about this. It's a great opportunity to get back out there. Who knows what it could lead to? *Finally!* Just pull over! Yes, here is fine. Geez. Why didn't I use a car service? Look, I'm at the Met. Gotta go. I'll e-mail you the particulars." And with that, the line went silent.

Hope clicked her phone off and held the handset close to her chest. Staring out into the night, with the twinkling stars above, she prayed she made the right decision.

"Woof."

Bigelow's deep bark drew her attention from the night sky and she looked at the dog. He was an unexpected addition to her life and now she couldn't imagine her life without him. She needed to keep a roof over his head and food in his bowl, so if contributing a couple of recipes to the cookbook could help her financially, then she'd happily contribute and promote the book.

The recipes needed to be perfect and she needed to start first thing tomorrow. Her gaze drifted back to the window. With her priorities rearranged, she needed to let the police investigate the fire and two deaths. She couldn't become any further involved. She'd done her civic duty by answering Reid's questions and by sharing her theory with Ethan.

Now it was time to focus on her career and leave the suspicious deaths to the police. After all, she was a blogger and not a detective.

It was official. Hope was out of her mind. What other reason could there have been for agreeing to participate in *The Sweet Taste of Success* cookbook? Oh, right, she was contractually obligated to participate. She moaned as she pulled her bedcovers closer to her chin. Darn, stupid contract. She opened her eyes and was greeted by just a hint of light. She stretched her full body from her fingertips to her toes, prompting Bigelow to lift his head. His tired eyes told her he wasn't ready to wake up yet, and she sensed her stretching wasn't appreciated by the dog.

"You hogged the covers last night," she told him as she reached for her phone to check e-mails. She found one from Corey, just like he promised, with the particulars of the cookbook deal.

Two recipes from each contributor. It wasn't the recipes she needed to develop and photograph that had Hope regretting her decision. It was the editor's name. She let out another moan. Maybe a lawsuit wouldn't be so bad after all. Publishing was a small world with a long memory. And nobody had a memory like Calista Davenport.

She'd come to Hope for a favor for one of her authors, and Hope had turned her down. Now the woman would be editing her.

*Good going, Hope.*

She shook her head. Of all the editors on the island of Manhattan . . . oh well. Focus on the project, not the editor. She'd develop and submit her recipes and pray for the best.

After she flung off the covers and climbed out of bed, she padded into her bathroom to get ready for her day while Bigelow remained curled up on the bed. Lucky dog. After Hope finished her morning chores and the administrative tasks for her blog were done, she patted Bigelow on the head. He'd settled on his bed in the kitchen and was gnawing on a chew toy and didn't seem to notice her leave for the library.

She pulled opened the main door of the Jefferson Town Library and stepped inside. The two-story stately brick building had housed the library since 1916 and served the community through a depression, wars, and the invention of electronic readers.

Quiet sitting areas were arranged in the front of the library, while the back section was filled with stacks and stacks of books. Fiction and the children's section were located on the first floor, nonfiction was housed upstairs, and meeting rooms were located on the lower level.

Hope threaded her way through the reading tables and displays to arrive at the circulation desk, where Beth stood conferring with a patron. Her light brown hair was pulled back by a floral headband and she wore a simple blue dress. Her style was understated and refined, and fitting for a head librarian. She patiently explained to the older gentleman how to access a website he wanted to visit. When she was finished, the gentleman thanked her and walked away from the counter with the aid of his cane.

Beth tilted her head sideways and her smile was replaced by a frown when she made eye contact with Hope. "How are you doing? I heard you tried to rescue Mrs. Olson from the fire. Is that true?"

Hope didn't want to discuss her ill-conceived, spur-of-the-moment idea to race into a burning building. In hindsight, it was a foolish move she regretted because she wouldn't have been able to save Peggy. Thankfully, there had been a levelheaded police officer nearby to stop her.

"Such a loss for Meg and her family and for Jefferson. Mrs. Olson was a kind, generous woman." Beth's frown slipped away as her face brightened. "I'm going to remember her that way." She gave a firm nod. "Now, how can I help you today?"

"I wanted to speak to you about a panel discussion for the library. It's last minute, but I think it's an interesting topic." Hope launched into her pitch about the blogger panel. Beth seemed intrigued and asked several questions, jotting notes as they discussed the event.

"It does sound fascinating." Beth reached for a calendar.

"What's fascinating?" Sally Merrifield asked as she approached the desk with a pile of books. Sally retired as the head librarian several years ago. Now she volunteered several hours a week wherever needed in the library.

"Hope and her fellow blogging students who were taking Cal's photography workshop have offered to do a panel discussion about blogging." Beth studied the calendar. "We do have a lot scheduled. But I think we can squeeze in your event."

"Given what has happened, perhaps now isn't the time to have another event." Sally had disapproval written all over her face. The seventy-plus-year-old woman followed rules, whether they were hers or long-standing rules steeped in tradition.

Beth, on the other hand, preferred to be flexible and, given she was a librarian in the twenty-first century, flexibility was an asset. A primary task for her was to create a place where readers of print books or e-books wanted to come and be a part of the community.

"It will be a challenge, of course." Beth nodded. "However, I think we have a rare opportunity by having four successful bloggers in town all at the same time."

Sally shook her head and made a *tsk-tsk* sound.

Beth looked at Sally and gave an "I'm the head librarian" nod. "I think this is a good idea. It'll give people something to focus on other than the tragedy." She turned back to Hope. "Can I call you in about an hour or so? I need some time to come up with a plan. We can post on our community Facebook page as well as the library's page and I can send an e-mail blast to our list."

"Sounds like this is all coming together," Hope said with satisfaction.

"Apparently so," Sally said with a sniff of disapproval. "I have work to do. Have a nice day, Hope." She ambled off to the rare books room.

Beth turned her attention back to Hope and she looked a bit more relaxed. "I also heard Maretta Kingston wants the spot now vacated on the P&Z Commission. You're hosting an event for her. An English tea party?"

Hope nodded. "Will you be able to attend?"

"I'm going to try. I'm surprised Maretta is looking to serve on a town board. She's never shown an interest before." Beth gave a casual shrug. "I guess she's full of surprises. Maybe she'll consider volunteering here. With Lily gone, we'll need to find someone to replace her for the annual book sale."

"Did you know her well?" Hope asked out of pure curiosity, since she'd made a promise to herself the night before to leave the investigating to the police.

"Not very well. We met to discuss the book sale. She was busy between her job and the P&Z."

"Did she ever talk about the commission?"

Beth shook her head. "No. Though, I did hear from another volunteer that the last vote about Lionel Whitcomb's proposed development irritated him. And what I just told you is the extent of my information regarding the P&Z board."

Hope tried to hide her disappointment, but her interest was piqued. Again. "I'll let you get back to work. We'll talk later."

She pushed herself away from the counter and headed to the main exit. From what Beth said, it sounded as if Lily decided to take on the bullish developer whom Hope had more than a nodding acquaintance with. She couldn't decide if it was a smart move on Lily's part or a foolish one. She also couldn't help but wonder how he was handling the forced delay.

# Chapter Eleven

Hope had always been the person who followed through on her promises. When she said she'd be somewhere, she was there. When she said she'd do something, she did it. So why was it so hard for her to keep the promise she made to herself? She promised she wouldn't investigate the deaths of Peggy and Lily. Yet, she had stood at the circulation desk asking Beth questions about Lily. She tried to convince herself she was simply curious. Who was she kidding?

She trotted down the front steps of the library and waited on the curb for a break in traffic so she could cross the street. Her cell phone rang and she pulled it out of her purse.

She swiped her phone on. "Corey, I got your e-mail. I'm working on the recipes. I mean, I'm brainstorming ideas."

"Good, good. Not why I'm calling. How come you didn't tell me about those two dead women? Seriously, Hope. You've got an angle that's perfect for television. We'd have a hit show," Corey said above the noise of horns blasting. He must have been walking to his office in midtown Manhattan.

"I'm only doing the cookbook. No more reality TV." She caught a break in the traffic and dashed across the street. Most of the businesses on Main Street were antique shops.

Antique lovers flocked to Jefferson year-round to shop. The biggest season for tourists was autumn, when the trees were blazing with color, there was a nip in the air, and the buzz of excitement for the upcoming holidays swirled.

"What's that old saying about protesting too much?"

Hope walked along the brick sidewalk until she arrived at the Red House Antique Shop. "What are you talking about?" The quaint red clapboard house was once the home to the town's first mayor and had since been converted to a retail space on the first floor and an apartment on the second floor. The large front window featured a display of Blue Willow dinnerware, with a rare soup tureen set in the center of the nineteenth-century mahogany table. She stepped closer to the store window and bit her lower lip. She wanted the table. Too bad its price tag had too many zeroes. Shoot.

"Your blog has a YouTube channel. You're not as camera shy as you claim to be. *Hey!* Watch it," Corey shouted. "Sorry. These drivers are unbelievable."

"What?" Hope blinked a couple of times. She'd been mesmerized by the table and barely heard what Corey had said. Something about YouTube? Oh, that old argument. They better be careful, they were becoming like an old married couple.

"Those videos are different. I'm doing them to demonstrate a recipe, not document every single moment of my life. Look, I have to go. I'll be in contact with Calista."

"Just think about it. One hour, amateur sleuth tracks down killers between recipes. I think it'll be a hit."

"I'm sure you do." She swiped the phone off and dropped it back into her purse. When she looked up again, she saw Milo Hutchinson inside the shop talking with Everett.

Milo was the current mayor of Jefferson, which meant Claire was going after his job. Even with the announcement of her sister's bid for mayor, Hope had run into Milo a few times and he was pleasant to her. He wasn't taking the situation personally, and she was grateful because they lived in a small town.

Hope pushed open the front door and the men immediately stopped talking as their heads swung around in her direction. From the looks on their faces, she'd interrupted a serious conversation. Before she could say anything, both men shared a glance. She couldn't read the expressions on their faces. Milo slapped Everett on the shoulder and said his good-byes, then strode to the door, quickly replacing his serious look with a friendly smile.

"Hope, good to see you." Milo's outstretched hand reached for the door to keep it from closing.

"Same here. Give Pamela my best. I haven't seen her lately."

"Yes, yes, of course. She's very busy. Have a nice day." The door closed behind Milo and he disappeared down Main Street in a hurry.

Hope turned to Everett. The amiable antiques dealer looked annoyed before he broke away and walked to the sales counter.

"I came in at a bad time, didn't I?"

"Nonsense. We were just discussing town business." He picked up a dustcloth from the counter. "Finally decided to take the plunge on the table you've been eyeing?"

She looked over her shoulder to the window display. Drooling over was more like it. Everett was changing the subject. If he and Milo were indeed discussing town business, it wouldn't be appropriate to discuss it with her. Though, she couldn't help but wonder if they were discussing the vacancy on the P&Z Commission.

"I wish. It's a little pricey for me right now."

"It would be perfect in your house." Everett busied

himself with wiping down a bronze glass lamp. "This would be also."

Hope moved closer to the lamp, which was beautiful but a bit too formal for her farmhouse. "You think so?"

"Of course. This is a slag glass lamp and you'll notice all sixteen panels are in excellent condition." He pointed to random panels. He must've noticed Hope's lack of knowledge. "These originated in the late nineteenth century in England. It was believed glass manufacturers of the time added slag from iron-smelting works to molten glass and the result was an incredible range of effects from tortoiseshell to marbling and quickly became popular for lampshades."

"Fascinating." Hope gave the lamp another once-over and concluded again it wasn't right for her home. Plus, the three-digit number on the price tag reaffirmed her decision. "You know your lamps."

"I should since it's my job. My passion. These lamps are exquisite and this one is in pristine condition. That's why it's pricey."

"Very tempting." Hope browsed the collection of antiques in the shop. While the table was far out of her budget, there were some smaller, less expensive pieces she coveted. "I'm sure you've heard that Maretta Kingston has applied to fill the vacancy on the P&Z Commission."

Everett stepped closer and inspected the lamp. Was there a speck of dust he missed? Hope glanced around the shop. Every nook and cranny was filled with something. As much as Hope loved a good cleaning session, she would have tossed in the dustcloth if she had so much to keep tidy.

"Yes. She'd be a welcome addition. She definitely has a passion for Jefferson."

That was one of the most interesting spins on Maretta she'd ever heard. "She does. Her joining the board probably wouldn't upset the composition of the board."

"What do you mean?" Everett walked behind the counter

and deposited the dustcloth onto a shelf. He fidgeted with a collection of knickknacks before resting his hands on the counter. He looked relaxed now. The annoyance that flickered on his droopy face earlier was gone and a lightness sparkled in his blue eyes.

Hope shrugged. "From what I've seen, I think Lily and Maretta shared the same vision for the town. Both women had demonstrated a respect for the town while keeping an open mind about new construction."

"What an astute observation and I believe a correct one. With Maretta, I don't believe there will be a change in the philosophy on the board."

"So you don't anticipate internal disagreements?"

Maretta could ruffle a person's feathers with a simple greeting. So, imagining her serving on a commission where she'd have to work with others was difficult.

"No, no, not at all."

"Lily didn't have any disagreements with the other board members?"

"Everybody loved Lily. Regardless of how she voted. That's why it's so shocking what happened to her. But . . ."

"But?" Hope prompted as she broke away from a display of salt and pepper shakers and joined Everett at the counter.

"Well, I guess there's no harm since our meetings are open to the public. There was an appeal a few weeks ago and Hans Vogel wasn't happy with us. Especially Lily. During the meeting she got a little confrontational with him, which was out of character for her. She told him he had nobody to blame but himself for allowing his property to become a blight."

Hope was surprised to hear Lily decided to pick a fight with Hans Vogel, of all people. He owned an acre of property just north of Main Street on a very busy street that, for the most part, was as charming as the main thoroughfare in town. However, the charm stopped dead at the rusted, damaged chain-link fence at what Hans referred to as his recycling business. The truth was, he collected junk and had piled the junk for decades. The ornery recluse didn't recycle, he just hoarded.

"He didn't take what Lily said well, did he?"

Everett shook his head. "I thought we were going to have to call the police, but he stormed out. Lily looked a little rattled but shrugged it off. She said he was just blowing off steam. You know as well as I do Hans doesn't like to be told what to do."

She did. She'd heard the stories. Luckily, she'd only had a few encounters with Hans over the years, and they were mostly from a far distance. He kept to himself, preferring not to become involved in community events and only showing up in town to mail a package, to vote, or to appear in front of the P&Z Commission.

"Why are you asking?"

Good question. She was supposed to be leaving the investigating to the police. "I guess I'm just trying to make sense out of all this. I won't keep you any longer. Thanks."

"If you change your mind about the table . . ." Everett called out as Hope exited the shop.

Hope moved from the refrigerator to the island to the double wall ovens with ease and precision, never missing a step or a dash of anything. She turned on the stand mixer to a low speed to combine the softened butter and lemon sugar. Within a few moments, she increased the speed and let the mixer do its magic. Before her very eyes, the butter and sugar became light and fluffy. Perfection. It was time to add the two eggs. She cracked one at a time and added them to the butter and sugar mixture until they were fully incorporated. The cookie baking was a well-orchestrated event, one that never failed to soothe her. The ritual of creating something yummy out of butter, eggs, sugar, and flour fed

Hope's creative side. It also distracted her from all the drama swirling around her lately.

Just as she scooped out her homemade ricotta from its container into the mixer bowl, the back door of her kitchen swung open and Claire entered with an unusually large smile plastered across her face. She looked like she was going to burst.

"You'll never guess what just happened." Claire approached the island and set her sleek tote bag on a stool. She was dressed in her real estate agent uniform—pencil skirt, silk blouse, and high-heeled pumps.

"Then just tell me." Hope scraped out the last remaining ricotta before discarding the container in a recycling bin.

Claire pouted. "You're no fun."

"I'm a little busy." After adding three tablespoons of lemon juice to the batter, she lined several cookie sheets with silicone liners to prevent the cookies from sticking.

"Testing a new recipe?"

Hope glanced up. "Yes." She immediately regretted her fib. She wasn't testing a recipe. The cookies were for Hans Vogel. She wanted to talk to him about his outburst directed at Lily.

She had promised herself she'd stay out of the investigation and work on the cookbook recipes, but who was she kidding? She couldn't help herself. She'd watched her friend's home burn down and two women were dead. Staying on the sidelines wasn't an option. Besides, she was only going to ask questions and whatever information she got from Hans, she'd take directly to Ethan. Having a batch of homemade cookies would be a good conversation starter. They'd never let her down.

Claire peered into the mixer bowl. "Looks and smells like your Lemon Ricotta cookies. Why are you testing that recipe?"

"Just trying something different with it." Darn, another fib. No, that was an outright lie, and her subconscious was kicking into overdrive, but if she told Claire the truth, she'd be subjected to a lecture on why her idea was a very bad one.

She added the dry ingredients to the mixture and said a silent prayer Claire wouldn't notice there was nothing different about those ingredients.

"Oh, I can't wait to taste one." Claire pulled back from the mixer. "Now, back to my incredible news. Matt has put in an offer for a house. The adorable Dutch Colonial on Crabapple Lane. You know, the one with the side porch set on two acres."

Hope turned off the mixer. "Good for him. It'll be a perfect weekend house to escape to from the city."

"Exactly what he's looking for."

"You came over here to tell me he's put an offer on a house?" Hope used a small ice cream scoop to drop the cookie dough onto the baking sheets.

Claire nodded. "I had to pass by here on my way to the office. I thought you'd like to know Matt is finally going to be putting down some roots here."

With the dough scooped out, Hope slid two baking sheets in each of the wall ovens and set the timer. The luxury of two ovens was a lifesaver when she was in a hurry. Within a few minutes, all of her baking would be done and she'd be ready to head out.

"Why did you think I'd like to know that?"

"Well, let's see. He's successful, handsome, and single."

Hope set the mixing bowl into the sink and filled it with warm soapy water. Her sister meant well, but she was too confused about her feelings toward Ethan to consider Matt a possible romantic partner. One minute Ethan was the friend she leaned on when she needed support and the next minute he was a sexy, hot cop. If she couldn't figure out her feelings, how could she possibly pursue a relationship with anyone?

"I don't need you to play matchmaker. I can take care of myself." She wiped her hands on a towel.

Claire scoffed. "I guess every family needs a spinster. Look at Mom's sister, Blythe."

"Hey! Pretty harsh."

Claire shrugged off her sister's indignation. "Sometimes the truth is. You know, maybe you shouldn't fight it, Sis. Embrace spinsterhood because that's the only thing you'll be embracing since you've sworn off men."

"Not true. I have Bigelow. Who is somewhere taking a nap."

"Maybe you should get a cat. Or two or maybe a dozen."

"You know, I'm done with this conversation." Hope checked the timer. Just a few more minutes to go before the cookies were baked and she could visit Hans. While she waited, she decided to find out what Claire knew about Lionel Whitcomb's proposed development. A bonus was that the change of topic would distract Claire from Hope's nonexistent love life and talking real estate was like dangling a shiny object in front of Claire.

"What do you know about the property Lionel Whitcomb owns next to the Village Shopping Center?"

"Why are you interested in that?"

"No particular reason." Hope shrugged off the question. "I heard someone mention it's in limbo right now because the P&Z Commission needed more information before giving it the green light."

"I'm sure he'll figure it out." Claire dug into her tote bag and pulled out her cell phone to check her messages. "I don't handle commercial properties, but Kent Wilder has been hot for the listing since Whitcomb announced the project. He's tired of selling starter homes. Too bad he doesn't have the chops to work with Whitcomb. That pompous jerk will chew him up and spit him out."

Hope's few encounters with Whitcomb, who relocated to

Jefferson a year ago with his trophy wife, led her to agree with Claire's assessment of the man. Whitcomb was a bully who blustered his way through everything. She'd witnessed him belittle and humiliate his trophy wife, Elaine, just months ago. He crushed her spirit and it made Hope's stomach turn and her heart ache for the woman. Why anyone would want to partner with him baffled her. But then, money was a strong motivator.

"I better get going. I have a few things to finish at the office." Claire pushed away from the island. "Then it's back home to work on the campaign."

"How does Andy feel about the campaign? About maybe becoming the First Husband of Jefferson?" Hope's brother-in-law had the heart of a saint, but he worked hard to attain a certain lifestyle and a significant cut in salary for Claire could affect their lives.

"Don't worry. He's secure enough to be the First Husband. And he understands this is important to me and fully supports me. He's as excited as I am about me beating the pants off of Milo."

The timer dinged and Hope moved over to the ovens. "You know I ran into Milo earlier at Everett's shop."

"You didn't buy the *table*, did you?"

"No, I still can't afford it." Though, with the money she'd earn from the cookbook, maybe she could purchase the table. She was loath to admit it, but maybe doing the cookbook was a good thing after all. "He and Everett were having a serious conversation. On his way out, I told him to tell Pamela I said hello. I haven't seen her lately. Have you?"

She pulled out the trays of cookies, setting them on a rack to cool. She inhaled the fragrance of the lemon and resisted the urge to bite into one of them.

"She's been MIA lately. Maybe she's having an affair." Claire feigned a surprised expression.

"Claire! What a terrible thing to say. You know, that's how rumors get started."

"It's already been started, and I heard it at the gym. I gotta go." She snatched a cookie off the cooling rack. "Ooh, hot, hot . . . hot." She blew on the cookie. "One for the road." With her other hand, she grabbed her tote bag and dashed out of the kitchen.

When the back door closed, Hope set to work putting together a cookie plate for Hans. From an upper cabinet she pulled out a scalloped floral plate. It was one of ten she purchased at a tag sale. She loved tag sales for budget-friendly finds for her house and for her blog. The set cost her seven dollars, and she used them for photos and for gifting baked goods. She hated using plastic throwaway containers.

Before securing the plastic wrap around the plate, she snatched a cookie and took a bite. The bright, fresh flavors packed into the small cookie burst in her mouth. There was no way Hans Vogel would turn her away when she handed him the plate of cookies. She was certain of that.

# Chapter Twelve

Apprehension bubbled in Hope's belly as she approached the gate of Hans Vogel's property. He wasn't a man known to welcome visitors unless they had cash to buy one of his *treasures* or junk, as it was commonly known around town. Though she'd heard he did indeed have an honest-to-goodness antique from time to time, the yard full of rusting artifacts didn't look promising. Holding the plate of Lemon Ricotta cookies, she said a silent prayer he wouldn't toss her and her cookies out on her bottom before she could ask about Lily.

She unlatched the gate and pushed it open. As she stepped onto Vogel's property, the gate closed with a heavy clank behind her. She followed the worn stretch of grass to the front porch of the old, neglected gray house and decided to use a ruse of being interested in one of his *treasures* if she sensed he was going to run her off. She reached the house. If she had to guess its style, she would have said plain farmhouse. There were no remarkable features about the modest two-story house with a narrow covered porch. She gingerly climbed the weather-beaten front steps.

So much stuff.

A wave of disgust rolled through her as she scanned the

cluttered space. An old ironing board, which served as a plant stand for dead plants, piled high storage bins, a rusty washing machine, and countless stacks of tied-up newspapers. How could Hans live among all that clutter . . . correction . . . garbage?

The front door swung open and unexpectedly Hans appeared. It wasn't his sudden appearance that stunned Hope; rather, it was the emitting odor of sourness and cigarette smoke that assaulted her nose. The smell was so pungent she almost gagged.

"What do you want?" Hans stood, filling the doorframe, and his dark gaze bore down on Hope. "What do you want? I'm not buying anything."

She'd forgotten how imposing Hans was, and it took Hope a moment to regroup. He was a beefy man with a ruddy complexion and messy gray hair. His thick hand held the door in place, keeping her out.

"I'm not here to sell something." She flashed a smile and hoped for one in return. None was forthcoming. Time to move on to the best tool in her arsenal. "I baked cookies. Lemon Ricotta." She thrust the plate toward Hans. "They're for you."

He scowled at the plate. "Who the hell are you?"

*Oh, boy.* Her best tool was failing her big-time. "Hope Early. I live in town. I heard you have some antique signs and I'm looking for one. I'm renovating an old house, and I want to fill it with treasures. I hear you have a lot of treasures."

If she wasn't scared right down to her toes, she would have been proud of herself for working her plan.

"What kind of cookies did you say they were?" His scowl softened as he reached for the plate. He wrapped his fat fingers around the plate.

"Lemon Ricotta Cookies." Her voice broke as the plate was ripped out of her hand. "They're one of my favorite recipes. I'm sure you'll like them."

Hans pulled back the plastic wrap and grabbed a cookie. He took a bite and chewed. His scowl completely disappeared as he finished the cookie.

Hope chided herself for doubting the power of a cookie. "Not bad."

Not bad? *Really?*

"My late wife used to bake cookies." Hans replaced the plastic wrap and set the plate on a surface beside the door. Hope couldn't see much beyond Hans, but the glimpse she stole revealed more clutter inside. "I have a few signs you may be interested in."

He stepped out onto the porch, pulling the door closed behind him. His large frame practically filled the space of the small porch.

They were in close quarters, too close for Hope, who turned and descended the porch steps, with Hans following her. She worried their combined weight on those treads would collapse them. Once they were safely off the porch, he took the lead and led Hope around the side of the house. Situated on the property were several small buildings, all in similar condition to the house. As she followed, she watched her step. There was junk littered all over the property—empty containers, piles of lumber mixed with overgrown weeds, and ripped tarps covering mounds of stuff Hope couldn't see. In the distance there were a few old rusty cars. She could understand Lily's frustration toward Hans for neglecting his property.

"You're probably too young to remember Tad's." Hans stopped at a clump of old signs and began digging through.

"Gas station, right?"

"Up and down the Post Road." The Boston Post Road was a main thoroughfare in its day and was America's first mail route. "Tad's was one of this area's first gas stations. The last one closed in the mid-sixties." He dragged out a sign. "This is a nineteen thirties enamel porcelain sign."

Hope inched closer to inspect the sign. In its prime, it must have looked magnificent hanging on the side of a gas station. Now, exposed to the elements, it was battered and its luster had faded. Though, still in one piece, with no other damage than the weather, it was still a great find.

Hans set the sign aside and pulled out another. "This one is from the same era. Enamel porcelain die cut. These are rare."

Rare meant expensive. "They're awesome. You have a lot of great stuff here."

"Most people think it's junk." Hans took a sweeping look around. "It's my collection of history from this area. Like a museum."

Hope looked around. Were they looking at the same piece of property? Selling that place as a museum would be a hard sell. And apparently Lily didn't buy it when she heard him plead his case.

"You mean like the P&Z Commission?"

Hans let go of the sign and it dropped to the ground. Hope cringed, worried the sign would be damaged. When she looked back up to Hans's face, she saw it had turned red and his dark eyes had hooded with anger. *Oh, boy*.

"Yeah. They gave me sixty days to clean up this place. It ain't right! The government telling you what to do with your property!"

"Lily Barnhart told you to clean it up, right?"

Hans's nostrils flared. "She had no business telling me what to do. She's some fancy-pants architect. She had a vision of what my land and home could look like. Guess she wanted my place to look like all my neighbors'."

"Mrs. Barnhart disappeared three weeks ago."

He scratched his head. "You don't say?"

"She was found dead two days ago."

Hans's body stiffened and a deeper shade of red crept up his neck to his face. "What?"

Hope jumped, startled by the loud, angry voice. She trembled as warning screams went off in her head to turn around and run. *Run fast!* She was foolish to confront Hans on her own. No one knew where she was, and a quick glance around revealed she could easily be disposed of and not found for a very long time. Especially if Hans refused to clean up his property.

"You think I had something to do with her death? You've got a lot of nerve, lady. Get the hell off my property!" Hans stalked toward his house and disappeared inside, slamming the door behind him.

It took Hope a few moments to regain her composure. When her nerves settled, albeit frayed, she turned and retraced her steps back to the front gate. She fumbled to undo the latch and crossed over to the concrete sidewalk, back to civilization. A feeling of safety flushed through her, and she exhaled a deep breath she hadn't realized she'd been holding. Before she continued to her car, she glanced over her shoulder for one last look at Hans Vogel's property.

He was a scary man with a reason to harm Lily. But she wasn't the only one. There were four other commission members and they could be in danger since they all voted to force Hans to either clean up his property or lose possession of it. They needed to be warned.

She pulled her cell phone out of her purse and tapped on the Internet app. She typed the address of Jefferson's website and when the site loaded, she searched for the P&Z Commission page, where she found the listing of members. Maybe she could discreetly inquire if any one of them had received a threat.

There was only one name vaguely familiar to Hope. Donna Wilcox. She was the mom of a friend from elementary school. Hope played at the Wilcox house all the time until the family moved to Boston. She'd lost contact with her friend, but Donna had returned to Jefferson the year

Hope moved to New York City. They hadn't spoken in years, and it was time to catch up with her. With her plan set, she began walking to her car, but a car horn caught her attention.

She glanced up as a Lexus eased into a space by the curb. She squared her shoulders and gave herself a mental slap for being distracted because this was how women were abducted right off the street. She came to a stop. Was that how Lily was snatched right out of her life?

The passenger window rolled down and, much to Hope's relief, she saw Matt Roydon.

"Hey there," he said with a big smile.

She walked to the vehicle, relieved to see a friendly face. The handsome criminal defense attorney wouldn't be kidnapping her anytime soon, though being swept off her feet by him didn't sound like such a bad idea at the moment.

*Whoa!* Claire's attempt at matchmaking was messing with Hope's common sense and her resolve to stay romance neutral. She and Matt were friendly, that was all. "I heard you put an offer on a house."

"I'm waiting to hear back. They counteroffered." Matt looked every bit the successful attorney enjoying a day off. The sleeves of his dark blue shirt were rolled up, revealing muscular forearms. He was tanned and his brown hair seemed a shade lighter from time out in the sun. The last time Hope had seen him was at her housewarming party when he brought her a dozen roses.

"Nail-biting, isn't it?"

"You know, with my job, I have to face a jury of twelve people and make a case for my client's innocence, but it's nothing compared to waiting to hear back about an offer on a house."

Hope shrugged. "It's an emotional thing. The house represents so much more than just shelter. I hope you get it."

"Me too. So, what are you doing here?" His gaze traveled

over Hope's shoulder to Hans Vogel's property and probably landed on the NO TRESPASSING sign.

Hope hesitated before answering. "I'm looking for antique signs." She wasn't technically lying, but she was omitting some, okay, a lot of the truth.

"Huh." He studied her like the criminal defense attorney he was.

His gaze swept over her, looking into her eyes, checking her facial expressions and traveling down to her hands, one of which was holding her cell phone. He even glanced at her feet. In a nanosecond, he was sizing her up, based on body language, to tell if she was being honest. How dare he not believe her. She was offended by his lack of trust. *Whoa.* Time to get off her high horse since she was being less than truthful about her reason for being there.

"You didn't find any you liked?"

She cringed at his tone. He knew she wasn't telling him everything. So, why start telling the truth now?

She shook her head. "No. Too pricey."

He leaned over the console between the two front leather seats. "Are you okay?"

"Yes," she answered swiftly. Too swiftly, she realized. No doubt he suspected she was up to something.

"Do you want to tell me what you're really doing here?"

"I did. I was looking at antique signs." *And getting thrown off a potential killer's property after bringing him cookies.*

"You know, a part of my job includes cross-examining people, and I'm a pretty good people reader."

"I'm sure you are." Hope pressed her lips together as she shoved a lock of hair behind her ear. No doubt the fidgeting was a huge red flag for the attorney. She desperately wanted to remain still.

"Since you won't share the whole truth now, how about we have dinner soon? When I come back to town for the closing, I'll give you a call."

"It's good you're confident."

"I met their counteroffer."

"No, I was talking about going out to dinner." Hope smiled as she stepped back onto the curb and waved good-bye to Matt, who shook his head and laughed.

He shifted his vehicle into gear and drove off. Her phone buzzed, notifying her that she'd received a text message. She swiped the home screen and found a message from Drew.

**Meet Jane & me at Village Shop Ctr. ASAP.**

Hope frowned. What was going on over there? She tapped her reply.

**What's up?**

Drew fired back an immediate response.

**Will explain when you get here.**

She thought for a moment and decided she'd go see Donna Wilcox after she found out what was going on at the shopping center. She replied back.

**On my way.**

# Chapter Thirteen

Jane waved Hope to an available parking space while Drew talked on his phone. After she navigated into the tight spot, with inches to spare between a hybrid and a minivan, she climbed out of her SUV and joined her friends beside a chain-link fence. Beyond the fence was an empty lot. On one side of the lot was the shopping center and on the other was a daycare center.

"What are we doing here?" The question came out harsher than Hope intended and she immediately regretted it. She was still agitated by her visit to Hans Vogel, and Drew's cryptic text message had added to her edginess.

"Is everything okay, dear? You seem tense." Jane's brows pinched with concern.

Drew removed his pair of aviator sunglasses and lowered his phone. He didn't give Hope a chance to reply to Jane. "This is the property Whitcomb wants to develop for a medical building." Dressed in a pair of white-rinsed jeans and a half-tucked pale green shirt, he looked casual yet polished and ready for any assignment.

"I know," she snapped. Hope needed to get a grip so she silently counted to ten. "I'm sorry."

"And the vote to proceed with the building was postponed

by the P&Z Commission," Jane added, so as to not be left out. She wore a turquoise floral dress with a coordinating cardigan. The color of the dress brought out her blue eyes.

Drew cast a sideways glance onto Jane and cleared his throat. "Now the concern is the impact on traffic because the medial offices would bring patients from surrounding towns. The vote was postponed because Whitcomb had to perform a few more fact-finding processes."

"Like a traffic study," Jane added.

Hope suppressed a laugh when Drew huffed. No doubt he was irritated Jane stole his thunder. She was starting to feel better and was eager to join the conversation. "Any idea how Lily was leaning regarding the vote?"

She walked closer to the lot, which was cleared for as far as the eye could see. Butted up against the busy shopping center, it was a prime location. The impact on increased traffic would be offset by the money the medical building could bring to the town, with increased business at the shopping center by employees and patients and the all-important property tax.

Drew looked to Jane before answering and she nodded her head, giving Drew the go-ahead. "No. Like everyone else on the commission, she asked a lot of hard questions. I think at one meeting I actually saw him squirm."

"Now, that must have been a sight," Jane said.

Hope laughed. "I need to get to one of those meetings." She would've loved to see Whitcomb in the hot seat for a change. The man was a blowhard and had gotten several free passes from the town for development in the past. It was about time he was challenged.

"You should. The last one with Hans Vogel was awesome. You should've seen him. He exploded at Lily." Drew's eyes bugged out and he gestured vividly with his hands. "It was as if his mind was blown."

"So I've heard." Hope dipped her head to avoid making eye contact. Drew didn't know she'd planned on visiting Hans.

"You know, I should go talk to him," Drew said.

Hope crinkled her nose and lifted her chin. "Maybe not now."

"Why, dear?" Jane asked.

"Yeah, why?" Drew chimed in.

"He's in a bad mood." Hope walked along the fencing and stared off into the distance. Just a few weeks ago, the rumbling sounds of heavy earthmoving equipment roared but now there were large piles of dirt and a big hole waiting for the foundation to be poured. Could Lily have been killed because of a piece of property?

"When isn't he in a bad mood?" Jane followed Hope.

"What did you do?" Drew asked.

Hope stopped walking and turned around. "I just came from his place. I visited him with a plate of cookies." She squeezed her eyes shut, bracing for the dynamic duo's reaction.

Jane reached out a hand and put it on Hope's arm. Hope opened her eyes and saw Jane's lips curve into a proud smile. "That's my girl."

Of course Jane would be proud of her. Give her a few seconds and she'd be comparing Hope's gumption to her fictional sleuth, Barbara O'Neill. Jane created Barbara, a curious college coed who solved mysteries, before she married. She'd written a total of five books before she retired from writing to raise her family. Even after all these years, Jane still had a nose for mystery and encouraged Hope to investigate. But the truth was, Hope didn't need that much encouragement.

"Everett told me about the meeting and how upset Hans was, so I went to talk to him about the vote. It didn't go well."

"Duh!" Drew threw his arms up in the air and held them there for a long moment.

"I know. I know. It wasn't the smartest thing to do, but I really didn't think about it. I just went."

"With a plate of cookies?" Drew asked.

"Lemon Ricotta."

"You had a feeling and you acted upon it. That's exactly what Barbara O'Neill would have done in her book," Jane said.

Almost a personal best for Jane. Though, Hope wasn't sure how healthy it was to be compared to a fictional sleuth.

"You know, if Reid finds out, he's not going to be happy." Drew brought the conversation back to reality and it hit Hope like a rock.

"When Hope solves this case, he'll be thanking her. Dear, do you think Hans is the killer?" Jane linked arms with Hope, and all three began walking away from the fence.

After checking his phone, Drew slipped it into his pants pocket. "He has motive and he can't possibly have an alibi since he's a recluse."

"I don't know. He's angry enough." Hope replayed the encounter with the recluse over in her mind. "He doesn't strike me as the type of person to plan something." She saw the confusion on Drew's and Jane's faces. "Lily was abducted and then found dead in Peggy's house. So, the killer had to grab Lily, probably killed her right away, then somehow hid her in Peggy's house and returned later to set the house on fire. No, Hans seems more like the type to grab, kill, and leave the body."

She shocked herself by saying that stream of consciousness thought out loud. When did she turn into the person who so matter-of-factly discussed murder?

"I believe you're right. What do you think?" Jane looked to Drew.

Drew sighed. "If not Hans, then who?"

"Kent Wilder?" Hope tossed out his name because, since her conversation with Claire earlier, she was curious how much he had to gain by Lily's death. "He wanted this listing." She pointed a finger at the lot. "We need to find out how Lily intended to vote on this project."

"How are we going to do that?" Jane asked.

"I'm not sure. I'm going to see Donna Wilcox to ask if she knew how Lily was going to vote. Perhaps they discussed the vote. I also want to find out if she received any threats, because if Lily's death is tied to the commission, all of the members could be in danger."

"Just be careful. If they're targets, any one of them could be next. Why don't we meet up later for dinner and you can fill us in on what you learn," Jane suggested.

Drew pulled out his cell phone. "My appointment just got rescheduled. Great." He looked up from the phone. "I'll follow you over there."

"Maybe it's better if I talk to Donna alone. Both of us confronting her could be a little overwhelming. . . . Oh, don't pout. I'll tell you whatever she tells me."

"Promise?" Drew asked.

Hope nodded and then set a time for dinner. They separated and when she reached her vehicle, she received another text message. It was from Cal.

Need to see you. Now.

Hope followed Cal into the living room and stopped at the sofa while he plodded to the wall of windows. He buried his hands deep into his pants pockets, his shoulders slumped, and he faced the vast expanse of the rolling hills.

"I appreciate that you came right over." His voice was shaky, as if Lily's death was finally sinking in.

Hope had seen it begin to settle in him earlier at her house, but at least he had a distraction—her photography. Now, all alone in his home, there weren't any distractions, just memories and reminders of his wife.

Cal's head dropped and he shook it. Hope's heart ached for him. In less than twenty-four hours, his world was ripped apart. Any glimmer of hope he'd had that his wife would return home safely was destroyed. Hope was familiar with those feelings. While her husband didn't die, she was left with memories and should-haves that still haunted her.

"I know you're busy, but I just needed a friend."

Friend? They barely knew each other. Surely he had people closer to him whom he could have called. "I'm glad you reached out."

He turned. His eyes were somberly hooded, with thick brows, and the crease lines that had given him an air of maturity before now were deeper and showed stress. "I have to make arrangements for Lily today." He pulled a hand out of a pocket and dragged his fingers through his hair as he stepped forward. "I thought I could handle this. I can't."

Hope moved toward Cal. "I'm so sorry." She reached out and rested a hand on his arm. "I can't imagine what this is like for you. Do you want me to go with you?"

Cal half smiled. "No, no. Lily's sister is going to be there. I just needed to see a friendly face. You know?"

Hope squeezed Cal's arm. "I know. I went through a divorce. It's nothing compared to what you're going through, but there were times when I just wanted someone with me. Not really to talk or do anything, just someone to be there. Someone I trusted."

"Who wouldn't blab to the gossip rags?"

"Exactly." Hope's divorce had made the gossip columns because her ex-husband decided her fifteen minutes of fame was the perfect launching pad for his new career. He went from financial adviser to reality TV star in the blink of an eye, trashing their marriage in the process. "You can trust me."

Cal covered Hope's hand with his and pressed firmly. "I know."

She wanted to be a good friend to Cal because he was a good person who was dealt a horrible hand. "How about some coffee or tea before you go?" She broke from Cal and started for the kitchen. "Have you eaten today? I can make you something."

"Brenda made an omelet for me."

Hope stopped. "Is she here?"

"She's running errands."

"I know this is a difficult time for you, but . . ." She hesitated to ask him about Lily's work on the P&Z Commission. Her mind was focused on solving the case and bringing the person responsible to justice, while Cal's focus was on planning his wife's funeral. How could she ask him questions?

"Hope, if you have something to ask me, go ahead. I'm an open book. Have been for weeks since Lily disappeared."

Hope chewed on her lower lip as she considered what to do. "Are you sure?"

He nodded. "Ask."

"Did you know how Lily was going to vote on Lionel Whitcomb's development? The one next to the Village Shopping Center?"

"No. She never discussed the projects brought before the board until after the vote. Do you think he had something to do with her murder?"

"I don't know. Did Lily discuss her work on the commission with anyone?"

"She talked about her work. She was proud of the houses she designed. But she was very quiet about the commission.

I guess it had to do with confidentiality and, to be honest, I really didn't ask a lot of questions about that part of her life." Regret flashed in his eyes. He'd never have the chance to ask her questions again.

Hope blinked back tears. "You talked to her about what really mattered to her. And she shared what was really important to her with you."

Cal scrubbed a hand over his face. "I'm not sure how to do this."

"Take it one day at a time."

"Sure." Cal glanced at his watch and shook his head. "I'm losing track of time. I have to meet with the funeral director."

"Of course. Before I leave, is there something you need help with?" After all, he did ask her to come over.

He scrubbed his face. "There is and I hate to ask. Lily needs an outfit. Would you mind selecting one for her?"

Hope's breath caught. Cal's request was unexpected and, honestly, a little awkward. She hadn't known Lily. The task of selecting the dress should have been done by someone closer, like her sister or best friend. "Are you sure?"

"I would ask Lily's sister, but I'm worried she won't be able to make it through the meeting with the funeral director. It would be a great help to me." He leaned forward and kissed her lightly on the cheek. "Please select the dress you think is appropriate. Our bedroom is at the end of the hall, left side. I need to get going."

"I'll make sure the front door is locked when I leave."

"Thank you." Cal walked out of the living room and, a moment later, she heard the front door close. Hope raised her hand and her fingertips touched the spot on her cheek where he'd kissed her. It was a friendly kiss. Just a peck between friends. So, why did the spot tingle with heat when his lips pressed against her skin?

She needed to get out of there. She didn't belong in the Barnhart house and definitely not in the bedroom. Besides, the thought of going through a dead woman's closet gave her a serious case of the woollies.

She swung around, determined to leave and not look back. She'd send him a text message and apologize for not being able to help. On her way out of the living room, she noticed a framed photograph of Cal and Lily on the coffee table. It wasn't there a few days earlier when Hope came in for coffee. He must've been going through photos, remembering their life together. They looked so happy in the photo. And Cal now looked so sad. How could she not help him?

She continued out of the living room and walked down the hallway, which led to the private quarters of the house. She opened the last door on the left and entered the master bedroom. Another wall of glass caught her attention first, followed by the expansive space of the room. It was huge. And like the public spaces of the house, the room was minimally furnished.

A king-size platform bed with a fabric upholstered headboard was the centerpiece of the room. Simple linens covered the bed, and two mirrored nightstands flanked either side of the mega-sized bed. Hope was drawn to the shiny and sparkly nightstand closest to her. She glided her hand over the beveled mirrored surface. Each drawer had a crystal pull. "Exquisite," she murmured.

Along the opposite wall of the floor-to-ceiling windows were two doors and a mirrored dresser with a charming shell inlay. She couldn't imagine the upkeep the furniture required. She'd be cleaning for hours every day. Shrugging off thoughts of housekeeping, she refocused on why she was there. She crossed the room and opened one door to find Lily's closet.

She stepped inside the closet. Smaller than she expected,

the space was well organized and tidy. Along one wall, clothing racks were hung at different levels and organized by garment type and color. Even all the hangers matched. Hope smiled. Lily was a kindred spirit. Shoe storage was built in at the deep end of the closet, while the wall opposite the hanging clothing was lined with shelves for folded garments and purses.

Lily's purse collection was minimal compared to Claire's collection. There were nine bags set atop a shelf. Nine. That was how many Claire had in black satchels alone. She couldn't imagine her sister surviving with only nine purses. She also couldn't imagine herself staying in the closet any longer than absolutely necessary.

She studied the clothing rack. A dress. Lily should be buried in a dress. Hope reached up and slid the hangers, studying each garment. One caught Hope's eye. A deep purple dress with a V-neckline and full skirt. She draped the dress over her arm and turned to the shoes. She chose a pair of nude pumps. Before she exited the closet, she stopped at the purses. Instinctively, she reached out to the snake print clutch but realized Lily didn't need a purse. As she returned the clutch to the shelf, she accidentally knocked over a tote and it fell to the floor. She scooped down to pick up the tote and noticed a small notebook had spilled out of the bag.

She heard footsteps outside the closet. She froze in place and listened. Footsteps again. "Cal?" she called out. Maybe he'd changed his mind about letting Hope select the outfit for Lily. When there was no answer, she called out again. Silence. She chided herself for being ridiculous. Her imagination was running wild. She scooped up the notebook and continued out of the closet.

She laid the dress and shoes on the bed, then dropped the two purses next to the dress. She opened the notebook and leafed through the pages.

Blank. All blank. Except for one page at the back of the notebook.

An address in the town of Westport, Connecticut, was scrawled on the page.

Westport was a coastal town located about an hour away from Jefferson and within commuting distance to New York City. Several of Hope's former magazine coworkers lived in Westport.

She flipped through the notebook again to make sure she hadn't missed something else written in the book. She hadn't. Except for the address, the notebook was blank. A little odd. Just one address. Why did Lily write it down? What was at that address? Did Lily go there? Was the address somehow connected to her disappearance and murder?

Hope debated on what to do with the notebook. Return it to the tote? Or take it and find out what was at the address? Since the house was probably searched when Lily disappeared, the police must not have considered the notebook and address of any importance. She slipped the notebook into her purse. She then grabbed Lily's tote and replaced it back in the closet. Could there be some other overlooked clues tucked away in the other purses? Just as she reached for the red satchel, she was interrupted by a creaking door. The little hairs on the back of her neck stood up, and a danger warning sounded loudly in her head.

There was someone in the house.

She had to get out of there.

Pulling the closet door closed behind her, she listened for other sounds, but there were none. Of course there weren't any noises. She was alone in the house. Her overactive imagination, combined with searching through a dead woman's closet, had her hearing danger where there wasn't any. If Jane could see her now.

"What on earth are you doing in Cal's bedroom?"

The unexpected voice of Cal's assistant caused Hope to jump and her hand covered her heart. "You startled me."

Brenda stood in the doorway, with her arms crossed over her chest and her shoulders squared. Displeasure was written all over her face. Her thin lips were pursed and her eyes cast a heavy dose of suspicion on Hope.

As Hope's pulse rate returned to normal after being scared out of her mind, she wondered how long Brenda had been lurking before she made herself visible.

"Why are you snooping?"

"I wasn't snooping." Technically she wasn't until she leafed through the notebook. "Cal asked me to select an outfit for Lily."

"He did? Why would he ask you? You didn't even know her."

Brenda's tone didn't encourage Hope to explain herself. "Perhaps you should ask him." She stepped forward. It was definitely time to go.

But Brenda blocked her. "I intend to protect Cal."

Weird vibes emanated off Brenda, and Hope sensed she was marking her territory, which had Hope asking herself if Brenda could have been involved in Lily's disappearance and death. Was Brenda in love with Cal and decided it was time he was all hers?

"Protect him from what?"

"From women like you who see an opportunity."

"I'm just a friend." Even though she didn't owe Brenda an explanation, she opted to try to diffuse the situation rather than escalate it. Brenda appeared to be a little unhinged. "If you don't mind stepping aside, I'd like to leave."

Brenda gave Hope one final look up and down before she stepped aside. Hope bolted out of the room and dashed down the hallway at warp speed. Visions of Brenda chasing her down the hall flashed in her mind and propelled her feet to move faster. She reached the front door and yanked it open.

Outside, she breathed a fresh gulp of air as she followed the path to the driveway. Against her better judgment, she glanced back at the house. She couldn't help but wonder if she had unknowingly inserted herself into a deadly love triangle.

# Chapter Fourteen

"Well, if this isn't a surprise." Donna Wilcox shaded her eyes with her gloved hand. Positioned precariously on a kneeling pad, she was knee-deep in spring planting. Empty plant flats were scattered around the garden bed and a bag of soil had toppled over, spilling out a small pile of rich, nutrient-dense soil. "I'm just cleaning up."

"I apologize for just dropping by, but I was on my way home and passing by your street." Hope wasn't lying. Arthur Lane was on her way home from Cal's house.

"It's good to see you." Donna stood and removed her gloves and gave Hope a big hug. "Looks like I'm very popular today."

Popular? The comment had Hope looking over Donna's shoulder and there was Drew standing next to a wheelbarrow, grinning like a Cheshire cat. He'd broken their agreement. She suppressed a frustrated sigh. She'd deal with him later.

"It's good to see you, too," Hope said.

"I'm so glad you stopped by. It's been too long. We all have so much to catch up on." Donna let go of Hope and she glanced at Drew. "Gosh, the last time you both were here was when you were just kids in high school. I'm so glad we never sold this place and just rented it instead. I can't imagine living in another house in Jefferson. All my memories are here. Come, I'm due a break."

She led her guests past the newly planted border of petunias to the back door. They passed through the ranch-style house out to the deck, where Donna told them to sit while she went inside for beverages.

Once the slider was shut, Hope leaned over the table. "What are you doing here?" she asked in a strained whisper. He hadn't parked his car in Donna's driveway. Sneaky.

Drew leaned forward. "My job."

"I thought we agreed I'd talk to her alone first."

"That doesn't work for me."

"Doesn't work for you? Seriously?"

"I need an exclusive interview. I need something for the front page. An interview with another commission member who could be a target of a killer will get me the front page." He glanced to the slider and then back to Hope. "Norrie's been kicking butt with her stories. I have to give something to my editor. Besides, I don't know why you're upset. It's not like it's your job to find the killer. You're a food blogger."

Hope cast a death glare at Drew and she could tell it was effective because he recoiled back into his chair and gone was the bravado on his face. "I see."

"Here's the lemonade." Donna stepped out of the house and onto the deck with a tray and set it on the table. She sat and served her guests their drinks. She seemed oblivious to the tension between Hope and Drew as she filled them in on her daughter's exciting career in Hollywood as a public relations specialist and her own divorce after thirty years.

Hope thought the breakdown of her own marriage, which was just over a year old when it ended, was rough, so she couldn't imagine what it was like for Donna after thirty years. All those years with the same person and suddenly to be on your own? Hope glanced around. It looked like

Donna landed well on her feet. She had her home, her garden was starting to come into bloom, and her excitement over her job as a patient advocate was contagious.

"Listen to me prattle on." Donna eased back into her chair. Her khaki capris and a floral short-sleeved shirt were smudged with dirt and her gray hair was pulled back into a ponytail. Her blue eyes beamed with life. Divorce looked good on Donna. "What's going on with you? Back home, too. I read your blog every day."

"It's been pretty amazing since I left Jefferson. But, I'm glad to be home." Hope sipped her lemonade. The tart and sweet liquid slid down her throat as she reflected on coming back to the place where she started. Resettling in Jefferson came with unique challenges. Some people thought she was settling, some people thought she was hiding out, and some people thought she'd finally come to her senses. Being back home was a lot like the lemonade, bitter some days, sweet other days.

"Your Gingerbread Muffin recipe you posted last Christmas was delicious. Don't get me started on your vegetable lasagna. Perfect for Christmas Eve. Thank you."

"You're welcome. I'm starting to work on the post for this coming Christmas."

"It's nearly eighty-five degrees. I can't imagine thinking about Christmas now." Donna laughed and then took a drink of her lemonade. "What about you, Drew? You're working at the *Gazette*, right?"

Drew nodded. "I'm a reporter."

"Good for you. I read an article in the paper about Peggy Olson's fire." Donna set her glass on the table and looked at Hope. "Terrible thing. She was a kind woman and your neighbor, right? I can't believe they found Lily Barnhart's body in her house. She'd been missing for weeks. How did she end up there?"

Hope shrugged. "Good question. Since you're on the

P&Z Commission, do you know if anyone had a problem with Lily?"

Donna stared off to her garden for a few moments before answering. "The only person I can think of is Hans Vogel. He was very upset at the last meeting. Lily did overstep her bounds by lecturing him, and he didn't take it well."

"That was unusual for her, wasn't it?" Drew asked.

"Yes, but she had her reasons."

Drew set his glass down. "And they were?"

Donna refilled her glass and offered to top off her guests' glasses, but Hope and Drew both declined. "Lily grew up in the house next door to Hans's. She told me she remembered the Vogels and how Mrs. Vogel always maintained a neat and tidy home and yard. Mrs. Vogel loved black-eyed Susans and planted a row of them one spring. Then when Mrs. Vogel passed, Hans let the property go to pot. He let junk pile up and didn't take care of the house. I think Lily felt it was disrespectful to Mrs. Vogel."

"I can understand that. I heard Lionel Whitcomb didn't receive the go-ahead to break ground for his medical office development," Hope said.

"We just want more information before we make a decision."

"In the past he's gotten the green light right away for his projects. How did he take the delay imposed upon him for this new development?" Drew asked.

"He was upset. Why are you two asking these questions?" Donna asked.

"I'm just curious." Hope took a sip of lemonade.

"Have you received any threats since those hearings?" Drew pulled out his phone and tapped on the power button.

"Drew." Hope leaned forward. "I don't think this is the time."

Drew didn't make eye contact with Hope. He kept his gaze locked on Donna. "I'd like your permission to record the rest of this conversation." Drew was waiting to press the on button.

"Record? Why? No!" Donna's blue eyes clouded with confusion. "What's going on? Do you think our work on the board caused Lily's death? Do you think we're in danger?"

"Oh . . . he didn't say that." Hope cast a second death glare at Drew.

"But you think that? That's why you're here." Donna looked ready to leap into defense mode. "You hear stories about this kind of thing, but you never think it'll happen where you live."

"Donna, please. I didn't mean to alarm you. I was just curious. If you haven't received any threats, then I think Lily's death wasn't related to the P&Z Commission." Hope reached out her hand and covered Donna's hand. "You haven't received any threats, right?"

Donna exhaled a deep breath. "No." But worry still filled her eyes. "Drew, you're not going to quote me for an article, are you?"

He frowned and tapped his phone again. "No. If that's what you prefer."

"That's what I prefer. Thank you for stopping by to visit. It was good to see you both."

Hope took her cue to leave and jerked her head for Drew to follow suit. They both stood and thanked Donna again for the lemonade. They stepped off the deck and walked in silence along the grass to the driveway. Hope's pace was faster than Drew's, primarily powered by her annoyance at him. He'd spooked Donna. Even though she'd said she hadn't been threatened, there was a chance she could have told them more.

"Hope! Wait up. Let me explain!"

She ignored him. Though she couldn't ignore the familiar car parked in the driveway or its driver, who was leaning against the hood.

"What are you doing here, Norrie? Are you following me?" For the second time in as many days, Norrie had shown up where Hope was. Was it a mere coincidence?

"Is this how you're getting your stories, Drew? You tag along with your friend?" Norrie asked, smirking.

Drew's eyes widened with outrage. "I don't tag along with anybody. How I get my stories is none of your business."

Hope considered telling him to fact-check that statement because he did kind of tag along, even though he got to Donna's house first. But she wasn't about say that in front of Norrie, no matter how miffed she was at Drew.

"You didn't answer my question," Hope said.

Norrie shrugged her shoulders. "I'm here to talk to Mrs. Wilcox, not the two of you."

"What for?"

"You'll find out when you read my article." Norrie pushed off from the car and started to walk up Donna's gravel driveway. "It'll be on the front page so you can't miss it."

"You see what I'm dealing with?" Drew asked in a whisper.

"You'll figure something out. I'm going home to work on my blog because that's what I am, a blogger." She walked to her car and pulled the driver's door open. She slid in behind the steering wheel.

Drew threw his arms up in the air. "I didn't mean it that way!"

Hope closed the door and started the ignition. She backed out of the driveway. A quick glance up to the rearview mirror showed Drew standing in the driveway alone. Good. Let him think about what he'd done. It wasn't the first time he put a story ahead of their friendship. But she didn't want to focus her energy on Drew. There was a killer still on the loose and that needed all of her attention. The one good thing she'd learned from the visit with Donna was that it appeared no one else on the P&Z Commission was in danger.

The killer was only after Lily, and Hope concluded Peggy was in the wrong place at the wrong time. That should have been some comfort for Hope, but it wasn't. If she'd called Meg right away then either Peggy would have been removed from the house or Meg would have either stayed or hired someone and most likely Lily's body would have been discovered.

Hope flicked on her turn signal. Where was Lily's body hidden in the house? Had she been dead the whole time? If so, how come there wasn't any odor? Hope certainly didn't smell anything other than the burnt peppers and onions when she was in the house the last time. If Lily was alive, was she tied up somewhere? If so, the killer had to have been taking care of her. But Peggy didn't mention seeing anyone else in her house. Just when she thought she'd gotten some answers, more questions popped up.

The timer dinged, signaling the baking was done. Hope grabbed two pot holders and prepared to be amazed. She loved her job. Food blogging was more than just writing five hundred words and adding a recipe at the bottom of the post. Every post she wrote came from her heart and soul. Food blogging was the documentation of countless trips down memory lane with her family, where food was shared to celebrate or to comfort. Food blogging was where she journaled the adventure of creating recipes, successes and failures. In a nutshell, her blog was where she shared her joy of serving meals to the people she loved.

With the pot holders in hand she pulled three cake pans from the oven and set them on cooling racks. Her eyes fluttered closed as she inhaled the heavenly aroma of hot-out-of-the-oven chocolate cake. She loved her job.

She really loved her job.

"Knock! Knock!" Jane called out as she entered through

the mudroom. She bustled in with her big purse, with Drew behind her. "I smell chocolate cake."

"Good grief. There goes my waistline." Drew dropped his messenger bag on a chair at the table. He approached Hope with the saddest puppy dog eyes she'd ever seen. Even his pout was sadder than usual. "Hope, I'm truly sorry for what I said about you being only a blogger. I didn't mean it."

Hope set the pot holders on the island, then rested one hand on her hip and glowered at Drew.

"What is going on between the two of you?" Jane asked. "What on earth did you say about Hope?"

"I went to visit Donna Wilcox," Drew said.

Jane's pale blue eyes narrowed as her confusion was starting to clear up. "I thought we all agreed Hope would speak with her first."

"We did. But I really need something to wow my editor. Right now, I'm barely showing up below the fold." Drew's cocky attitude from earlier had faded. "I can't lose my job. I don't have the kind of résumé a big city newspaper is looking for and, besides, Jefferson is my home. I can't leave."

Jane studied Drew for a few moments and then turned to Hope. "He's truly remorseful. Go on, forgive the poor boy."

Hope's hand dropped from her hip. "Fine. I forgive you."

Drew's face brightened and he ran to her and wrapped her in the biggest hug ever. "Thank you. Thank you. Thank you."

Hope's arms were pinned to her side. "You're welcome . . . I can't breathe."

"Oh, sorry." Drew let go of Hope. "I'm starving. What's for dinner?"

"Chicken and wild rice casserole." Hope glanced at the lower oven. During her drive home, she'd run through a list of dinner ideas. She craved comfort food. Spending part of her day in a dead woman's closet selecting a dress for her to wear had overwhelmed Hope, and it wasn't until she pulled into her driveway that the grief slammed into her. A heaping bowl of mac 'n' cheese or a thick slab of meat loaf would hit the spot. Short on time, she opted for her tried-and-true chicken casserole. The dish was easy and fast.

"One of my favorite dishes you make." Jane sat at the table just as Bigelow ran into the kitchen at full speed, coming to an abrupt stop at Jane's feet. "What a cutie pie." Jane patted the dog's head.

Hope rested a hand on her hip. Where was that dog-training book? Chapter three covered running inside and she needed to reread it. "He has to learn not to run in the house."

"He's just energetic. Give him time to mature," Jane assured Hope.

Bigelow settled by Jane's chair and lowered his head onto his front paws.

Hope raised an eyebrow to Jane's statement. Bigelow had boundless energy and showed little sign of maturing anytime soon. When the oven timer buzzed, Hope grabbed the pot holders and pulled out the Le Creuset skillet. She set the hot dish on a trivet and covered it with a sheet of aluminum foil. "This needs to rest for a few minutes. Drew, could you slice the ciabatta bread while I set the table?"

"Sure." Drew slid out a serrated knife from the block on the counter and sliced the long loaf of bread. "So, how did the rest of your day go? Tell me you have something I can use for the paper."

"Cal texted me and asked me to come over. I was at his house before I showed up at Donna's." Hope folded three cloth napkins and set them next to each place setting.

"Why didn't you tell me earlier?" Drew carried the basket of sliced bread to the table and sat.

"Excuse me?" After the stunt Drew pulled at Donna's house, she wasn't sure she'd be updating him with her whereabouts anytime soon.

Drew offered a half-shrug. "Sorry. What did he want?"

"He asked me to select a dress for Lily." Hope returned to the island and checked their dinner. It needed a few more minutes and then she could serve her guests. She secretly hoped they weren't too hungry because she loved the leftovers of the casserole.

Jane lowered her head. "Tsk. Tsk. Such a tragic situation."

"While I was in her closet, I accidentally knocked down a couple of her purses and this fell out of one of them." Hope snatched the notebook off the island and brought it to the table. "There's only one thing written in this notebook."

"What? What did you find?" Drew reached across the table and tried to snatch the notebook out of Hope's hand, but she pulled it close to her chest. "Come on!"

"It's an address in Westport." Hope flipped open the book and showed the page to Jane and Drew.

"How mysterious," Jane commented, and stood. She went to the refrigerator, took out a pitcher of water, and then returned to the table.

"Nothing else?" Drew slouched back into his chair.

"This could be important. Now, I took the notebook, but I didn't tell Cal about this. I probably should tell Ethan. Though, the police must've searched the residence when she disappeared, so either they missed it or they didn't think it was important."

"My guess is a thorough search wasn't done," Jane offered.

"Or, someone hid the notebook in there after Lily disappeared," Drew speculated. "I can track down this address. I'll get back to you on this. If we're lucky, it's a lead. Or it could be a dead end, like every other angle I've tried." Drew typed the address into his phone and then stood. "I'm going to wash up before supper." He trudged out of the kitchen.

Bigelow's head swung up and then he popped up and trotted after Drew.

"Poor Drew. That Norrie girl has him doubting his own abilities." Jane helped herself to a slice of bread.

"I think a little competition with Norrie is a good thing for Drew." Hope moved to the counter and removed the aluminum foil from the casserole. With pot holders, she carried the skillet to the table.

"I suppose you're right. It's never good to get too comfortable. We must always be reaching for a new goal. Like the cookbook you're contributing to. It's very exciting. Who knows, it may lead to your own cookbook one day." Jane's eyes beamed at the golden dish of chicken and wild rice topped with sliced almonds and loaded with melted Swiss cheese.

"I have to admit, it is a little exciting. And a lot nerve-racking." Hope spooned a large portion onto Jane's plate.

"The address you found is very curious."

"There's more." Hope filled Jane in on her weird encounter with Brenda as she scooped out servings for Drew and herself.

"She sounds like she's in love with Cal and sees you as a threat. Love can easily turn to murder." Jane bit into a forkful of the casserole.

Hope stared at Jane as chills skittered along her arms. Had Hope just been alone, face-to-face with the killer?

# Chapter Fifteen

Hope entered the lobby of the Jefferson Country Club. The automatic door slid closed behind her. Kent Wilder, the real estate agent who had desperately wanted to represent Lionel Whitcomb, was somewhere in the club. It was amazing how eager Kent's secretary had been to share his whereabouts after Hope produced a box of Lemon Ricotta Cookies. Extras were always a good thing to have handy.

She scanned the club. Members passed by her, busy chatting and hurrying off to their golf carts or to the tennis courts. A comfortable seating area was off to her left and included a towering stone fireplace. To her right, the dining room's waitstaff were busily preparing for the lunch crowd. Out of the corner of her eye, she spotted Kent walking in her direction from a hallway. He looked crisp in a pink and white polo shirt paired with khaki trousers. As he approached, he adjusted the white visor he wore.

"Hope? What are you doing here? Thinking of joining?" He flashed his trademark smile. The same smile he had when he showed Hope a house for sale that was a total money pit. He played her emotions like a violinist on a Stradivarius, all the while knowing she'd go broke trying to make the house livable. But it did have charm. Claire had intervened just in time and talked Hope out of the purchase. The house was later condemned.

"Maybe. You've been a member for a while. How do you like it?"

"It's adequate. But for a real golf experience, there's an awesome club down in Florida. Though, for a beginner like yourself, this place is good enough."

"Thanks for the tip. I think learning to play will help me relax. It's been stressful these past days with everything happening in town. You must feel the same way." She'd hoped he'd agree and she could then guide their conversation to the direction of Lionel Whitcomb.

Kent's gaze shifted to over Hope's shoulder and she turned her head to see what had caught his attention. Three men, all dressed for a day of golf and carrying gym bags, were approaching. So much for guiding him into a conversation. "Yeah, good idea. I hate to rush off, but I'm meeting people." He hurried past her to join the three men. A few slaps on the back and the four of them headed to the lounge area.

"Wait!" The loudness of her voice surprised her, but it did get Kent's attention. He stopped and looked over his shoulder. With her voice a little lower, she asked, "Is it true you're trying to get the listing for Lionel Whitcomb's new commercial development?"

"Why do you want to know?"

"Someone who wants the listing and its sales commission may be willing to do anything to make sure it was approved for development."

Kent stalked back to her. His trademark smile was gone and in its place was a hardened look that made her question her decision to confront Kent. He stood ramrod straight and towered over Hope. A slight curl to his hips indicated his height advantage over her bolstered his ego. "Do you have any idea of what you're implying?"

She swallowed. She wouldn't be intimidated by Kent. "Yes."

"Good. Then if I hear you've repeated this to anyone, I will sue you for slander. Do you understand me?"

"Come on, Kent!" one of the three men called out.

Kent looked over his shoulder and nodded. Before he broke away to join his friends, he looked back at Hope and stared at her for a long moment. She fortified her stance and met his gaze. He gave a curt nod and then stepped away, back to his buddies.

Kent went from uninterested to infuriated in a matter of minutes. Quick to temper. Now she was even more curious about how far he would have gone to secure the listing. The chances of him talking to her anymore were slim, actually slimmer than slim, and he'd probably call his attorney if she approached him with more questions. Her work there was done.

She spun around and started for the exit but was intercepted by a young man wearing a baggy, dark navy blazer with the club's logo embroidered on the breast pocket.

"Miss Early, so good to see you." He held out his hand for Hope to shake. "I am Eli Wheeler. Would you be here for a tour? There are many amenities available to members, including privacy, something a celebrity like yourself may be interested in."

Celebrity? Hope's fifteen minutes of fame was over a long time ago, but she guessed once in the spotlight, always in the spotlight. Of course, the club representative must have associated celebrity status with wealth. Eli would be disappointed to learn Hope's brief stint on television didn't pad her bank account. She received a meager runner-up check. Her divorce drained most of her savings and her home was mortgaged to the hilt. She was far from wealthy.

"Actually, I came to see one of your members. Kent Wilder."

Eli's mouth twitched and he broke eye contact with Hope

for a moment. She sensed he had a less than favorable opinion of Kent. And she wanted to know what it was. There was a way to encourage him to talk, but it would be wrong. Sort of. However, if what Eli knew could help solve the murders, then using the only tool available to her wouldn't be so terrible.

"It was nice meeting you, Eli. I don't think this club is right for me. If you have one troublesome member, who knows how many more you have, and you're right, I'm looking for privacy and a peaceful environment." She adjusted the strap of her purse on her shoulder and made like she was stepping forward, very, very slowly, all the while hoping her ruse worked.

"I assure you we don't have troublesome members." Eli shuffled next to Hope. He wasn't about to let her get away. His eagerness to sell Hope a membership was written all over his thin face. "Mr. Wilder has been dealt with."

*Ah-ha!* Hope contained her excitement. She was right in reading Eli. Maybe she was getting the hang of this sleuth thing.

"How bad was the infraction?" Hope asked in a whisper.

Eli leaned forward and in a low voice said, "Our members come here to relax. Take in a round of golf, have a nice meal or drinks with friends. They do not come here to be hounded."

"He hounded someone?"

Eli nodded cautiously.

"Let me guess. Lionel Whitcomb."

Eli's eyes widened in surprise at Hope's accurate guess.

"I know Kent is a real estate agent and Lionel is a developer." Truth be told, Kent was an aggressive real estate agent who considered the death of a colleague a few months ago as a bonus for his bottom line.

"I can't spread gossip," Eli said.

"Of course not. I appreciate your discretion."

"Thank you. Now, if you'd like a tour, I'd be happy to show you around."

Tour? Right. Eli was under the impression Hope wanted to join the club. "Perhaps another time. I'm running late for an appointment." Hope stepped away from Eli, who looked disappointed he wasn't going to sign a new member. Even though guilt tugged at her, she stood firm with her answer.

She continued to the exit, her mind replaying the two conversations she'd had. The distraction of dissecting Kent's words caused Hope to miss the person approaching her, but the woman's voice stopped her in her tracks.

"What are *you* doing here?" Elaine Whitcomb stopped and placed one hand on her hip, jutting the other out. Her bright red wrap dress was tied snugly around her waist, and she could've used a little fashion tape at the plunging neckline, which revealed a lot of cleavage for daytime. Her golden blond hair was styled and sprayed to stay in place and her makeup was flawless, highlighting pouty full lips and high cheekbones.

Hope ignored Elaine's less-than-friendly tone. "Hello, Elaine. It's good to see you."

Despite living in a small town, they'd managed to avoid each other for several weeks, but it was only a matter of time before they'd run into each other. At the beginning of spring, Elaine had unfriended, unfollowed, and unsubscribed from all of Hope's social media after she accused Hope of snooping around her house. Hope hadn't been searching the house. She was trying to find the bathroom in the Whitcombs' mansion and got lost. It was hard to build a friendship on that foundation.

"I can't say the same."

"I didn't expect you to. I've already apologized and I do hope someday you'll accept the apology because I meant it." Hope wasn't going to beg Elaine to be her friend, even though she knew the trophy wife needed one. Most of the women in town didn't trust the flirty blonde and if Hope had a husband, she'd be cautious too. Maybe one day they'd be friends.

"This is a private club so you should leave before I inform Eli." Elaine tilted her head and stared Hope down. Her four-inch stilettos put Hope at a height disadvantage.

"Actually, I was just discussing a membership with Eli." Hope couldn't help herself because Elaine's smugness was reaching a level that needed to be knocked down a tad.

"What? How could . . ." Elaine sputtered.

Her husband arrived by her side and wrapped an arm around her waist. His beady eyes zoomed in on Hope. "What the hell are you doing here?" Lionel Whitcomb wasn't known for small talk. Rather, he was known to be rude, impatient, and bossy. His short-sleeved shirt revealed chubby, hairy arms, and his black pants pooled at his dull loafers. He couldn't even get his pants hemmed? Lionel in no way looked like the successful businessman he was. His thinning hair was combed over and heavy, bushy eyebrows rimmed his angry eyes. What did Elaine see in him? Oh, right, he was wealthy. From her time in New York City, Hope knew some women could and would look past a lot of flaws as long as the credit card had a high limit.

"Can you believe they're going to let her join?" Elaine squealed, almost showing a hint of outrage on her heavily injected face.

"She ain't joining." Lionel pointed a stubby finger at Hope. "I pay a lot of money to this club. And I have a lot of weight around here."

Elaine closed the small space between her and Lionel and patted his chest. "My husband is a powerful man."

"Yet, the P&Z Commission didn't give his commercial development their stamp of approval. From what I heard, Lily Barnhart was undecided. There was a chance she would have voted 'no.' I wonder what's going to happen now that she's gone."

Lionel untangled himself from his wife. "Are you imply-ing I had something to do with her death?" His voice was loud and harsh and caused people to look in their direction.

"Honey, you have to watch your blood pressure. Don't let her upset you. She's just a busybody."

"She's something, all right." Lionel stormed off toward the lounge, leaving his wife and Hope alone.

Elaine crossed her arms over her ample chest. "You're a busybody. Maybe I should tweet it since you're such a social media butterfly with your blog. Hope Early, pound sign busybody."

"Hashtag," Hope corrected. "It's a hashtag on social media."

Elaine blinked. She guessed Elaine was confused but, since her face was as tight as a drum, there weren't any facial expressions to decipher.

Hope shook her head. She didn't have the time nor the inclination to school Elaine on how social media worked. "Good-bye." She passed the trophy wife and headed for the exit.

The afternoon had warmed and a hint of humidity landed on her when she stepped outside. She followed the curvy path bordered with lush, fragrant flowers. The dense plant-ings attracted butterflies and bees and provided coverage for a chipmunk who nearly cut Hope off as it darted across the path.

After she regained her footing, she pulled out her cell phone. The garden beds were perfectly balanced between color and definition and the mix of shapes and sizes was genius. Just the inspiration she needed for her garden. She took several photos and then continued to the parking lot.

She had stepped off the curb and was walking toward her

car when her ears perked up at the sound of laughter. She looked over her shoulder, in the direction of the sound, in time to see a man slap Everett Cranston on the back. Everett was in the middle of two men and glanced in her direction. She waved, but he didn't acknowledge her. Before she could approach him, a horn blared, startling her. A sedan had stopped just a few feet away from her. She was blocking traffic. She waved and said sorry, though the driver probably didn't hear her. She moved out of the way and, by the time the car had passed, Everett had disappeared into the club. Not wanting to risk another run-in with Kent or the Whitcombs, she shoved her phone back into her purse and continued to her car. She dug into her purse for her key fob and unlocked the door. She slid behind the wheel. Her next stop was home.

Her cell phone buzzed, and she reached into her purse to pull the phone out. She glanced at the message. It was from a contact at a local cooking magazine confirming a feature in an upcoming issue. An e-mail with details would follow.

Hope smiled. Being featured in *Cooking Now!* magazine would be a big boost to her blog. The magazine had a reputation for only publishing recipes from established food writers or professionals. They rarely featured bloggers. She squeezed her eyes shut and savored the moment.

Her moment of revelation was shattered when someone struck the driver's-side window. She jumped as her head snapped around to the window.

Lionel was standing outside her vehicle, glowering at her.

With a shaky hand, she pressed the window's power button and the window lowered. "What's the matter with you? Sneaking up on me and hitting my window."

"Listen, lady. I'm gonna give you a piece of advice. Mind your business or you'll be sorry."

Her heart was still racing but she managed to steady her nerves. "Sounds more like a threat than a piece of advice."

He grunted as he turned away and marched back to the country club. Hope leaned back into the headrest and took in several deep breaths. *What the hell was that all about?*

# Chapter Sixteen

Hope pressed the delete key hard on her laptop computer until the long string of words she'd just typed disappeared. Rereading the words, she had no choice but to admit they were forced and contrived and definitely not her. With the sentence gone, she fell back into her chair and stared at the laptop screen. Her lips pressed together in frustration. She wanted to shut the computer off and go soak in a bath. But she couldn't. She had work to do. She released her shoulder-length dark hair from its elastic band and ran her fingers through her hair. What she'd give for a salon shampoo. The vigorous massage of the stylist's fingertips on her scalp, the extra-long rinse of pulsating water, and the gentle rub of a fluffy towel. Between her blog and the home renovation, she took whatever pampering she could squeeze into her schedule. And a little bit of pampering would have felt good right about then.

Maybe she should play hooky and dash off for the salon since she couldn't concentrate on the post she was supposed to be writing. Her mind was distracted by recent events and what lay ahead in the coming days. There would be two funerals, a tea party for Maretta and a panel discussion at the library, and two recipes were due for a cookbook she had little enthusiasm for. Not to mention Lionel's threat veiled as a piece of advice. No wonder she couldn't concentrate.

She straightened up, gathered her hair back into the elastic, and put her fingers back on the keyboard. Time to work.

"There are days when the last thing I want to do is cook. Yes, you read correctly. It's a little-known secret among food bloggers. We enjoy an evening of take-out. I've found those are the precise moments when I need to tie on an apron and pull out a mixing bowl and get to work. The simple ease of gathering ingredients and turning them into a nourishing meal helps clear my mind and somehow rights whatever I felt was off."

Hope's fingers flew at record speed as she continued to write. Inspiration had sparked and she did her best to keep up with the flow of words spilling out of her head, until her mind drifted back to the two deaths.

She stopped typing.

Darn it.

She just needed to finish the post. Just a few hundred more words.

With her fingers repositioned on the keyboard, she began typing.

"Perhaps it's the familiar rhythm of cooking that settles my mind when it's racing a mile a minute with thoughts. Thoughts like could Kent Wilder be so ambitious that he would kill two women?"

Hope stopped typing and huffed.

She repositioned her fingers on the keyboard and started typing again.

"There is also comfort found in making recipes given to me from my mother, grandmother, and aunts. We share the same blood, the same genes, and the same moments in our kitchens cooking for our loved ones. While we cooked in different eras, we all shared the same experience of tying on an apron and preparing the recipes the exact same way. A connection to my past. Was there a connection between Kent and Lionel Whitcomb? Could she find out?"

Hope huffed louder as her fingers stopped typing. It was no use. She couldn't focus on her post. She might as well set the work aside until her mind was cleared. She stood and walked to her office to retrieve a composition notebook.

Years ago, when Hope was a member of the mystery book readers club at the library, led by Jane, she used a notebook to jot down notes on the story she was reading. Because she was so involved with the story, she usually deduced the killer before anyone else in the group did.

Back at the table, she pushed aside the computer and opened the notebook. She wrote a list of names—Kent, Hans Vogel, Lionel Whitcomb, Cal. Four men who could've had a reason to kill Lily.

A knock at the back door was followed by Bigelow's deep bark. The dog leapt from his bed and dashed to the mudroom. She closed the notebook, then stood to chase after her dog. She seemed to be doing a lot of that since she adopted him. Through the glass in her mudroom door, she spotted two of her neighbors. Once she shooed Bigelow back, she opened the door.

"Hi, Hope," Dorie Baxter and Leila Manchester said in unison. Both women were dressed for their daily walk, which normally didn't include a stop at Hope's house.

"What brings you ladies by?" Hope tugged on Bigelow's collar to keep him from jumping on her neighbors.

"We're not catching you at a bad time, are we?" Leila stepped over the threshold.

"Well . . ." Hope struggled with Bigelow, who was determined to break free of her hold and greet their visitors.

"Oh my, he's very friendly." Dorie followed her walking buddy into the mudroom and was on the receiving end of a playful jump from Bigelow.

"No!" Hope grabbed hold of the dog again and gave him a command to sit. She needed to repeat it twice more before he listened and sat. "I'm sorry. We're still working on his training."

"Not an A student?" Leila reached down and patted the dog's head.

Hope shook her head. Bigelow was far from an A. In fact, she doubted he rated a D at that point. With her pup under control, she shifted her attention back to her neighbors. "What brings you two by during your walk?"

"It's so awful what happened the other night. None of us can believe Peggy is gone." Dorie shoved her hands into her pants pockets. Her lightweight trousers were paired with khaki walking shoes and a bright yellow T-shirt. She was the model for active seniors. She swam twice a week at the gym and took yoga classes three times a week and supplemented those activities with long walks.

"You're doing such a lovely job with this house." Leila didn't seem to share Dorie's concern with the fire. She seemed more interested in Hope's remodeling. She walked past Hope and Dorie and continued into the kitchen. It appeared Leila wasn't one to stand on formalities, like being invited in.

Hope let go of Bigelow's collar and allowed him to follow Leila. She then gestured to Dorie to enter the kitchen.

"Simply lovely." Leila hesitated for a moment when the floor creaked.

"The pumpkin pine flooring is over a hundred years old,

so it's a little creaky." Topping Hope's wish list when she made the offer on the house was to replace the uninspired flooring in the kitchen and family room once those two rooms were joined together. On a weekend trip up to Vermont just weeks after buying the house, she found the antique floorboards and had them shipped to Connecticut. That was just one of the many buying excursions she'd made since moving back to Jefferson. She spent countless Saturdays at flea markets and tag sales looking for pre-loved treasures to add to her home.

"This is beautiful." Dorie approached the giant side-by-side stainless steel refrigerator. "I wish I was thirty years younger and had your energy. I think I'd have a blog too."

Leila walked around the island and stood beside the table. She propped her hands on her hips and took in the entirety of the space. Hope couldn't help but join her in scanning the room. Every day she wanted to pinch herself to make sure it wasn't all a dream. The fireplace, complete with a cooking hearth, stood solid and proud. It dated back to the original homeowner and the mantel was crafted from reclaimed wood taken from a home built in the eighteenth century. The row of twelve over twelve paned windows on the south side of the room looked out onto the property's three acres. The room, the house was everything she dreamed of when she decided to come back to Jefferson.

"I've been following your progress on the house on your blog. When do you ever find time to sleep?" Leila looked back at Hope. Her cheeks were dotted with pink blush she hadn't blended well, while her rose-colored lipstick bled into the fine lines of her upper lip. It seemed she never left the house without being made up, even for a power walk.

Not giving Hope time to answer Leila's question, Dorie stepped forward. "It's so hard to believe something so terrible happened the other night. Why on earth was Lily Barnhart in Peggy's house?"

"The police are trying to find that out." Hope considered offering tea to her unexpected visitors, but she did have work to do and they had a walk to take.

"What has Chief Cahill told you?" Dorie asked.

"Nothing," Hope answered.

Both Dorie and Leila cast dubious looks her way.

"Really. It's an ongoing investigation so he can't talk about it."

"It just seems like he spends so much time here . . ." Leila left the rest of the sentence unspoken since it was clear as crystal what she was alluding to.

"We're just friends," Hope said.

"There's nothing to be ashamed about. You're both consenting adults." Leila winked.

Hope's cheeks warmed. Good grief, she was blushing.

"We're not trying to pry into your private business." The grin on Dorie's face contradicted what she'd just said.

"I don't have any private business." What was Hope doing? She didn't need to defend her personal life or lack thereof to Dorie or Leila.

"Certainly your ex doesn't have any private business. He's flaunting his model girlfriend all over town." Leila's lips pursed in disapproval.

Hope inwardly cringed. Her neighbors read those gossip websites? There was barely an ounce of truth to any of the stories those sites published. Since her time on *The Sweet Taste of Success,* she'd been often asked if she would do it again. Some days her answer was a firm "no" and other days it was a definite "yes." There, looking at her two inquisitive neighbors who knew all about her ex-husband's dating exploits because she went on national television to bake some cupcakes and pies, her answer would be a firm "hell no." Unfortunately, there weren't any do-overs in life. She had made her choice and she had to deal with the consequences.

"What Tim does is no longer my concern." Letting go of

the idea that she could control Tim's behavior was one way Hope was dealing with the consequences.

"Darn right." Leila nodded, and her dyed black hair cut shoulder length bounced. "I got rid of husband number one years ago and never looked back. He was nothing but bad news. Maybe sometimes it takes a second try to find your true love. I know it did for me."

"We didn't come over to discuss your love life," Dorie interjected. "We wanted to talk to you about starting some kind of neighborhood watch."

Leila joined Dorie at the island. "With what happened at Peggy's house and Dorie's break-in—"

"You had a break-in?" Hope interrupted.

Dorie's head bobbed up and down. "A few weeks ago. We went away for a couple days and when we got back, we found someone had broken in through the kitchen door."

"I didn't know." Hope rested her hands on the island. First a break-in and then a fire. It appeared her road was a bit unlucky. "Was anything taken?"

"No. If the door hadn't been damaged, we wouldn't have known someone came into our house."

"Why would someone go through the trouble of breaking into a house to take nothing? Perhaps something scared him off," Hope suggested.

Dorie shrugged her shoulders. "Maybe."

"When exactly did it happen?"

Dorie looked thoughtful. "Let me see if I can remember."

Leila rolled her eyes. "Really, Dorie, it's not so hard to remember. You and Harold left the morning Lily Barnhart disappeared. I remember because when I heard that she'd gone missing, that night I went to call you but remembered you'd left town."

"That's right." Dorie sounded confident. "Anyway, let us know if you're interested in the neighborhood watch. We're planning on having a meeting and we're going to ask a police officer to join us." Dorie turned to Leila. "We should get going. I have to feed Princess."

"Peggy's cat?" Hope had forgotten about the white stray Peggy took in months ago. She didn't see the cat when she went over to turn off the smoke detector.

"I've been cat sitting since Peggy went into rehab. Meg is allergic, so I volunteered to keep her. My husband is also allergic, so the poor thing is relegated to the sunroom. Thank goodness I didn't have the chance to return her to Peggy or she could have perished in the fire. She's a love."

"Come on. We have to get our three miles in." Leila was already on her way to the back door.

Dorie said good-bye and followed her friend out of the house.

Hope turned to go back to the table but stopped and pivoted. Considering what Dorie had just said about her break-in, Hope decided to err on the side of caution. She went to lock the back door. She returned to the table, pushed the notebook to the side, and pulled the computer toward her. She should be working rather than brainstorming theories of the murder. She stared at the computer screen and tapped her fingers on the table. There was no way she could concentrate on work.

She reached for the notebook and flipped open the page with the list of names.

"'We share the same blood, the same genes, and the same moments cooking for our loved ones,'" Drew read aloud from Hope's computer.

"Hey! What do you think you're doing?" Hope closed the refrigerator door and frowned at Drew. "Why are you reading my post?"

Drew had dropped in after the senior walkers left and he

was famished, as usual. Hope reheated leftovers from recipe testing—grilled chicken and roasted potatoes. She was trying a new spice rub on the chicken and she had finally found a combination she liked.

Drew lifted his head and held a cupped hand to his ear. "Do you hear that?"

Hope set the plate in the microwave and pressed the start button. "Hear what?"

"The crashing of traffic to your blog if you publish this. What are you thinking? You're supposed to be writing about food and recipes. Not ancestry. It's *Hope at Home*, not *Hope's Blog of Family History Boredom*."

Ouch. Hope was never one to shy away from constructive criticism, but Drew had just leveled some pretty harsh feedback at her post. "It's a work in progress."

"Take my advice, stop the progress."

"Like you're an expert?"

"Well, I do know something about writing attention-grabbing copy. It's my job as a reporter."

"Right," Hope conceded. His feedback was accurate. Her prose was too flowery and boring. She'd have to delete the whole mess and start over again. "Do you want to tell me why you stopped by?" The microwave beeped and she retrieved the plate and took it to the table. She set the plate down and shifted her computer from Drew's view. She'd had her quota of criticism and advice for the day.

"Only after you tell me why you have a composition notebook out." Drew pierced a chunk of potato with his fork. He swallowed his mouthful. "Leftovers make the best lunches."

"Yes, they do." Hope sat across from Drew. Maybe she should work on a series about leftovers. Cook once, eat twice. Of course, the leftover meal wouldn't just be a warmed plate of the same meal served the night before.

That would be as boring as the words she'd just typed. No, she'd have to create a second way to serve the meal without requiring too much work but just enough to make it a little different.

Drew snapped his fingers. "Earth to Hope."

"Oh, sorry. I was thinking of an idea for a new series on the blog."

Drew raised a questioning eyebrow.

"It has nothing to do with my family tree."

"Good."

"Why are you here?"

Drew's eyes twinkled. Hope knew that look. He had something juicy to share. He set his fork down and took a drink from his water glass. Then he dabbed the sides of his mouth with a napkin. He then carefully folded and replaced the napkin on his lap.

"Would you just tell me," Hope ordered.

Drew became slightly deflated. "You're no fun. But I'll still tell you. I tracked down the address from Lily's notebook."

Hope perked up. "You did?"

Drew gave an exaggerated nod. "I did. It's called the Day Spa in Town."

"A day spa?" The surge of adrenaline that had pumped through her body a moment ago dissipated. She wasn't sure what the address would turn out to be, but a day spa in Westport wasn't a lead. She kind of hoped for the killer's address, as unrealistic as it sounded. "Maybe she planned on booking an appointment."

"I did a little checking. It's in a prime location, which means big bucks. Lily probably could have afforded services there. What's intriguing is who the owner is."

Hope inched to the edge of her seat. "Who?"

"Pamela Hutchinson."

"The mayor's wife? She owns the spa?"

Drew nodded. "She opened it about four months ago." He picked up his fork and continued eating his lunch.

"In Westport? Why not around here? Someplace closer? Doesn't it seem odd she wouldn't tell anyone? It's a big deal opening a business." Hope's mouth twitched. Why the secrecy? Was there something Pamela was hiding? Then she recalled a recent news story of a day spa owner who was arrested for running an illegal prostitution ring out of the shop. "What kind of day spa is it?"

Drew's mouth gaped open and he dropped his fork. He must have remembered the brothel story from the news too.

"Now there's a reason why she would open it so far away and kept it a secret."

"Believe me when I tell you, if it's a brothel, I'd have one heck of an exclusive story. 'Mayor's Wife Runs Prostitution Ring.'" Drew clapped his hands together. "The story practically writes itself."

Hope raised a cautionary hand. "Don't get ahead of yourself."

"You're the one who suggested it."

"True. But we don't know for sure." Hope studied the back of her hand. Her fingernails were bare of polish and a little ragged from all the work she'd been doing around the house. "I think I need a manicure. Maybe a facial."

"You're going to Westport now?"

"I certainly am."

Drew pouted. "I can't go with you. I have a press conference to go to."

"I'll fill you in. I promise."

"Well, if it's not really a spa for ladies who lunch, be sure to get some photos on your phone and send them to me."

"Of course I will." The last thing Hope wanted to find at the address was a brothel.

# Chapter Seventeen

The Day Spa in Town was nestled among some of the priciest, trendiest shops in Westport. The heavy glass door with gold lettering closed quietly behind Hope as she approached the sleek reception desk. The spa oozed expensive from the marble floor to the one-of-a-kind light fixtures to the over-the-top floral arrangements displayed throughout the reception area. Pamela's clientele were accustomed to the best and the spa did not short-change them.

Hope had hustled Drew out of her house as soon as he finished eating his lunch so she could get ready for her trip to Westport. She changed from her khaki shorts and tank top into a sleeveless taupe dress and stepped into a pair of nude pumps. She twisted her hair into an updo and applied a little makeup. With a final sweep of translucent powder, she remembered not too long ago she'd prepared for work the same way—professional dress, heels, and makeup. Now those clothes and accessories were for the occasional meeting with brands, interviews, and apparently a facial.

The receptionist greeted her with a cool smile. "Welcome. Your name please?" Her pale green eyes broke from Hope to look at the computer screen as her fingers prepared to tap on the keyboard.

"Hope Early."

The receptionist nodded as she typed.

"I don't have an appointment."

The typing stopped and the receptionist lifted her chin. "How may I help you today? Would you like to schedule an appointment?" Her face was flawless, and her dress appeared well tailored, perhaps a bit too pricey for a receptionist, but Hope didn't doubt a certain appearance was required to greet the wealthy clients.

"Is there any chance I could get a facial? I know you may be booked, but I've been working all day and I need a little pampering. You understand?"

The receptionist nodded. "Of course. You're right about us being booked, though."

"I see." It was a long shot. The place didn't look like it took walk-ins like the Hair-O-Rama in Jefferson. She had considered calling to book an appointment before she left her house but worried Pamela would have seen her name on the schedule. She wanted to look around before Pamela found out she knew about the spa.

"I'm sorry. I didn't put it together at first. You're Hope from *Hope at Home*. Right?"

Hope nodded.

"I love your blog. The other day I watched your video on making pie crust. Up until then, I believed pie crust was the enemy." Her lips eased into a relaxed smile.

Before Hope could reply, a brunette dressed in trendy athleisure wear emerged from the hallway Hope assumed led to the treatment rooms. She was followed by a tall woman dressed in a white lab coat. They said their goodbyes and the client waved to the receptionist on her way out.

"I'm happy to hear you've made peace with pie crust. I won't take up any more of your time." Hope did her best to hide her disappointment. A little part of her was hoping to find a brothel. Then Hope could understand why Pamela

wanted to keep the spa a secret. But everything looked on
the up and up. So, why the secrecy?

The receptionist leaned over the desk. "Gigi just had a
cancellation, and I'm sure she'd be happy to give you a facial.
Just give me a moment."

"That would be fantastic." Hope brightened. Things were
turning around and hopefully she'd get a chatty esthetician
like the gal who usually waxed Hope's brows at her salon.
Or would the esthetician be tight-lipped due to the level of
clientele the spa serviced? When the receptionist reappeared, she waved for Hope to follow.

Chatty was an understatement. By the time Hope settled
onto the facial bed, wrapped in a plush robe with her hair
pulled back by a headband, she'd learned Gigi was recently
married to the love of her life, had honeymooned in
Bermuda, and had just bought a condo in Norwalk. While
Gigi, a bubbly twenty-something with high energy and the
most luxurious blond curls Hope had ever seen, did a quick
inspection of Hope's skin, she shared how the drama of
eight bridesmaids nearly wrecked her wedding day. Hope
wanted to ask her what she expected by having eight women
in her bridal party. For her wedding, Hope had two, her
sister and best friend, and they were a handful, so she
couldn't imagine eight women. Gigi complimented Hope
on her skin and then set to work as low classical music
played in the background.

Every inch of Hope began to relax. Her shoulders let
go of the weight of all the projects she was juggling. Her
muscles loosened the grip of everything she was holding
on to. And her mind stopped racing with the endless to-do
lists. Her breathing settled into a calming rhythm, and
every breath was deep and cleansing. Her eyes fluttered
shut as she eased into the most relaxing state she'd been in
for months.

"Where do you live?"

"Jefferson." Hope's voice was low, and one eyelid slit

open. She was in the Zen zone and didn't want to interrupt that. She just wanted quiet. She shut her eye and tried to get back to the zone.

"Cute town. My favorite antique shop is now there. The store used to be closer to me, but it closed after a fire and reopened up by you. Too far away now."

A buzzing sound drew Hope's eyes open.

"Just a little light exfoliation." Gigi held the device to Hope's forehead and dragged it across, tugging at the skin and removing dead skin cells. "Do you know Pamela?"

"Yes." She blinked a few times. She needed to stay awake because she was there for information, not for a nap. "Lily Barnhart told me about the spa. Do you know Mrs. Barnhart?"

Gigi shook her head. "The only other client from Jefferson I've worked with is Elaine Whitcomb. Do you know her?"

*Oh, yeah.* "Sort of." Hope kept her reply neutral so whatever Gigi wanted to say about Elaine, she would. So far Gigi didn't require much encouragement to talk. Exactly what Hope had wanted when she punched the address for the spa into her GPS.

"I'm not one for gossip." Gigi glided the exfoliating device down one side of Hope's face. "But Pamela and Mrs. Whitcomb must be best of friends."

"Why?"

Gigi transferred the device over to the other side of Hope's face. "Because all of Mrs. Whitcomb's services are complimentary and, let me tell you, she receives a lot of services." When Gigi finished exfoliating, she set the device down and reached for a jar. She slathered a rich cream over Hope's face and, with her fingertips, she gently massaged it into Hope's skin. "The woman is dripping in money, but she pays a big fat zero. That must be the reason why she's so rich. Lucky for me she does tip—nicely." She giggled as she continued to work on Hope's face with her expert hands.

Hope laughed along with Gigi, but her mind raced with

the question of why Pamela would provide Elaine free services. Maybe they were good friends. It was possible. Though, Hope doubted it because Elaine didn't make female friends easily, due to her flirtatious personality around men, and Pamela was known to have a jealous streak when it came to Milo. Just a few years ago at a party, Hope witnessed Pamela nearly assault another woman who had had too much to drink and made a pass at Milo. No, Hope couldn't see Pamela letting Elaine anywhere near her private life. So, why would she give carte blanche to Elaine at the spa?

"We're almost at the end of our session." Gigi's hands rested on Hope's shoulders and she began to massage deeply. Her fingers kneaded into Hope's muscle tissue.

Hope's eyes fluttered closed again. "Ah."

Gigi's hands worked their magic on her tense shoulders. And Hope drifted back into the euphoric state where her mind was blank. No recipes to develop. No garage or political events to organize. No dead bodies.

"You are now ready to face the world. How do you feel?" Gigi removed her hands from Hope's shoulders.

Hope reluctantly roused from her relaxed state to join the real world again. Bummer. "I feel great. I needed this. Thank you."

Gigi said her good-byes and left to allow Hope to dress. Hope then paid her bill and as she reached the front door, she heard Pamela's voice. She turned around and there was Pamela speaking with the receptionist. What good fortune.

"Pamela! I was hoping I'd see you before I left." Hope crossed the reception area quickly, so Pamela couldn't escape to the back. Pamela straightened up at the mention of her name, but then her eyes narrowed as she saw Hope.

"Hope? What on earth are you doing here?" Pamela released the file she held and then clasped her hands together. Petite with impeccable taste in clothing, she was wearing a navy suit, and her silver hair was cut into a chic bob. Add in the glint of haughtiness in her hazel eyes, and she looked every bit the owner of a chic day spa.

"I just got the most amazing facial." If Hope's wallet could afford monthly appointments, she'd book Gigi in a heartbeat. For now, she'd have to make due with at-home facials for the foreseeable future.

"How did you find out about my spa?" Pamela stiffened and her line-free face tensed.

"Lily Barnhart, of course. You've been keeping this gem of a spa a secret. You really shouldn't. It's fabulous."

"Lily told you?" Pamela's voice softened as a half smile formed on her plump, glossed lips.

Not in so many words, but Hope kept that little nugget to herself. "I'm surprised you haven't told anyone about this place. It's fabulous. Drew has to write a profile about this spa."

Pamela's smile faded as her eyes clouded over with panic. "No, no, no, he doesn't have to."

Hope shrugged. "You may be right. After all, the spa is a good distance from Jefferson so not everyone will be able to make an appointment. If you don't mind me asking, why did you open your business so far from Jefferson?"

"For the clientele, of course. If you'll excuse me, I have to call a distributor about a delivery." She turned and disappeared into a back office.

Hope thanked the receptionist again for her assistance and left the spa. All of Pamela's polish and poise couldn't disguise she was unnerved by Hope's presence. The door of the spa closed behind her as she stepped out onto the sidewalk.

Why was the spa such a secret? What was Pamela hiding and why?

* * *

Hope's fingers flew over her phone's keypad as she typed a text to Drew. She wanted to tell him about her visit to the spa. Maybe he could get away from the office and join her at the Coffee Clique. When she finished typing, she set her phone down, reached for her double latte, and waited for Drew's reply.

"I'm so glad I've run into you." Norrie Jennings approached the table and, without hesitation, pulled out a chair and sat.

Hope arched an eyebrow. "Please, do join me."

"Thank you." Norrie set her coffee cup on the table and dug into her large tote for a notepad and pen. "I love coffee shops. There's such a sense of community in them. You know, where everybody knows your name. It's so charming."

Norrie took a sip of her coffee, then flipped open her notepad and studied the page before lifting her head. "The other day when we ran into each other at Mrs. Griffin's house, I didn't have the opportunity to ask you what it was like when you came upon Mrs. Olson's burning house."

"Are you asking for a quote for a story you're writing for the newspaper?"

"Yes. It's going to be another front-page story."

When Hope worked in magazine publishing, she'd mentored young assistants and groomed them for editorial positions. She encouraged them to promote their accomplishments and not be ashamed of having professional goals. Norrie was someone Hope would have admired for her ambitions if she weren't running over Drew to make a name for herself.

"I appreciate you have a job to do, but I'm not comfortable discussing the fire." Hope reached for her latte and took a drink.

Norrie regarded Hope for a moment. "Of course. I understand."

Hope expected the reporter to push back since she was

looking for an exclusive. Why had Norrie given up so easily? Hope's phone buzzed and a message from Drew appeared on the screen.

**Can't meet. Catch up later.**

*Great.* She was stuck with Norrie. The last person she wanted to have coffee with.

"Could you then tell me about your relationship with Cal Barnhart?"

Hope's head swung up. "What?!"

"Mr. Barnhart visited your house the afternoon he learned his wife was dead. Why was he there?"

The hairs on the back of Hope's neck stood up. "Are you watching my house?"

"No, of course not. But I do have sources."

"Who?"

"I'm sorry. I can't reveal my sources."

"You have no right to pry into my personal life."

"So, Cal Barnhart is a part of your personal life?"

"Don't twist my words. I have a right to privacy."

"You went on national television, a reality show, and now you write a blog about your home and your family. Do you think you can have privacy?" Norrie challenged.

Norrie's words stung Hope for a moment. She had put her life out there on *The Sweet Taste of Success* for many weeks, but it was only a sliver of her life—baking. Yes, in the confessionals she'd mentioned her previous life as a magazine editor, her mother and sister briefly when she spoke about how she learned to bake, and how much she missed her husband because she was living in a hotel during the competition. It was only after the show her personal life made the newspapers and gossip websites because of Tim's philandering. She'd never commented publicly on her marriage and she'd never sought interviews to tell her side of the divorce story. Rather, she had kept her head down, worked hard, and prepared for her move back to Jefferson.

"Cal Barnhart and I have a professional relationship, and I will not comment on a police investigation." Hope collected her purse and coffee. "And one more thing, Miss Jennings, I do believe everyone is entitled to privacy in their lives and you should be ashamed of yourself for prying into mine."

She marched off, weaving between the tables to get to the exit. The woman had some nerve ambushing her and twisting very innocent actions into something scandalous. God, she hated reporters. Except for Drew, of course.

"There you are. I was able to sneak away." Drew leapt onto the curb and dashed to Hope. "What happened in Westport? I just got an earful from my editor."

"It's not a brothel. Wait, what's going on with your editor?" Hope took a drink of her latte, so much more enjoyable away from Norrie.

"He called me into his office, shut the door, and told me I wasn't to write an article on Pamela's spa. What's going on?"

"Why did you pitch the article? How come you didn't wait for me to get back?"

Drew sighed. "I didn't pitch the article. So how come my editor knows? He's no psychic."

Good question. She shot a glance over her shoulder. Norrie had said she had sources. Did one of her sources tell her about Hope's trip to Westport? Or maybe it was as simple as a phone call from Pamela.

"I saw Pamela at the spa and I mentioned you could write a profile on the spa. She looked a little wary and said it wasn't necessary. She must've called Milo after I left."

"He must've called my editor. What's going on? What's with this spa?"

"Good questions, Drew." Anxiety churned in Hope's

stomach as she tried to wrap her head around Milo having a newspaper story killed. Though, she couldn't rule out Norrie and her confidential sources.

"Are you going to talk to Ethan?" Drew asked.

"About Pamela owning a spa? And Milo not wanting any publicity for it?"

"Gotcha. We don't have enough."

"Not yet. You keep digging. There's obviously something the Hutchinsons want kept quiet."

"First, I need a coffee." Drew reached for the door handle.

"You should know Norrie's in there." Her cell phone buzzed and she checked the caller ID. Calista Davenport. "I have to take this call."

Drew sighed again. "Guess I'll pass on coffee. I better get back to the office anyway. Call you later." He turned and walked to the curb and waited until a car passed, then crossed the street.

Hope headed to her car with the phone to her ear. "Hi, Calista."

"I'm calling to touch base about the recipes for the cookbook." Calista's words were rapid. She spoke as fast as she walked the streets of midtown Manhattan.

"Great." Hope cringed. She'd barely had time to brainstorm ideas, much less develop the recipes. "I'm narrowing them down and will have the recipes to you by the end of the week."

"Perfect. Now, just one more thing about the recipes. I need five."

"Five?" Hope arrived at her SUV. "Corey told me two."

"Corey isn't the editor of the book. I am and I need five recipes by the end of the week. Shouldn't be a problem for you, right?"

Calista's question was left hanging in the air as Hope tried to wrap her mind around having to develop five recipes within just a few days. "No, not at all. I'm looking forward it."

"Good, that's what I like to hear."

What Hope would have liked to hear from Calista was good-bye.

"One more thing."

That wasn't what Hope wanted to hear.

"I heard about what's happening up there. Cal Barnhart's wife being found dead after disappearing. You're in his photography workshop?"

"Was," Hope corrected. "It's been cancelled."

"Don't be too disappointed. He's a good photographer but there are better ones to learn from and, for what it's worth, I suggest you keep your distance from him."

Hope wasn't surprised to hear Calista knock Cal's skills. She was a hard-nosed editor who demanded perfection and often clashed with photographers and food stylists.

"Why? What's his story?" Hope grimaced as she said the words. Didn't she just a few minutes ago tell Norrie everyone had a right to privacy and now she was asking about Cal's personal life?

"A rumor was circulating he was involved with someone from a recent shoot for *Dessert Time* magazine." There was no hint of embarrassment or shame in Calista's voice for passing along gossip. In her mind, she was just passing along information.

"I appreciate your concern."

"Well, you can show your appreciation by sending me those recipes ASAP."

Before Hope could reply, their call was disconnected. She pulled the phone from her ear. "Bye, Calista," she muttered. Considering their relationship, perhaps brief conversations were the best.

The drive home took less than five minutes and as soon as she hopped out of her SUV, she slipped off her pumps and wiggled her toes in the grass. She couldn't believe she used to wear high heels every day to work. She grabbed her latte and purse. Barefoot, she crossed the lawn to the front porch.

All the relaxation she felt after her facial was wiped away by her run-in with Norrie and the weird thing at the newspaper. Why would Milo want to suppress an article on his wife's business? Why did the editor agree to it? What happened to freedom of the press?

Bigelow's loud and piercing bark jogged Hope out of her thoughts. He was always excited when she came home, but there was something different in the tone of his bark she couldn't identify.

Her eyes darted around as she climbed the porch steps with a keen sense of alertness. She was looking for something out of the ordinary. And when her gaze landed on her front door, she found something out of the ordinary.

She crept forward. A torn sheet of notebook paper was nailed to her door. The block lettering read: PLAY WITH FIRE AND YOU'RE GOING TO GET BURNED.

# Chapter Eighteen

Hope steadied her hand as she poured a glass of iced tea. She tightened her grip on the pitcher's handle just to make sure she didn't drop it. At a noise from the mudroom she looked up, startled, and then realized the noise was Ethan's footsteps approaching. Finding the sinister note nailed to her door had sent a powerful message to her. Someone wanted her to stop inquiring about the deaths of Lily and Peggy.

Ethan's stride into the kitchen was purposeful, and he exuded authority in his uniform. The gun holstered to his belt was added reassurance for Hope. "Are you okay? You still look a little pale."

"I do?" Gosh, what had she looked like when he'd first arrived? He'd come speeding down the street with his lights flashing and swerved sharply into her driveway. He'd jumped out of his car and pulled her into a protective hug for a long moment, until she felt safe again.

"Iced tea?" She raised a glass.

When he nodded, she came out from behind the island and set the glass on the table. He followed, pulled out a chair, and sat. He dropped his notepad and pen on the table. There was a bunch of scribble on the page.

"Are you sure you're okay?" His heavy brows knit together and the lines around his mouth deepened. He was worried about her, *again*. He was always there for her when her life turned upside down and unraveled.

"I'm better now." She was. Ethan was there.

"What else can you tell me?" He clicked his pen, ready to write. When he arrived, he took her initial statement and then sent her back inside the house while he collected the note and nail as evidence.

"Nothing really." Hope returned to the island and took a sip of her iced tea. She had considered spiking her drink, giving it a kick that would calm her nerves faster than just letting time do it. Though, she should probably keep a clear head to answer Ethan's questions. "I came home and there it was."

After discovering the note, she'd rushed through the house to make sure the back door and all the windows were locked. Bigelow thought it was a game, so he'd playfully trotted after her room to room. She couldn't explain to the dog it wasn't a game, it was a warning to back off.

"You have no idea who could have left the note?" Ethan cocked his head sideways. His espresso brown eyes hinted he didn't believe her earlier when he'd asked the same question.

"Like I said before, I don't know who would've nailed that note into my newly refurbished door." She was so proud of the door—a great find at a tag sale last year, which Ethan had helped her transport back to her house. She'd spent a long weekend sanding, priming, and painting, and all of her hard work had paid off. The black door was a striking contrast to the white painted porch and really set off a pair of wall-mounted lanterns she'd refurbished.

"You can fix the nail hole," Ethan said, as if reading her mind.

"I know I can." Her stomach growled, reminding her she

hadn't eaten in hours. She grabbed a block of Vermont Cheddar cheese from the refrigerator and a box of crackers. Still under Ethan's scrutiny, she assembled a cheese plate.

"A little putty and it'll be as good as new."

"A little putty? That's not the point. I spent days working on the door and then some lunatic rams a nail into it to try making some kind of point."

"What point?"

Hope pressed her lips together. The most obvious point would be the lunatic wanted Hope to stop asking questions about Lily Barnhart and the fire. "You're the police, what do you think?"

"I think you're doing it again. I think you've gotten your-self caught up in this murder investigation and you're making someone nervous. Very nervous."

Before Hope could respond, the back door opened and Claire called out a greeting. Saved by her sister. "You won't believe the day I had. Running for mayor is an exhausting job." She entered the kitchen. For someone who was com-plaining about how tired she was, she looked far from run-down. From her three-inch pumps to her gray dress to her rosy cheeks, she exuded poise and radiance, which was far from what Hope looked like when she was exhausted.

"Hi, Ethan." Claire waved as she caught sight of Hope. "Wow! You look great!" She grabbed Hope's hand and twirled her around to get a full look. Her eyes scanned Hope from updo to nude pumps and then nodded approvingly. "Hot date?" she asked, winking.

"Date?" Ethan echoed.

"No, no, no date." She had no dates planned. Well, there was dinner with Matt, but it wouldn't be a date. It would be a celebration of his new house.

"Oh, I forgot. You went for a spa treatment." Claire let go of Hope's hand and then dropped her designer monogrammed purse on the island.

"How do you know about the appointment?" Hope asked.

"Drew told me. Why else would you be all dressed up? After all, you can't go for a facial dressed in your yoga pants."

Hope propped her hands on her hips. "You make it sound like I live in yoga pants. You know, I do wear other clothes."

Claire shrugged. "If you say so."

"What spa did you go to?" Ethan asked.

"It's called Day Spa in Town." Hope grabbed a cracker and nibbled as she considered how much to tell Ethan. Was it a coincidence a threatening note was left for her upon her return from a visit to the address she found in Lily's notebook? She doubted it. But, she had no evidence to prove they were connected and, without evidence, whatever she said was nothing more than speculation.

Claire joined Ethan at the table. "She should get a facial more often. What about you? Manicures? Pedicures? You know they're not just for women anymore."

"Do I look like a mani-pedi kind of guy?"

Hope stifled the laugh erupting in her throat, but it was no use. The image of Ethan sitting for a manicure was the most ridiculous thing.

"Just trying to make conversation. What are you writing there?" Claire gestured to Ethan's notepad.

"An incident report."

"Why are you writing it here? Don't you have an office . . ." Claire paused for a nanosecond before she swiveled her head to Hope. "What kind of incident?"

"Nothing. Barely an incident."

"A threatening note was nailed to her front door," Ethan said.

Hope shot Ethan a "really, did you have to say that?" look.

Claire's eyes widened with horror as she jumped up from the chair. "What?!"

"Calm down." Hope walked around the island to her sister. "Like I said, it's no big deal."

"Don't tell me to calm down. What have you gotten yourself into?"

"Now that's a very good question," Ethan chimed in. "I know you're snooping around trying to find the person who set the fire and you need to stop." His lips set into a grim line.

"Is she safe here?" Claire asked.

"I'll put on extra patrols and I'll be back." Ethan stood and shoved his notepad and pen back into his shirt pocket. He walked to Hope and squeezed her arm gently. "Keep the doors locked."

"That's it?" Claire's voice was edged with worry. She crossed her arms over her chest and her stance indicated the arrangements Ethan was setting up weren't satisfactory.

"For now. Let me get back to work. The sooner we close this case, the better it will be for all of us." He pulled his hand off of Hope's arm and left the house.

Hope stood there, suddenly feeling alone.

"Now, do you want to tell me what you've done to receive a threat?" Claire whispered.

Hope jumped, startled. She'd been so focused on Ethan and his leaving that she didn't hear Claire approach from behind.

"Nothing really. I've just asked a few questions. And I searched Lily's closet." Hope darted around Claire and dashed back to the island.

"What?!"

"Cal asked me to select a dress for Lily—"

"Wait. You saw Cal?"

"Yes. He called and asked me to come over to his house."

"Don't you read the newspapers? Nine out of ten times the husband is the murderer when a wife is killed."

"Nine out of ten times? Where did you get that number from?"

"Never mind." Claire sighed. "What I'm trying to say is you shouldn't be involved with him."

"I'm not involved with him. He just needed someone to talk to. Claire, his wife was murdered. He's devastated."

"It could be an act." Claire approached the island.

Hope shook her head. She didn't believe the grief she saw in Cal's eyes was fake. He was hurting, she had no doubt. "He asked me to select a dress for Lily. He couldn't do it himself."

"He placed the burden on you? You barely know him or Lily."

"It wasn't a burden. Anyway, while I was looking through her closet, I accidentally knocked down a purse and a notebook fell out. There was only one thing written in the notebook. It was an address for a spa in Westport."

"You looked through her private belongings? You're getting as bad as Jane." Claire nibbled on a piece of cheese.

"I picked it up. I was curious, okay? I admit it. I flipped through the pages, but there was only one thing written in the notebook. The address in Westport. Odd, right?"

"You're asking me to agree with your snooping?"

Hope heaved a sigh. "You wouldn't have done the same thing?"

"No, because I wouldn't have been in Lily's closet because I wouldn't have gone running over there because Cal could've killed his wife." She popped another cube of cheese into her mouth and chewed.

Hope hated when Claire sounded logical. "Fine. I see your point. Now, let's move on to the address."

"And who writes things down in notebooks these days. My cell phone has a notes app."

"Not everyone is digital only. You still use a paper planner."

Claire shrugged. "So, the address was the spa you went to?"

"The spa is owned by Pamela Hutchinson. Did you know she opened a spa?"

"No. Why did she open her business in Westport?"

"She said for the clientele."

"When did you see her?"

"On my way out. She didn't look that happy to see me."

"Imagine that?"

"Ha-ha." Hope topped a cracker with a cube of cheese and devoured it. She was starving and needed something more than just an appetizer. "I'm going to start dinner."

"What are you making? The kids are out and Andy is working late."

It looked like Hope was going to have a dinner companion. "Chicken quesadillas. I have some leftover chicken from recipe testing."

"Sounds good. No cheese on mine. This is enough." Claire finished the piece of cheese she'd just snatched off the plate.

"Of course." Hope grabbed an apron and began preparing their dinner while Claire pulled out her organizer and reviewed the to-do list for Maretta's tea party, which was tomorrow.

Hope half-listened as her sister prattled off the list of to-do tasks while the day's event played through her mind. While she didn't want to admit it to Claire or Ethan, she was a little scared. If the person who left the note was the person who abducted Lily and then set the fire to Peggy's house, he or she had gotten too close to Hope's home for her comfort.

Had she stumbled upon something that could direct the police to the killer? Had she spoken to the killer?

# Chapter Nineteen

Hope yawned while her hens vocalized their desire for some free-range time, with Helga the loudest. The four-pound Hamburg hen didn't like confinement. She preferred roaming in the yard. Hope chuckled at the chick's independent streak. She admired it. After the water bottles and feed bowls were filled, she opened the door from the barn stall to the enclosed space outside. The hens could come and go as they pleased and still be protected. But, the chickens liked to free-range and Hope believed she benefited from better eggs when they did so. She opened the door of the pen to allow the chickens to venture out to the yard.

In her research, she learned having a dog on the property would deter predators, but it could take months of training the dog not to be a predator himself before he could be left alone with the chickens. However, when Bigelow came to live with Hope, he took to the chickens right away, never once chasing them. Now, if she could get him to take to his obedience training as well as the chickens, she'd be happy.

Another yawn escaped as the last of the hens darted through the doorway and out to the bright, sunny morning. Too bad she didn't feel as bright and sunny or energetic as her hens. She'd been up past midnight working on her neglected blog and baking scones for Maretta's tea party. When her alarm went off, she considered hitting the snooze button, but reality hit—she didn't have time to snooze.

While the White Chocolate Chip Scones and the Lemon Blueberry Scones were made the night before, she still had two more varieties of muffins to bake. Once out of bed, getting dressed was a mad dash. She grabbed a pair of torn jeans and a plaid shirt and slipped into her barn boots before heading out to the chickens. On her way to the barn, she tied her hair into a sloppy ponytail and was grateful no one was around to see her.

When the last hen was out of the coop, she exited the stall and deposited her feed bucket by the grain bin. She took off her work gloves and grabbed the water bottle she brought out with her. She took a drink and as she turned to walk out of the barn, she caught the silhouette of someone standing at the barn doors. Startled, she dropped the water bottle and splashed water over her boots. The silhouetted person came rushing forward and Hope instinctively stepped back, raising her hands. Just when she was about to yell, she recognized the person.

"Brenda? What are you doing here?" Hope bent down to pick up the water bottle and tipped it so the remaining water drained out. Jane's cautionary words about how Brenda could see Hope as a threat echoed in her ears. She wasn't about to let down her guard until she found out the reason for Brenda's surprise visit.

"I'm here to find out what you're up to." Brenda waved a rolled-up newspaper in her hand. "What exactly do you want from Cal?"

"What are you talking about?"

"Like you don't know? You haven't seen the newspaper this morning?"

"No, I haven't." She usually read the newspaper after

finishing the barn chores. Hope stepped forward and held out her hand. "May I?"

Brenda gave her the newspaper and waited while Hope unfolded the newspaper and scanned the front page. She gasped at the photograph of her and Cal hugging. Her mind searched for when the photograph could have been taken and recognized it was on the second day of class when she stayed for coffee. Cal had walked her out to her car and they hugged good-bye. Her eyes darted to the byline. Norrie Jennings. How on earth did Norrie get the photograph? Arrgh! Her grip on the newspaper tightened.

"Care to explain?"

"Explain?" Hope was taken aback by Brenda's nerve to show up at her house uninvited and demand an explanation. As Hope explained to Norrie the day before, she didn't owe anyone an explanation about her life, much less Cal's assistant. However, alienating the woman wouldn't help Hope get the answers she desperately needed in order to find the person responsible for Lily's and Peggy's deaths.

"It's not what you think. It was completely innocent. I assure you I have no romantic feelings for Cal. None. We're just friends." She wasn't even sure if they were friends, but she knew what they weren't, and they weren't lovers.

Brenda's lower lip quivered and tears filled her eyes. Her body began to crumble. She was on the verge of a breakdown.

Hope lunged forward and wrapped an arm around Brenda's midsection. "I have coffee and tea, whichever you prefer. We can talk. Okay?"

Brenda nodded and Hope led her out of the barn. Once they were inside Hope's kitchen, she settled Brenda at the table and went to heat the teakettle. She snatched a Lemon Blueberry Scone off a tray she'd assembled and plopped it on a plate for Brenda. She'd have to rearrange the tray later since now there was one missing scone. Great, one more thing to do. She shooed Bigelow away from Brenda's side by tossing him a chew toy to keep him occupied.

"Are you having a party?" Brenda broke off a piece of scone and popped it into her mouth.

"Yes. It's an English tea party for Maretta Kingston." The kettle whistled and Hope dropped a tea bag into a mug and then added the hot water. She carried the mug over to Brenda and set it in front of her. She then took a seat opposite Brenda and glanced at the *Gazette*. She unfolded the paper. While Brenda sipped her tea and composed herself, Hope read the highlights of the article, which recounted the events of the fire, Hope's visit to the P&Z Commission members, and how she was instrumental in solving a previous murder in early spring. She had to admit, Norrie did a thorough job writing the article.

"I'm sorry. I shouldn't have come at you the way I did. I saw the photograph and I saw red."

Hope studied the assistant. Brenda wasn't young. She was closer to forty than twenty. Her appearance was meek. A drab hair color that didn't highlight her olive complexion, and shapeless clothing that didn't show off her figure. Brenda was one of those women you didn't notice when they entered or left a room.

"How long have you been in love with Cal?"

"From the first day I met him. Foolish, huh? He's a really good man." Brenda lifted her chin. "He loved Lily, even though there have been other women."

Brenda had confirmed what Calista told Hope yesterday. "Sounds like they had a complicated marriage."

Brenda let out a mirthless laugh. "That's one way to put it."

Hope caught a glimpse of the wall clock in the family room. She was running out of time to finish preparing for her guests. There was a strong chance she'd be hosting in her torn jeans and plaid shirt. "Did any member of the P&Z Commission ever come to the house?"

Brenda looked perplexed by the shift in conversation. From adultery to zoning.

"It's important, Brenda," Hope urged.

"Not when I was there. But I did overhear a brief part of a telephone conversation a few weeks ago."

"What did you hear?" Hope didn't have time to frame the question in a more tactful way. Her guests would be arriving soon, and she was behind schedule and there was a murderer on the loose.

"I didn't mean to eavesdrop. Lily said she was concerned about the project and couldn't vote for it in good faith."

"Did she mention which project?"

Brenda shook her head. "No."

"Did she ever mention a spa in Westport?"

"Not really. Though, the day before she disappeared, she told me she may be late coming home because she was going to Westport."

"Did she say where she was going?"

"No. And she was late getting home that evening." Brenda pushed the teacup away. "Hope, I'm truly sorry for coming here this morning the way I did. I was completely out of line."

"Thank you for your apology."

Brenda sounded sincere and a small part of Hope felt sorry for Brenda. It must've been hard being in love with your boss while he was married and dating other women. Not only did Cal have a complicated marriage, he had a complicated life. And it was going to get more complicated once Norrie Jennings got a whiff of his infidelities.

"I guess I shouldn't let the article get the better of me." Brenda broke eye contact and her gaze lowered.

Hope's gaze also lowered and landed back on the article. Norrie had crossed the line, flinging allegations and innuendo sprinkled with just enough facts to get it by her editor so they could sell more copies of the newspaper. She searched deep inside for an inkling of forgiveness toward Norrie, but none was forthcoming.

Brenda stayed a little longer to finish her tea and scone. While they talked, Hope baked the four dozen muffins she needed for the tea party. As she mixed the batter and filled the muffin tins, she did her best to give Brenda a pep talk and encouraged her to spread her wings and find a new job in a new town. The suggestion was well received, and Brenda said she'd consider it after Lily's funeral. By the time the muffins were cooling, Brenda was at the door saying good-bye and then Hope dashed upstairs to shower and dress for the tea party, with just a few moments to spare before the guests arrived. For the past few days, whenever she thought about the tea party, images of the Mad Hatter and a rabbit flashed in her mind. Not good.

Showered and changed for her guests, Hope surveyed the setup. Along the wall of windows in the family room, tables were arranged for the food, teapots, and pitchers of juice. A mix of heights of the serving pieces added interest to the buffet. She used cake pedestals and square bowls turned upside down to hold large white porcelain platters. She arranged the scones and muffins on the cake pedestals and platters, while freshly cut fruit was artfully arranged on a large tray. Two crystal bowls sat next to each other on the table. Greek yogurt in one, homemade granola in the other.

She stepped back and took in the whole setup. She'd chosen a delicate floral tablecloth for the buffet and tucked vases with tulips between the trays and bowls.

Perfect.

Until she noticed a few of the Lemon Blueberry Scones

sat slightly askew. She leaned forward and gently rearranged the scones.

Now it was perfect.

"Quit fussing. It looks beautiful." Claire approached the buffet with a cup of coffee. "Where did you find all of these?" She pointed to the collection of mismatched teacups with silver spoons nestled together.

"Tag sales mostly." She'd also set out a stack of plates purchased at a flea market a few weeks ago, along with cloth napkins she snagged at an estate sale in Roxbury.

"Why can't you shop at a store like normal people?"

"I love the hunt." Hope scanned the buffet again. Good thing she did because the symmetry was off on the tray of apple cinnamon muffins. She adjusted the spacing of the muffins. She could tweak all day, but her to-do list was already too long. She needed to stop obsessing over the buffet. "We have to talk before people start to arrive." She glanced at her watch. The guests would be arriving within just a few minutes, so she didn't have much time to fill Claire in on the front page story in the *Gazette*. Before she could get the newspaper, the doorbell rang.

"Don't move. It's important that we talk." Hope hurried out of the family room to the front door. She didn't have to worry about her rambunctious dog as the ladies arrived. She'd arranged a playdate for Bigelow with Buddy at the Madisons' house. She pulled open the door and found the first arrival was the guest of honor herself, Maretta Kingston.

"You're the first one here. Please come in." She held the door for Maretta to enter the foyer. "Claire is in the family room."

"Good. We need to talk." Maretta looked at Hope. Deep-set lines between her overly plucked eyebrows accentuated the scowl on her drawn face. Her grayish hair was dull but nicely cut into an age-appropriate style. Without another word, she headed for the family room. The full skirt of her polka-dot dress swooshed as her sensible shoes barely made a sound as they marched across the antique wood floor.

Hope shut the door and went after Maretta. Images of the Mad Hatter flashed in her mind. She had a sinking feeling the tea party was doomed.

"Good morning, Maretta." Claire set her coffee mug on the island. "Hope has everything ready for the guests."

"Your sister has been a busy bee." Maretta's voice was laced with accusation.

"What are you talking about?" Claire asked as Hope reached Maretta's side.

Maretta gave Hope the once-over. "I saw the newspaper this morning."

"The *Gazette*? What about it?" Claire looked to Hope with bewilderment.

Hope stalked over to the magazine basket on the hearth and pulled out the newspaper. She handed it to her sister.

Claire unfolded the newspaper and gasped when she saw the front-page story. "What did you do?"

Hope put up her hands in surrender mode. "Nothing. I swear."

Maretta wagged her finger at the newspaper. "Scandalous. It's not fitting for the next mayor of Jefferson to have her sister involved with a suspected killer."

"Hold on, Maretta. First, Cal and I aren't involved. And second, he's not a suspected killer."

From Maretta's response to the article, Hope had no doubt the knot forming in her stomach was going to get tighter as the day progressed. She was confident others would have the same reaction. She predicted a lot of explaining on her part.

"It's always the husband," Maretta said with conviction.

"I can't believe this. Do you know how this looks?" Claire let out a loud, exasperated sigh. She folded the newspaper and shoved it into Hope's hands. "As much as it pains me to say, I have no choice but to agree with Maretta. This is scandalous."

Hope's mouth gaped open. Her sister was siding with Maretta Kingston, of all people? How could she?

"We just hugged. I was leaving his house after we had coffee and talked. Nothing else happened. It was just a hug!" Hope used Drew's dramatic hand gestures to get the point across. "Just a hug!" The doorbell rang again. *Thank goodness.*

Hope stomped away to let in the first of the guests. Before she reached the front door, she ditched the newspaper and pasted on a warm smile. As the ladies entered her home, she was on the receiving end of several sly smiles and curious glances. Yep, they'd all read the newspaper with their breakfasts. The stream of guests trailed off, with a few running late. Just as she was about to close the door and join everyone in the family room, one last-minute guest showed up, and Hope was surprised by her arrival.

"I'm happy you were able to come today." As she closed the door, she caught a whiff of a citrusy perfume Elaine Whitcomb had apparently bathed in.

"Lionel does business with Maretta's husband, so I'm here in that capacity." Elaine gave Hope a cool look and her voice was icy. They wouldn't be exchanging girlfriend bracelets anytime soon.

"Whatever the reason, I'm glad you're here. Everybody's in the family room, and we're about to get started." Hope gestured for Elaine to proceed ahead.

Elaine's hips swayed as she walked through the foyer in high-heeled strappy sandals. Her leopard print wrap dress hugged her hourglass figure and a clutch bag dangled carelessly in her fingers.

Claire passed Elaine as she entered the foyer. "She came?" she mouthed while pointing her thumb at Elaine.

Hope shrugged.

"All they're talking about is the article and photograph. How could you, Hope?" Claire asked.

"I didn't do anything." She whisked past her sister and went to the family room, where her guests mingled. Some were at the buffet, others were grouped into seating areas, chatting. She heard bits of conversations as she passed through the room. They were discussing her, Cal, Lily, and the fire.

"These White Chocolate Chip Scones are delicious. I must have the recipe for the inn." Sally Merrifield approached Hope, a half-eaten scone on a plate.

Sally was equally enthusiastic about town politics and baked goods. She always asked for a recipe of something she enjoyed, and Hope was happy to oblige. "I'll e-mail it to you later today."

"Good. Good. Now, I think you should know everyone is buzzing about the photograph in the newspaper."

Before Hope could reply, Maretta rushed past her. "Finally, the press has shown up."

Hope glanced over to Claire. "Press?"

"I sent a press release to the *Gazette*. This is news." Claire followed Maretta to the foyer.

"Your sister is correct. This is news." Sally bit into the remaining half of her scone before turning to walk away.

It was only eleven in the morning, but Hope was exhausted. First, Brenda, and now, the circus in her home. She wanted to get the event over with so they'd all leave and she could crawl back into bed. Just when she thought her day couldn't get any worse, Claire and Maretta returned with Norrie behind them.

"Hello, Hope. You have a great house." Norrie smiled brightly as she surveyed the open space. "You're really doing all the work yourself?"

"I'm sure you didn't come here today to talk about DIY

projects," Maretta interrupted. "Let's get started. I have an announcement to make."

Hope ignored Norrie and Maretta and zoomed in on her sister. "What is she doing here? She's not welcome in my house."

"Calm down. We don't need a scene." Claire led her sister away from Norrie.

"I think it's a little too late for that advice," Hope said.

"Everybody, please. If I could have your attention." Maretta clapped her hands together as she took center stage in front of the fireplace. She lifted a pair of reading glasses to her face as she prepared to read from a sheet of paper.

The guests quieted down as they turned their attention to Maretta. Elaine sat on the sofa next to Jane. She crossed her legs and jutted out her ample bosom. Jane shifted. She looked as if she was trying to get comfortable again. Claire dropped onto the edge of an ottoman while Hope stood off to the side, where she had a good view of Norrie. The reporter positioned herself across from Maretta to take photographs. Hope wanted to keep an eye on Norrie, to make sure she didn't disappear and snoop through her house.

"Thank you all for coming here today," Maretta said. "I've given much thought about the opportunity the Planning and Zoning Commission offers. The commission has great oversight when it comes to the development in town and, with that, great responsibility."

Hope scanned the room. Heads nodded in agreement and Claire smiled with pride. So far, so good. The speech should take just a few more minutes, then everyone would help themselves to more food, chat about Maretta's speech, and head out the door.

"I've also given much thought to how I could best serve my hometown of Jefferson." Maretta lowered the hand that held her glasses. She stopped reading from the paper. "I feel serving on the P&Z Commission doesn't afford me the best opportunity to serve Jefferson."

Hope looked around the room. The heads stopped nodding, and Claire's smile faded as confusion glazed over her face.

"I feel the best way to serve the town I love is by running for the office of mayor. Jefferson needs me, and I'm ready to serve. Today, I officially announce my candidacy for mayor." A triumphant smile stretched across Maretta's thin face.

*Oh, boy.* Confusion gave way to anger. Redness spread across Claire's face, and Hope dashed to her sister just in time to stop her from jumping up from the ottoman.

"No," Hope said.

"But . . . she . . . what . . . ?" Claire muttered, unable to complete a thought.

"Take a deep breath and count to ten and take another breath. Remember, we don't want to create a scene." Hope held a firm grip on Claire's shoulder, despite her death glare. Their mother would be so proud of Claire's master of the facial expression because Hope was certainly scared by it, but not enough to let Claire do something foolish.

"Sounds like good advice." Norrie approached with her camera poised for a photograph. "And here I thought this was going to be one of those dull teas for ladies who lunch. I love my job."

"Good for you," Hope snapped. "Do you mind giving us a moment?"

"Sure. Right after I get a quote. Mrs. Dixon, how do you feel about the announcement today? You were under the impression Mrs. Kingston was seeking the open position on the P&Z Commission and then she pulled the rug right out from under you by announcing her bid for mayor."

"My sister has no comment." Though, Hope had a few

choice comments of her own for both Maretta and Norrie, but they would remain private. Just like any comments Claire had at the moment.

Claire jerked her shoulder free of Hope's grip and stood. She squared her shoulders and took a deep breath. "Actually, I do have something to say."

"No, you don't." Hope gave her sister a stern look.

Norrie inched closer to Claire. "What is it you want to tell the people of Jefferson?"

Hope inserted herself between Claire and the reporter. "She doesn't have a comment at this time. Now, please leave my house."

Norrie's mouth opened to protest but before she could say a word, she was cut off by Sally, who came to Hope's side. "Let me show you out, Miss Jennings."

"I still have more questions," Norrie said as Sally wrapped an arm around her and led her toward the foyer. Her protests eventually faded as the two women disappeared out of the room.

Not only would Sally get the recipe for the White Chocolate Chip Scones, Hope would bake her a special batch as a thank-you for showing Norrie the door. With the reporter situation taken care of, Hope wanted to focus on her sister's situation.

"I can't believe Maretta! Where is she?" Claire bolted in search of her opponent.

"Looks like your little tea party is over," Elaine said. "I for one am glad Maretta has thrown her hat into the ring. Looks like you won't get to be the First Sister of Jefferson."

"The what?" Hope asked.

"You know, like the First Lady, but you're her sister. Guess you shouldn't have counted your chickens before they hatched."

"I haven't counted anything. I need to check on Claire."

Hope shook her head in confusion as she wove through the guests. The one good thing that came out of Maretta's unanticipated announcement was there was a new topic of conversation. The chatter shifted from the photo in the *Gazette* to Maretta's surprising news.

"Seriously?!"

Meg's loud voice broke all the conversation hubs and had all heads turning to the entry into the family room, including Hope's. Meg stood holding a rolled-up newspaper. The *Gazette*, Hope guessed.

"You're at it again!" Meg stormed into the room, making a beeline for Hope as mouths gaped open and eyes widened with a mixture of horror and excitement.

"I'm sure we can calmly discuss whatever has you upset." Hope reached out, but Meg recoiled. A calm discussion didn't seem likely.

"You're turning my aunt's murder into a fiasco. The article is all about you. Your blog. Your amateur sleuthing abilities. Your relationship with Cal. You. You. You. What about Aunt Peggy? She's the victim." Tears streamed down Meg's cheeks. Her eyes were puffy and her face was blotchy. She must've been crying since the newspaper arrived at her house.

"I had no idea Norrie was writing the article. Most of what she wrote isn't true."

"Playing innocent again? Just like when you got the role of Dorothy in *The Wizard of Oz* after you pestered Mrs. Collins about it for days and then claimed you had no idea why she changed her mind. That role was mine! I ended up being the Wicked Witch of the West. I had to wear that stupid green face makeup and I had a breakout for weeks and that's when we had our class photographs taken!"

"Do you hear yourself? You're holding on to something that happened decades ago. Look, if you don't believe me about the article, there's nothing I can do about it. But don't come barging into my home and yell at me." Hope's spine was straight, her shoulders squared, and she wasn't backing down. There'd be no more apologizing.

"Meg, honey, how about a cup of tea?" Beth Green swooped in and led Meg to the buffet.

Hope nodded her appreciation. As much as she was angry with Meg, she still had empathy for the woman because of the loss she'd suffered.

Once Meg was settled with tea, the rest of the guests returned to their conversations and Hope continued to look for Claire.

She found her sister on the front porch with Jane. A soft breeze swept by, and the clucking of her hens off in the distance harkened to what should have been a lovely spring English tea party, not a fiasco of cutthroat politics.

"Her car is gone." Claire pointed to the line of parked vehicles. "She left. Just like that. She dropped the bomb and then hightailed it out of here. Can you believe her?" Claire dropped her arm and paced the length of the porch.

"She never mentioned an interest in running for mayor?" Jane asked.

"No, never. If she had, I certainly wouldn't have hosted this tea for her. I expected to have an opponent, but I didn't think it would be her. What am I going to do?" Claire stopped pacing. Her shoulders sagged and her gaze searched Hope's eyes for answers.

Her sister needed support and reassurance. Hope gladly stepped up to the plate. "You're going to go back in there and put on a happy face." She pointed to the front door.

"Happy face. Really?"

Hope squeezed Claire's arm. "Really. You're not going to let anyone see you're upset. You're their candidate. They came here today because you're the woman they want as their mayor."

"They came here because I asked them to support Maretta."

"Support her for the P&Z Commission."

Claire nodded. "Okay. You're right. I've got this."

"You've got this." Hope let go of her sister and was about to turn to go back inside her house when the sound of approaching vehicles caught her attention. Two Jefferson police SUVs pulled into her driveway. A moment after the engines were turned off, Ethan exited one vehicle. She could've used a police officer earlier when the tea party took a downward turn. Even though he was a little late, he was a welcome sight. Though, the driver who exited the second vehicle wasn't.

Detective Reid. What now?

"Ethan, we're in the middle of a crisis at the moment." Hope gestured for Claire and Jane to go inside, but they stood firm. Whatever the reason for the visit from the police, she was going to have an audience.

"We need to talk. Now." Ethan's voice was stern and official sounding as he climbed the porch steps.

Dread whooshed through her and yet she still asked, "What's going on?"

Reid followed Ethan up to the porch. He looked grim, as usual. "We'd like to know what you were doing at Hans Vogel's house." Reid reached into the breast pocket of his navy blazer and pulled out a notepad.

"Hans Vogel. What were you doing at his house? The man is a recluse, a hoarder, and a nasty person." Claire stepped forward, next to Hope. "But his lot is a good size. If it got cleaned up, he could sell for a decent price."

"I don't think he's interested in selling because he's dead," Reid added.

Claire gasped. "Oh, my."

Hope dragged in a breath. She'd just seen him a few days ago. How could he be dead?

"Is that so?" Jane's blue eyes widened with a hint of curiosity.

Hope could tell Jane's wheels were turning about the news. Like Hope, she was probably trying to piece together the sequence of events.

Hope spoke with Hans about Lily and then he ended up dead. A coincidence? Or murder?

Jane had agreed with Hope the hoarder didn't seem to be a likely suspect in Lily's disappearance and fatal fire because he lacked the sophistication to plan out those events. However, he could have known something about the crimes and the killer wanted to make sure he didn't tell anyone.

"You're here because you think Hope killed Hans?" Jane asked.

# Chapter Twenty

"What have you gotten yourself into?" Claire paced the length of the kitchen. "Why did you go there? To clean?" She was channeling their mother in her tone of voice and cadence, and she'd nailed the disapproving head shake.

Detective Reid raised a hand. "Mrs. Dixon, please. I need to ask your sister a few questions." When Claire complied, he sat across the table from Hope, with his notepad open and pen in hand.

For the first time, Hope appreciated the detective. Though, she was confident the newfound appreciation wouldn't last for long, not once his attention turned back to her. When it did, the questions were routine about her visit to Hans Vogel. She was a little distracted as she answered because she kept glancing to Ethan, who was leaning against the island with his arms crossed over his chest and his face furrowed in deep thought. It didn't take a detective to know what was on his mind. Three deaths in less than one week. That was a lot for a police department the size of Jefferson's to investigate, and it had to be taking a toll on Ethan.

"How did you know I was there?" Hope asked.

"We found a plate of cookies in the kitchen," Ethan said. "Lemon Ricotta. I recognized the plate and the cookies."

Hope nodded. She'd dropped off a plate of cookies a week earlier for Ethan at the police department and she'd used one of those plates she'd purchased at the flea market. "How did he die? And do you have a time of death?"

"We're the ones asking the questions, Miss Early," Reid answered.

"That's because they're the police and you're not." Claire passed behind Hope, continuing to pace.

Reid ignored Claire's comment. "What time were you at his house?"

"Wait one minute." Claire halted and her tone changed to protective. "If you suspect my sister of having any involvement with Vogel's death, then I want to call Matt Roydon."

"No, Claire, we don't suspect Hope of murder." Ethan unfolded his arms and shoved his hands into his pants pockets. Hope could tell his patience was waning once he started to shift.

"You don't?" Hope asked.

"Should we?" Reid asked.

"No!" None of this made sense to her. "Then why are you here?"

"We want to know why you were there," Ethan said.

Hope stood and walked around the island. She poured a cup of coffee and stirred in a dash of cream as she considered what to tell them. A motion outside on the patio caught her eye. It was Elaine strutting past the French doors and then she disappeared. After Ethan and Reid entered her house, her guests were ushered outside by Sally and Jane, where they could finish their tea and gossip about the newest turn of events.

"Why were you there?" Claire propped her hands on her

hips and gave Hope their mother's powerful "you better spill the truth now or else" look.

"I went to look for an old sign. I heard he had a collection." Hope took a drink of her coffee and chided herself for not being completely forthcoming, but all she had so far were hunches and gossip. Nothing concrete. Nothing solid. Nothing she could prove. At least not yet.

"Did you buy a sign?" Reid inquired.

Hope pulled her attention back to the matter at hand. "No."

Reid jotted something down on his notepad. "What did you two talk about beside his sign collection?"

Hope shrugged. "He mentioned his wife and we briefly discussed the mandate the P&Z Commission made regarding his property. He'd had an outburst at the last hearing and was very angry with Lily."

"I knew it!" Claire had her own little outburst. "You're sleuthing again! This is why some psycho left the note yesterday."

"Claire, please," Ethan said.

Claire shook her head vigorously as she marched over to the sofa and dropped down with a huff.

"What happened next?" Reid asked.

"I told Hans Lily was dead, and he got angry and demanded I leave. I did right away. I don't think he knew Lily was dead."

"Yeah, he's a recluse," Claire chimed in.

Ethan leveled a warning glance on Claire, and she huffed again.

"I'm not sure how many times I need to warn you about interfering in an official investigation. Perhaps some time in jail would help you remember you're not a police officer but a blogger." Reid snapped his notepad closed.

Hope set her mug on the island. "All I did was inquire about some signs and make a little conversation with Hans."

"Humpff," Claire muttered from the sofa.

Apparently, her sister wasn't going to help her. Claire wouldn't be Hope's one phone call after she got fingerprinted.

"Were you just making conversation with Donna Wilcox?" Reid asked. "She called me right after your visit."

"I can explain," Hope offered, but Reid's intense glare made it clear he didn't want an explanation.

"On top of the murder investigations, I now have members of the Planning and Zoning Commission calling because they're worried they could be a target."

"I didn't mean for that to happen." It wasn't her intention to cause hysteria among the commission members. If only Drew hadn't shown up, Donna wouldn't have panicked. "Do you think they're targets?"

"You should be more worried about who's going to post your bail," Reid countered.

"You're arresting me?" Hope set her cup on the island with a thud. "You can't be serious. I didn't do anything."

"You're not being arrested, Hope," Ethan interjected. "We're just asking questions."

"Your call, Chief." Reid stood, with his notepad and pen. "Guess it's your lucky day, Miss Early. I'll show myself out." He exited the kitchen and, within a moment, she heard the front door close.

Lucky day? The detective couldn't have been more wrong. Not one thing went as planned and the day wasn't even half over yet.

"I don't know how many more times I can stop him from arresting you." Ethan went to the coffeemaker and poured a full cup. He liked his coffee black and strong, and he gulped a large drink. If he wasn't on duty, he'd probably pour something stronger, and Hope couldn't blame him. To think, he'd left the Hartford Police Department for a less stressful job in the country. Hope wondered if he regretted his choice.

"Ethan, I'm so sorry. I don't know anything about Hans Vogel's death. He was alive and very angry when I left."

"I believe you. I know why you're doing what you're doing. I also know that nothing I say will stop you."

Hope picked up her coffee mug. "You know me too well."

"Maybe you should arrest her so she'll stay out of trouble," Claire said.

"Why are you still here?" Hope walked to the sink and rinsed the mug. Then she surveyed the family room. There were a few scones and muffins to wrap, dishes needed to be loaded into the dishwasher, and the buffet tables needed to be taken down. Any other day those tasks wouldn't have felt so daunting. She'd happily shift into clean-up mode, pulling out a large trash bag and her cordless vacuum and get to work. But at the moment, all she wanted to do was crawl back into bed. As if reading her mind, Claire slipped out of her stilettos and padded barefoot across the room to retrieve a trash bag from a bottom drawer, then began tossing stirrers, sugar packets, and any other garbage left over. Hope smiled. Even though she encouraged Ethan to arrest her, Claire still had her back.

"Now, I have one question for you." Ethan closed the space between them. "What's with the photo of you and Cal hugging?"

Hope stared up at him, searching his eyes, and found a mix of fatigue, worry, and hurt. She guessed the hurt came from unfolding the newspaper and finding that photo glaring back at him. Even though the hug was innocent, it was positioned as something salacious. She couldn't blame him for questioning it. If the situation was reversed, she'd be curious.

"The photo was taken as I was leaving his house. After the workshop we had coffee and talked and then I left. He hugged me good-bye. I swear there's nothing going on between us."

"I believe you. Just to be clear, because his wife's death has been ruled a homicide, he is a person of interest. It's a matter of course."

"Cal couldn't have killed Lily."

"You know this how?"

"Well, I just do. Just like I know you could never do such a thing."

"Thanks for your confidence." His tone was light as his lips curved into a relaxed smile.

Hope's pulse zipped a little bit as she thought how kissable his lips were.

"You've gotta be kidding!" Claire shrieked from across the room.

Both Hope's and Ethan's heads jerked up to find Claire dashing across the room with her cell phone in hand.

"What's wrong?" Hope had switched from thinking about kissable lips to bracing herself for more bad news.

"This." Claire shoved the phone into Hope's hand. On the screen was an article on another news website about Cal, and it featured the photograph of him hugging Hope. "This is now officially a scandal, and I'll lose the election to Maretta."

"Good grief." Hope shook her head and handed the phone back to Claire. She had no interest in reading the article.

"Maretta's running for mayor?" Ethan asked.

"She made the announcement earlier." Claire took another look at her phone. "Why do you always have to find the strays?" She turned and stalked out of the room.

"Wow, you've had a hell of a day." Ethan's cell phone buzzed. He pulled it out of its holster and took the call. "I'm on my way."

"Duty calls?"

"Yes. Try and stay out of trouble." He kissed Hope on the forehead like he'd done so many times before, but never had the simple kiss left her wanting more.

\* \* \*

A knock at the back door drew Hope's attention from stacking the plates she'd just removed from the dishwasher. She walked through the mudroom and glanced through the glass to find Mitzi Madison. She pulled open the door. "You know you're late."

"I know. Sorry. A friend of ours was rushed to the hospital. I went to be with her husband until their children arrived. Where is everybody?" Mitzi peered over Hope's shoulder.

"They're gone. Come on in." Hope led her neighbor into the kitchen. "There are some muffins and scones left, and I still have coffee."

Mitzi's face brightened. "I'd love a scone." She walked over to the table and sat while Hope went to the counter. "Coffee, too, please."

"Coming right up." Hope poured a full cup of coffee and added three teaspoons of sugar and milk. Light and sweet, just the way Mitzi liked her coffee. After the tumultuous morning she'd had, preparing a snack for Mitzi was exactly what she needed. The simple act of plating a scone and pouring coffee calmed Hope's nerves and settled all the thoughts that rattled her mind. All of the clutter in her head fell to the wayside. "I'm sorry to hear about your friend. I hope she's going to be okay." Hope approached the table with the plate and the cup of coffee.

Mitzi bit into the scone and moaned with delight as she chewed the light and airy treat. "These are so good. I think my grandson would say they're stupid good." A smile stretched across her face, lines forming along her lips and the corners of her brown eyes. Her silver hair brought out flecks of amber in her eyes, and wispy bangs gave her a youthful look. She wiped her mouth with a napkin, then took a drink of her coffee. She set the cup on a coaster, which Hope appreciated. "I can see something's wrong. What happened?"

"I don't even know where to begin."

"Go all the way back to the beginning. I'm not in a rush."

All the way back to the beginning? If Hope did that, Mitzi would be sitting in the kitchen for days. She began just after Brenda left and the guests started to arrive for Maretta's event. She gave her neighbor all the gory details of the party, which had Mitzi shaking her head. She had a hard time wrapping her mind around the turn of events, just like Hope did. In a strange way, Hope found Mitzi's reaction somewhat comforting.

"I can't believe I missed all of that." Mitzi finished her scone and pushed the plate away. "I'm still in shock over the fire."

Hope nodded in agreement. "I think everyone still is."

"You know"—Mitzi leaned forward—"Peggy said something very odd the night I went to check on her after she burned the peppers and onions."

"She did?" Hope asked.

"She said some of her things seemed out of place, but she couldn't be sure. You know, she was getting on in age. Heck, sometimes I forget where I put something." Mitzi laughed before she took another drink of her coffee. "She probably was just confused."

Hope nodded. "I guess you're right. She'd been away for a while and Meg probably came over to tidy up once in a while."

"Exactly what I thought." Mitzi finished her coffee and then stood to carry her cup and plate to the sink. "I better get going. I'll have Gilbert bring Bigelow home."

"Thanks. I appreciate all your help with Bigelow." Hope followed her neighbor to the mudroom.

"We're happy to help. That's what neighbors are for. He's a sweet boy. Full of energy." Mitzi gave Hope a big, reassuring hug. "Peggy will always be with all of us," she whispered into Hope's ear. She then disappeared out the door.

Hope closed and locked the door. Even though her morning had been a disaster and she was overwhelmed by the craziness of it all, the threatening note left nailed to her front door wasn't too far from her mind. She did a double check on the lock before she went back into the kitchen. And a triple check.

# Chapter Twenty-One

"You've had quite the morning." Jane closed the hardcover book she had been reading when Hope entered the inn.

"Somehow, I'm still standing." Hope dropped her purse on the reception desk. She was beyond exhausted. Her body felt like she was a dead woman walking, and if she sat down to relax for a moment, she'd fall asleep. As appealing as napping sounded, she couldn't give in to the tiredness that dogged her. She still had a full to-do list to tackle.

"Is everything all right with Ethan and Detective Reid? Neither looked happy when they were at your house." Jane set the book down. She spent her afternoons reading. In the morning she fussed over her guests, making sure they had good breakfasts and their itineraries for the day were set before venturing out to the northwest corner of the state. Aside from antiquing, which Jefferson was known for, the area had great trails to hike or bike, art galleries, farm stands, vineyards, and breweries. There was something for everyone, and Jane knew where all the good places were. Once her guests were out the door, she settled with a cup of tea and a good book in the wingback chair angled so she could see the comings and goings in the foyer. There she recharged before her guests returned later in the day. "The police are being very hush-hush about Hans Vogel's death."

"No gossip?"

Jane shook her head as she stood and joined Hope at the desk. "Not a peep."

"Hey, Hope." Louis jogged down the staircase. His plaid shirt was untucked and his khakis were baggy and wrinkled as usual.

As tired as Hope felt, she still had an urge to steam a crease into his pants.

"Heard you had some excitement at your house this morning."

Hope glared at Jane, who blinked innocently. "There wasn't any gossip about Hans. But you, on the other hand? Loads of gossip."

"Thanks." Hope grabbed her purse off the desk. Felicity arrived at the top of the stairs, so their meeting could start. "Where's Elena?"

Jane shrugged again. "She left right after breakfast. I hardly recognized her."

"What do you mean?"

"The mouse turned into a vixen. The hair, the makeup, the short dress. She looked like she should have been getting back from somewhere rather than leaving first thing in the morning. The girl has a secret," Jane said.

Felicity reached the bottom of the staircase, her phone still glued to her ear. "Tell him I'll provide the photographs. He just needs to send me the products." Felicity turned away from the group but talked loudly enough so they couldn't help but hear her.

"She's on the phone with her agent, again." Louis arrived by Hope's side. "Saw the photo of you and Barnhart. You two close, huh?"

"If class hadn't been cancelled, she'd be getting an A-plus."

Felicity pulled the phone away from her ear. "I know I did in college when I cozied up to the professor."

Somehow, Hope wasn't surprised by Felicity's statement or candor. "Do either of you know where Elena is?"

"She said she had to go out and was fine with her topic for the panel discussion." Louis started walking to the living room.

"Jane said she was all dressed up when she left." Hope followed Louis.

"She looked smokin'. I didn't think she had it in her." Felicity tossed her hair.

"It's only us three, so let's get started," Hope suggested.

The group got comfortable in the living room as the early afternoon sun flitted through the sheer window panels. A soft breeze came through the open French doors to the patio, while melodies of wild birds drifted inside.

In between brainstorming, Felicity and Louis shared what they'd been up to since the workshop was cancelled. Rather than return home, they decided to stay and visit local businesses and participate in the panel discussion. Their outings would provide fresh content for their blogs. They'd found farm stands and restaurants and even visited a brewery. To Hope, it looked like Jefferson was growing on them.

"I need coffee." Felicity popped up from the deeply cushioned armchair. Her long, slim figure seemed more fitting for a fashion blogger than a food blogger. A twinge of envy pricked at Hope as she discreetly glanced at herself. She was still in good shape, thanks to remodeling her house, the daily chores for the chickens, and her semi-regular runs, but she wasn't as taut or firm as she had been when she practiced Pilates four times a week and sweated it out in the gym the other days. Living in the country had made her soft.

"Hope, do you want a cup?" Felicity asked.

Hope lifted her gaze. "Yes, a big cup, please."

"Be right back." Felicity walked out of the living room, the thick carpet cushioning her high-heeled sandals.

Louis jumped up and joined Hope on the sofa. "I'm glad we have a moment alone." He pushed his glasses up the bridge of his nose.

"Really?"

"I want to ask you something. I'm thinking about auditioning for the next season of *The Sweet Taste of Success*." Enthusiasm danced in his cocoa-colored eyes as a smile stretched from ear to ear. "Do you think it's a good idea?"

"It's a baking competition and you're not a baker."

"Right. But it's done wonders for your career," Louis countered.

"It's also done nothing for some of the other contributors. Only a handful of us were able to capitalize on the show. Honestly, I think your time and energy is better spent working on your blog rather than putting yourself through the audition process and learning how to bake."

Hope wasn't sure if Louis could handle the rigors of the competitive cooking show. He'd be dropped into a relentless cycle of near-impossible baking challenges and never-ending and highly encouraged backstabbing and he'd be isolated from friends and family for an extensive period of time. Had she known about those conditions before she signed the contract, she wasn't sure she would have participated.

"Have you considered writing a cookbook?"

"Yeah, every now and again." Louis slumped back onto the sofa.

Hope hated dashing his dreams of stardom, but he did ask for her opinion.

"I just feel stuck. I don't even have an agent."

"You have a brand you've built from your first post, and it would be a shame to toss it because you feel stuck right now." She patted his knee as she stood. Where was Felicity with the coffee? "I'm going to see what's keeping Felicity."

Hope stepped out into the foyer. Jane had left the desk unmanned and Felicity was leaning against the doorframe of the dining room talking on her cell phone. Her back to the foyer.

"Your article was amazing . . . I would have given anything to have seen the look on her face when she saw it . . . Oh, you're welcome. I had to wait so long for her to come out of the house, but it was so worth it when they hugged."

Hope stopped where she was and Felicity's words repeated over in her mind. Felicity took the photograph of her and Cal hugging? She was working with Norrie? They were friends? They were conspiring together against her? Or Cal? It had to be Cal. It was all about chasing the story for Norrie. She didn't care who she trampled over as long as she got a front-page story on Cal Barnhart and her byline was seen by everyone. In Norrie's world, Hope was what was called collateral damage. Hope had a word for people like Norrie and Felicity and she was going to share it.

Hope was ready to confront the underhanded Felicity Campbell, until the inn's front door swung open and two guests came rushing in, giggling and jostling their shopping bags. *Shoot*. Hope retreated and bumped into Louis, who had come up behind her.

The two women dropped their bags beside the desk, waved a hello to Hope and Louis, and then headed for the dining room, where a beverage cart held snacks for guests to help themselves to.

"Is our meeting over?" Louis stepped into the foyer.

Hope turned and nodded. Boy, was it ever over. She doubted she could remain civil toward Felicity, and it was best for all of them for her to leave the inn. "Yes. I have to go."

She dashed into the living room, grabbed her purse, and

fled the inn. Outside, she inhaled a deep, cleansing breath. She felt like she'd been sucker punched. She knew she and Felicity weren't friends and there was some competition between them, but to do something so low and subversive was outrageous. Hope felt ill.

"What are you up to, Hope Early?"

The question dragged Hope's head up and she came face-to-face with Elaine Whitcomb. Her day just kept going downhill, didn't it?

Elaine propped a hand on her hip. "I know you spoke with Gigi."

"Yes. I spoke with Gigi when I went for a facial. I'm allowed to get a facial. It's a free country. So, I got a facial. And she's the one who brought you up, not the other way around. I didn't mention you. I didn't ask about you. She's the one who told me you get all of your services for free. I didn't ask!" She exhaled a short, aggravated breath after spewing out all her pent-up frustration of the day. She thought she'd feel better, but nothing changed.

Elaine just stood there. She looked stunned, well, as much as she could, given her facial enhancements. "Hope, are you okay?"

"Do I look okay?" Hope snapped.

"No, no, you don't." Elaine hesitated. She looked around, as if looking for help. There wasn't anyone else nearby. "Why don't we get some coffee?"

Elaine swept an arm around Hope and led her into the Coffee Clique. She guided Hope to a table and sat her down on a chair while she rushed to the counter to place an order. She returned with two coffees and a cinnamon roll. "The kid said this is your favorite." Elaine set the pastry down, along with the cups.

Hope eyed the pastry. It was her favorite. But did she really need the extra calories? A few minutes ago, she envied

Felicity's figure and accepted the move to the country made her own body less firm. Soft, she had decided on. Maybe it had. But at least she didn't go around sabotaging other women out of petty jealousy or whatever motivated Felicity. Hope reached for the cinnamon roll. Yeah, her body might not be firm, but her soul was kind. That had to be more important than a six-pack. Justified in indulging, she bit into the pastry, and the warm flavors of butter, cinnamon, and velvety sugar icing swirled in her mouth. *Heaven.*

"I got you a decaf." Elaine sat across from Hope and placed her clutch bag on the table. She took a sip of her coffee. "You're having a bad day?"

Hope glanced up from the cinnamon roll.

"You could say that," Hope said after swallowing her bite. She went to take another bite but stopped. Oh, God. What was she doing? She was consoling herself with a pastry and having a meltdown in front of Elaine Whitcomb, of all people. *Get it together, woman.* She couldn't take another bite. Not one more. She pushed the plate away. All she wanted to do was run home, snuggle with Bigelow, and forget this day ever happened. But she was an adult who couldn't run from her public meltdowns. She squared her shoulders. It was time to pull up her big girl panties and apologize to Elaine.

"I'm sorry for my outburst. I shouldn't have raised my voice. You've been very *kind.*"

The last word was a struggle to say, but she got it out.

"We all have our bad days. I guess yours is pretty bad." Elaine sipped her coffee again.

Now there was something they both could agree on. "I swear I wasn't at the spa to snoop on you." No, she was there snooping on Pamela Hutchinson, but she didn't want to burden Elaine with the details. "Gigi asked where I lived and then she started talking about her other client from

Jefferson, which is you. She continued to say you don't pay for the services you receive."

"She does like to talk." Elaine circled the rim of her cup with her manicured finger. "I don't know why Pamela doesn't charge me for the services I receive. She called me one day and invited me for a facial. I went. It was nice to go back. I used to live in Westport."

"You did?"

Elaine nodded. "With my second husband."

"Second?" Hope sputtered on her coffee. After swallowing, she wiped her mouth with a napkin before asking, "How many times have you been married?"

"Not many. Lionel's my fourth."

"Fourth? That's a lot of husbands."

"It's hard finding the right one."

Now there was something else they could agree on. Maybe there was a chance for a friendship between them after all. Four husbands was a lot. She couldn't help but wonder what happened to the other three husbands. The question was right on the tip of her tongue, and she was dying to know, but asking would be rude. She took a sip of coffee and let the question go . . . at least for the time being.

"Anyway, I went for the facial, and Gigi was great. I booked another appointment. I tried to pay, but Pamela said the services were complimentary."

"Did she say why?"

"No. It felt weird, but when I told Lionel, he said to accept the gift. I didn't want to go back. I felt funny about it. You know? But Lionel said since it's free, he wouldn't pay if I went somewhere else. I had to keep going back there for my facials and all the other treatments. I simply can't do without them. You know, it's not easy maintaining all of this." Elaine batted her eyelashes as her unnaturally plump lips curved into a smile.

"I can't begin to imagine."

"I'm sure there's a perfectly good reason why Pamela is being so generous." Elaine's smile slipped. "Something has been bothering me."

"What's wrong?" Hope asked cautiously.

"It seems like you're always trying to pin a murder on my husband. Why don't you like him?"

Talk about a loaded question. Hope laced her fingers around her coffee cup as she tried to find a way to phrase her answer. "It's not about me liking or disliking Lionel."

"It's not?"

Hope was relieved Elaine didn't push her to say how she actually felt about Lionel. "On the surface, it appears he could've had a motive for murder."

"That's silly. My husband isn't a murderer. Sure, he has a bad temper and sometimes says things he shouldn't, but he wouldn't hurt anyone. He's a teddy bear."

Hope wouldn't ever have described Lionel as a teddy bear. Maybe a grizzly bear. "I've learned the P&Z Commission delayed the vote for his newest development and it appears Lily wasn't in favor of voting for the project to continue. So, if there's anything you can tell me to change my opinion, please do."

Elaine waved her multi-ringed hand and it nearly blinded Hope. How many diamond rings could one woman wear at once? "Oh. Okay. This will be easy to clear up. Lionel told me he didn't have to worry about Lily's vote because it was taken care of."

"What did he mean by that?"

"He wasn't specific. He just said the project would get the go-ahead and not to worry. So you see, Lionel didn't have a reason to kill Lily. She was going to vote in favor of the development."

"How can you be sure?"

"Because Lionel told me."

Hope leaned back. Unfortunately, what Elaine said made sense to her. If Lily was swayed to vote in favor of the development, then Lionel wouldn't have had a motive for murder. But everyone Hope had talked to said Lily wasn't inclined to vote in favor of the development. How could Lionel have been so certain of Lily's support?

"So, we're good? Lionel didn't murder anybody, and I'll start paying for my spa services. I'm confident I can convince Lionel to pay going forward." She twirled a strand of her bleached blond hair. "I can be very persuasive."

Hope didn't doubt Elaine's ability to persuade Lionel to part with a few bucks.

"Thanks for the coffee," Hope said.

Elaine stood and lifted her clutch bag off the table. "Anytime." She flashed a broad smile before sashaying out of the coffee shop.

Hope drained the last of her coffee and eyed the cinnamon roll. As tempting as the pastry was, she remained steadfast. She pushed the plate away and thought about what she'd learned so far but only came up with questions.

Why would Pamela offer up hundreds of dollars' worth of services to Elaine for free? Why did Lily go to Westport the day before she disappeared? Did she find out Elaine was getting free services? Was there something else about the spa Hope was missing? Or was Lily's death not connected to the spa or Lionel Whitcomb?

"Do you want the pastry wrapped to go?" the kid from behind the counter asked as he walked to Hope's table.

Hope stared at the cinnamon roll. She wanted to say yes, but she knew she wouldn't enjoy it. "No, thank you."

"Okay." Before he turned to go back to the counter, he left a register receipt on the table. "The other lady said you'd be paying."

*Seriously?*

"Of course she did." Hope grabbed the receipt. To think she thanked Elaine for her coffee. She was a piece of work. She reached into her purse for her wallet, mumbling to herself about being stuck with the bill. She opened her wallet and then heard her cell phone ring. She pulled the phone out and there was a new text message from a blocked number.

Burn baby, burn. Is that the way you want it?

# Chapter Twenty-Two

Hope leapt out of her seat with the phone still in her hand. Panic pulsed through her as she surveyed the coffee shop. Was her anonymous texter there? There were just a few other customers clustered into small groups engaged in conversations. She slapped down a ten-dollar bill on the table, grabbed her purse, and raced out of the shop. She stepped out onto Main Street and the afternoon sun beat down, yet a chill snaked its way through her body. The person could be anyone. Anywhere.

*Burn, baby, burn.*

She had to call Ethan to let him know she'd received another threat.

*Burn, baby, burn.*

She stopped walking and cast a wide glance over Main Street.

Everything looked normal. Businesses were open, locals came and went while tourists flocked to the antique shops. Spring drew visitors from all over Connecticut for day trips and from out of state for serious antiquing. With a stretch of lovely weather, business was booming in Jefferson. Not even the recent turn of events in the case of Lily Barnhart seemed to dampen tourism. Hope had an unsettled feeling

Lily's case actually boosted tourism. She guessed morbid curiosities were good for the economy. Her own curiosity at the moment was trying to figure out who sent the threatening text and how the person got her phone number.

A tap on her shoulder nearly sent Hope swinging around, ready to throw a punch.

Matt raised his hands in surrender. "Whoa! Is everything okay?"

Hope caught her breath. "You scared the daylights out of me." She shoved her phone back into her purse.

"I'm sorry. What's going on? Are you okay?"

"Yeah. I'm just a little jumpy." Her admission had Matt cocking an eyebrow. "Okay, a lot jumpy."

"I heard about the threatening note left nailed to your front door. I suspect you're playing detective again."

"Yes, I am. And you can save the lecture. I've already heard it. Several times." Her heartbeat was returning to its normal rate and her nerves were settling down. Whoever sent the text probably wasn't watching her. Or, at least she hoped not. Her chest felt tight just thinking that someone had eyes on her and was waiting to strike again.

"I wasn't going to lecture you. You're a grown woman and if you insist on making foolish decisions, it's your right."

"Foolish? Thank you for understanding. I have to go."

"Hope." Matt reached out and grabbed her arm. "You know what I meant. Doing what you're doing is dangerous. I'm not saying any more on the matter. But still on the subject of the murders, I've been retained by Cal Barnhart."

"He's been arrested?"

"No. However, it's a smart move to have legal representation. He should have actually done it earlier."

"Wouldn't he have looked guilty?"

"He would have looked smart. Far too many times the police will gravitate to the path of least resistance and an innocent person can be arrested, tried, and convicted of a crime."

"You're generalizing and I'm not a juror." She knew Ethan wouldn't sacrifice the freedom of an innocent person just to close a case. Though, she wasn't too sure about Detective Reid. The jury was still out on him.

"Perhaps, but it doesn't hurt to have an ally on your side. I saw the photograph of you two in the newspaper. What exactly is your relationship with Cal?"

Hope rolled her eyes. "Not you, too. There's no relationship. We barely know each other!"

"You're wound pretty tight today."

"Am not." Who was she kidding? She was ready to punch him a moment ago. She took a deep breath to calm herself. "You're right. I am. I'm sorry. I think I'm going to be apologizing a lot today."

Matt rested his hands on her shoulders, tugging her a little closer but not too close. The last thing she needed was another candid photo of her in a man's embrace or in the vicinity of his broad chest. "How about dinner tonight? We won't talk about Cal or anything related to the murders. We'll just celebrate."

Hope smiled. Not talking about Cal or the fire or the threats on her life sounded perfect to her. "Celebrate what?"

"My new house. My offer was accepted."

Mental face palm slap. She'd completely forgotten he'd put in an offer on a house. "Congratulations! Yes, I'd love to have dinner with you tonight to celebrate."

"I'll call you later."

He released her with hesitation before continuing on his way. He was concerned for her and, truth be told, so was she. He reached the curb and looked both ways before crossing. She smiled. Safety first. She reveled in the first light moment she'd had all day and let her gaze follow Matt to the Jefferson Town Real Estate office. He sure was a fine specimen of a man—his confident swagger as he walked, his broad shoulders and his glutes. She wiggled an eyebrow. Yeah, he had good glutes.

After he disappeared into the building, Hope lingered for a moment as she considered what to do next. There wasn't any shortage of options for her. She had to report the text message she received, she had a pile of work to do, and, even though she tidied up after the tea party, the house needed a good cleaning. Her gaze drifted along the line of shops and homes and landed on the Red House Antique Shop. Her day was about to get a whole lot better.

When she caught a break in traffic, she dashed across the street and made a beeline for Everett's shop. Before she could reach the front door, she was intercepted by Drew.

"You'll never guess what happened." He beamed. He didn't give her time to respond. "Maretta called me. Me! I have an interview with her. I'll be back on the front page!" His hands were expressive as he shared his comeback story.

"Congratulations," Hope mustered. She was too emotionally and mentally drained to rally any more excitement.

"That's all I get? Not for nothing, but my career has been circling the drain since Norrie joined the newspaper and now I have an exclusive. Could you show a little more enthusiasm?"

Her friend was right. What was she thinking? Of course she should've been more excited. Forget there was an arsonist/murderer stalking her or the tea party she hosted was turned upside down and ended with an official visit by the police. How selfish of her.

She forced a smile. "Congratulations!"

Drew smiled gratefully in return. "Thank you. It feels good to be back." He glanced over his shoulder. "Doing a little shopping?"

"I need some retail therapy."

"I heard about the tea." Drew grimaced. "Maretta, Meg, and the cops. You throw a hell of a party."

"Not funny. Either get out of my way or open the door."

"Touchy, touchy." Drew shifted and opened the door of the antique shop for Hope. He followed after Hope entered.

"Good afternoon, Hope, Drew," Everett greeted as he looked away from a display of china he was arranging on a hutch. When he wasn't telling the story, or provenance as it was known in the antiques world, of an antique, he was busy fussing with the shop's merchandise.

Hope drifted to the mahogany table she'd been drooling over and dreaming about for months. Financial sensibility had kept her from making an offer on the table, even though the price on the table wasn't the final price. Everett would negotiate like he always did, and she actually enjoyed that process of haggling. However, the final cost would still be in the four figures.

"I heard what happened at your house this morning." Everett looked over his shoulder. He was the consummate antiques dealer—keen eye, inquisitive, knowledgeable, and discreet. He'd never reveal who gave him all the salacious details on the tea party. "Looks like we need to find another candidate for the commission since Maretta is now running for mayor."

"Looks like you do." Hope was still focused on the table. At least she was trying to focus on the table. The stress of the past few hours overwhelmed her and, as much as she knew it was wrong, making a purchase would help her feel better. She needed a little pick-me-up.

"I wonder what prompted Maretta to run for mayor. I've never heard her mention an interest in politics before," Everett said.

"That's one of the questions I'm going to ask her." Drew drifted away from the table, but not too far. A gilded mirror caught his attention. "I have an interview with her today."

He leaned forward and smiled into the mirror. He combed his fingers through his blond hair and adjusted his striped tie.

"Speaking of the commission, did you know someone assured Lionel Whitcomb he didn't have to worry about Lily's vote?" Hope asked Everett as she lifted her gaze from the table. What Elaine had told her over coffee left her more curious. Who was Lionel's source about the vote?

Everett raised his eyebrows slightly. "This is the first I'm hearing of it." The shop's telephone rang and he excused himself to answer the call at the sales counter.

Drew slid back to Hope's side and tugged on her arm. "What are you talking about? Lily was going to vote in favor of the development? Since when?"

"Elaine told me," Hope whispered as she craned her neck forward.

Drew's eyes almost bugged out of his head. "Seriously? When?"

"A few minutes ago, when we had coffee."

"Coffee? You and her?"

"Long story. Anyway, she said Lionel didn't have a reason to kill Lily because Lily was going to vote in his favor. My question is who could've assured him?" She thought for a moment and an idea wriggled in her brain. "The killer. Of course the killer would have because there'd be a vacancy on the commission and filled by someone in favor of the development."

Drew looked unimpressed. "Good theory."

"You have another?"

"As a matter of fact, I do. There's another way to make sure someone does what you want them to do. Bribery."

"You're way off base. Lily didn't seem to be the type of person who would have taken a bribe. And she's dead. If she accepted the bribe, she wouldn't have been killed."

"Unless her death had nothing to do with the commission." Drew's cell phone buzzed and he pulled it out of his back pants pocket. "Maretta. Gotta take this." He spun around but tossed a look over his shoulder. "Oh, I'm still looking into who owns that property in Westport." He continued out of the store.

"Is there anything in particular you're looking for today?" Everett asked from behind Hope.

Hope startled. People kept sneaking up on her. "Yes, there is." Her fingertips glided across the table's polished surface. Not a scratch. Pristine condition. Hence the price. Should she buy it or be financially sensible and leave empty-handed?

"Ah." Everett's eyes twinkled. "You won't regret this purchase."

She looked at the beautiful table. It'd been calling her name since it arrived in the store. She placed a palm on the surface. She really wanted it. Really, really wanted it. She'd be receiving an advance payment for the cookbook soon and she was finishing up an e-book on frozen desserts she'd be selling on her website in a few weeks. What the heck. Throwing caution to the wind, along with her financial responsibility, she made an offer.

She and Everett haggled a little bit and finally got to a price they both agreed upon. She was slipping her credit card back into her wallet when he said, "You and Drew had your heads together before he left. Is everything okay? You seemed a little distracted when you came into the shop." His face was pinched with concern.

"I was a little distracted. So much is going on. Maretta's surprise announcement, the fire, and Hans is dead, did you know that?" When Everett nodded, she continued. "And I heard Whitcomb had been assured he had Lily's vote."

"The only way anyone can be assured of our vote is when we actually vote. It's probably just gossip." He stepped out from behind the sales counter. "But I will make some inquiries. If something is going on, I'll make sure to find out." He guided Hope to the door. "I'll deliver the table tomorrow."

"See you then." Hope turned, refusing to second-guess her decision. Just as she stretched her arm out to open the door, she noticed a new item in the shop and it jogged her memory from her visit to the country club the other day when she confronted Kent.

"Hickory-shafted clubs in their original nineteen-twenties' canvas bag." Everett joined Hope by the antique golf clubs and pulled one of the clubs out of the bag.

The clubs appeared to be in good shape; their heads were clean and their leather wrap grips were in fair condition for their age. Hope was familiar with golf clubs because her dad often asked for a new set for Father's Day.

"You play golf, right?" she asked Everett.

"I do. Are you thinking about taking up the sport?" He admired the club like Hope admired a perfectly risen soufflé.

"No. But I saw you the other day at the country club. I was leaving and I waved but you didn't see me. Oh well, I better get going. Great set of clubs." She glimpsed at the price tag and frowned. It was much less than her table. Maybe she should collect golf items rather than furniture.

Outside the shop, she glanced over at the Jefferson Town Real Estate office and remembered her dinner plans with Matt. Was it a date? No, he said it was to celebrate his new home. It wasn't a date. But what if it was a date? She hadn't been on a date in ages. If it was a date, what should she wear? Did she really want it to be a date? They were friends, kind of. Not like her and Ethan. Maybe it was better that way if it was a date. She and Matt didn't have a history or anything to risk if the date didn't go well.

She needed to stop overthinking. Her plans with Matt were for dinner. Dinner. Period. With a firm nod, she picked up her pace to get back home. She had a dinner to get ready for.

It wasn't a date.

Hope followed a count of three on the way down and a count of one on the way back up for her fifth squat out of twelve. Two fifteen-pound dumbbells rested on her shoulders, and she went down for another three counts. The move was slow and controlled, with a burst of energy on the way back up.

"So, what time is the date?" Claire set her twenty-pound weight on the rack. She'd just finished an overhead triceps extension.

"It's not a date." Hope concentrated on her form to make sure her knees didn't extend over her toes.

"Then why this emergency workout?" Claire patted her forehead with a towel and then took a swig of water from her bottle.

When Hope returned home after dropping a small fortune on a table she shouldn't have purchased, she panicked. Again. And not about the table or the threats but about Matt. In the back of her mind, she couldn't help but think the dinner was really a date and, after her earlier assessment of her body, she had an unrealistic need to firm it up within just a few short hours. Even though she knew it wasn't possible, she had to try. So, a quick call to her sister for a guest pass to the gym and Hope changed into her workout clothes and hit the weights.

"Come on. Admit it. You're attracted to him. It's okay. He's single. You're single." Claire grabbed two ten-pound weights and began doing a set of upright rows.

"He's handsome and I like his company. He's smart and funny." Hope stopped squatting. "But what about Ethan?"

Claire gave Hope a sympathetic look. "It's only dinner. You're not marrying him."

Hope squatted again. "You should have seen the look on Ethan's face when he showed up the other day and Cal was helping me with my photography."

"Jealous?"

Hope shrugged. "I think so."

"Good. The two of you have been doing this little dance for too long. You either need to let him dip you or let someone else cut in."

Hope traded down to twelve-pound weights. "Dip me?"

Claire stopped lifting her weights. "Look, you both needed each other's friendship after your marriages ended. And you both needed the little flirtation to rebuild your self-esteems. Your exes have moved on, so you both need to move on also, either with each other or with other people."

Hope absorbed her sister's solid advice. She hadn't realized how detrimental the divorce had been to her self-esteem until recently when she realized Tim's behavior stemmed from him not feeling he was good enough as a husband, friend, and person. He looked outside their marriage for validation, admiration, and love. Hope would never be able to fill the void he had. The time had come to let go of the past and move forward, and not just with her career. The blog was in a good place. She'd just signed with an agent and was connecting with more brands. She had the opportunity to participate in a cookbook and, rather than dreading being pulled back toward the past, she now saw the potential for her future. She had a beautiful home, a loving family, friends, and a faithful dog.

Claire was right. It was time to move forward and open herself up to finding love again.

"Just don't stand there. You have six more squats to do," Claire barked.

Hope laughed. "Yes, sir." She went back to her workout

and, for the next thirty minutes, sweated and moaned her way to feeling less stressed. She didn't know how much firmer she was, but her head was clearer and the dreadful morning was in her rearview mirror.

After they finished working out, they hit the showers and dressed.

"Smoothie?" Claire asked as she touched up her makeup. "And you can finish telling me about your coffee with Elaine. I can't believe you two had coffee."

"Neither can I." Hope slipped on her ballet flats and stood up from the bench. She grabbed her gym bag and followed Claire out of the locker room. At some point, she was going to have to tell Claire about the second threat she'd received. But, she didn't want to think about it at the moment. As nervous as the threat made her, she wasn't going to allow the person behind it to get inside her head and change how she lived her life.

At the beverage bar, they each ordered a green tea smoothie. They grabbed a couple seats at a table and Hope filled Claire in on what happened after the tea party but left out the detail of the table purchase. She knew Claire would jump all over her for spending that much money. Since the table was being delivered the next day, she'd have to fess up to the purchase eventually, but that would be a problem for another day.

"I want to hear everything." Claire took a long drink of her smoothie as Hope began recapping her one-on-one time with Elaine. It felt good to spend a little girl time with her sister and it almost had her forgetting about her date with Matt. Almost.

# Chapter Twenty-Three

"I'm happy you were able to get reservations here." Hope tucked her chair under the table for two while Matt walked around to the other side and sat. The Avery Bistro was a popular restaurant with a small menu. "I was here a few months ago to celebrate Claire's anniversary."

"She's the one who suggested this place. She said you love the food here." The candlelight on the table flickered. Its glow softened Matt's chiseled jawline. He gave a slow, knowing smile that Hope felt all the way down to her toes.

"I do." She lifted her menu to give her mind something else to concentrate on, other than Matt's sexy grin. She perused the menu, even though she was certain of what she was going to order. The list of entrées was a distraction and gave her a chance to get a grip before she made a complete fool out of herself. The resulting silence between them made her uncomfortable, so she peeked a look over the top of the menu.

Matt was studying the menu.

"You'll find, once you're settled, a lot of great places for dinner. There are also a few wineries." When did she become a walking, talking, breathing tour brochure for Jefferson?

"Someone mentioned a brewery nearby."

"Yes. Northwest Hills Brewery. They have a great pub menu. You should definitely check it out."

"Maybe you'll be able to join me," he said over his menu.

*Oh, boy.* So, they were on a date. A first date. Hope cleared her throat. "Maybe," she squeaked out.

Matt closed his menu. "I know what I want." His gaze was intense, and she prayed he was talking about food. "What about you?"

"Linguini with clam sauce."

Matt let out a hearty laugh. "Great minds think alike." He closed his menu and relaxed back into his chair. "You look lovely tonight."

Hope's cheeks warmed from the compliment. She'd shimmied into a little black dress and stepped into a pair of strappy sandals. Simple yet elegant and perfect for dinner with a friend or a date. She'd added a shimmery wrap over her shoulders and put her hair into a more polished updo than the one she wore the other day to the spa. Which reminded her she hadn't heard from Drew. He was going to look further into Pamela's spa. She'd have to call him later when she got home.

"Thank you. It's been a while since I've been out to dinner. It's kind of nice to dress up. Most days I'm in jeans and a plaid shirt between working on the house and recipe testing."

"You always look great, no matter what you're wearing."

Hope reached for the water glass at her setting and drank. She needed to cool off and change the subject. A little part of her liked the idea of a date with Matt, but the truth was she wasn't ready for a date. Dating required her to be willing to risk being hurt again. And, she wasn't sure she was up for that. The hurt from Tim's betrayal was starting to fade with each passing day but it was still there, a reminder to be careful with her heart. Was Matt a man she could trust with her heart? On paper, yes. But, then again, Tim looked good on paper too.

She lifted her gaze from her water glass and found Matt looking at her, his expression curious, and she couldn't blame him.

She'd just gulped half a glass of water. "Thirsty." She set the glass down.

Their waiter arrived and took their orders.

After the waiter walked away, Hope leaned back. She was going to stop the craziness in her head and enjoy her evening with her friend Matt.

"I'm dying to see your house. I remember seeing it in the newspaper when it was first listed. It looks charming."

"And I'd love for you to come over. You know, I'm a pretty good cook. Maybe not food blog worthy, but I do make a mean chicken Marsala."

*Oh, boy.* A third date? If he kept it up, they'd be planning their wedding reception by the time dessert came. Even with what Claire had said about her relationship with Ethan and her own worries they could never move past anything but a friendship, she still wasn't ready to enter into a romantic relationship with someone else. Okay, now she was just being silly. Of course she had to consider other men because she and Ethan were just friends. Weren't they? Looking across the table at Matt she was completely confused. She gave herself a mental shake and what dislodged was a small, hopeful thought that she and Ethan could be more than friends.

*Whoa!*

The waiter reappeared with a bread basket and then moved to another table. More patrons were coming in, and the din of conversation was starting to fill the room. Grateful for the distraction from her thoughts, Hope reached for a slice of bread just as Matt did, and their hands brushed.

His skin was warm and their contact lingered for a moment before she yanked her hand back. So much for a distraction.

He offered her a roll and she accepted. As she buttered her roll, she wondered if she should say something about any future dates. Or should she just leave it alone and enjoy their dinner tonight?

"Do the police have any leads on who left that note nailed to your front door?"

Hope set her butter knife down and said a silent *thank you* for the change of conversation, even though it was about a threat made on her life.

"No. And it isn't just one threat. I received another threat earlier today." She took a bite of her roll.

"What? Did you tell the police? What did the threat say?"

Hope shared the specifics about the text message with Matt and told him she reported it to Ethan. The niggling suspicion that Ethan would want to lock her in her house once he learned about the second threat was correct. When he realized she wouldn't agree to his suggestion, he tried to assign a police officer to her, which she promptly declined. She didn't want a shadow and, besides, she was having dinner with Matt so she'd be safe.

"Why on earth did you turn down police protection? Hope, those threats are very serious. There are two people dead."

"Three," Hope corrected. "Hans Vogel was found this morning. I spoke with him just a few days ago."

Matt shook his head as his face darkened. "I'm very concerned for your safety." He reached across the table and rested his hand over Hope's and squeezed gently. "I don't want anything to happen to you. You're a very special woman."

*Special?* "Matt, I think we should talk about something. About us."

"Us?"

Hope nodded. "You and me. What's happening between

us? I just think you should know I'm still sorting things out from my divorce. I have to admit I'm a little gun-shy about entering into a new relationship . . . I think that's why Ethan and I haven't moved past our friendship . . . I'm not saying we've talked about it and decided we want to but are just waiting . . . Maybe we should talk about it. We talk about everything else except us."

"You and Ethan?"

Hope nodded again. "I talked to Claire earlier about us. . . ."

"You and Ethan or you and me?"

"Ethan and me. She thinks I should let him dip me."

"Dip you?"

Hope giggled. "She meant we've been doing this dance around our relationship and it's time to find a new partner or let him dip me. Silly, huh?"

"And the new partner would be me? Us?"

"Exactly. Maybe we're just meant to be friends."

"You and Ethan?"

"Yes. I mean, after all this time, nothing has happened between us romantically so maybe it never will and I should look for a new partner. I just don't think I'm ready. You're a very nice man. Very attractive, I have to admit you're kind of sexy for a lawyer, but I don't want to lead you on."

The waiter reappeared with their salads.

Hope murmured a thank-you and once the waiter was out of earshot, continued, "I don't want you to think this dinner is going to turn into a second date at the brewery or a third date in your house over pasta."

"Good to know." Matt lifted his fork and jabbed at a slice of cucumber. He chewed. "The dressing is very good."

"Is it?" Hope lifted her fork but set it down. It landed with a clink against the plate. "That's all you have to say after everything I've just said?"

"Hope, I'm not looking for a romantic relationship with

you. Tonight's dinner is to celebrate my new house. And I mentioned dinner at the brewery because besides Claire, you're the only friend I have up here."

"I see." Hope lifted her fork again and stabbed at a chunk of lettuce. "My mistake." And what a big mistake it was. Huge. Gigantic. Stupid. She didn't consider he might have been involved with someone else. A girlfriend. A fiancée. Heck, he could have had a wife stashed someplace. If so, what was he doing going out to dinner with her without telling her? The nerve.

"Wait." Matt reached out and drew Hope's attention back to him. "I think you have the wrong idea. I just got out of a long-term relationship, so I'm not ready to date anyone."

Hope's shoulders slumped. He'd had his heart broken. Thank goodness he wasn't a cad. "I'm so sorry. Breakups are hard. If you ever want to talk about it, I'm here for you."

While she did sympathize with him, a small part of her was relieved to know the reason why he wasn't interested in her romantically. With her pride restored, she lifted her fork again. Maybe she didn't make a complete fool out of herself after all.

"Rodney and I had been together three years last month."

Rodney? Oh, God. Any chance of her not making a fool out of herself was gone. She wanted to bang her head against the table and then crawl under it.

"His career was more important than our relationship. He was offered a position in Oregon and moved out."

Hope cringed inwardly as an uncomfortable silence descended upon them again. She didn't know what to say to Matt. What could she say? She pierced a slice of cucumber with her fork and took a bite. "This dressing is really good." She finished chewing and wondered if she could get her linguini to go.

"There you are." Drew rushed to Hope's table, coming up short. He knocked the table with his legs.

Both Hope and Matt reached out to secure their water glasses.

"Sorry," he mumbled.

"What are you doing here?" Hope was confused by his appearance and even more embarrassed than she was just moments ago because now heads were turned in their direction and looking on with curiosity.

"Why aren't you answering your phone?" Drew asked.

"Because I'm having dinner." Hope's jaw was clenched. People were watching them.

"We need to talk. Hi, Matt." Drew gave a small wave.

"Hey, Drew. What's going on?"

"I need to steal her for one sec." Drew reached out and assisted Hope up from her chair.

She swatted off his handling, but he grabbed her again to lead her toward the front of the restaurant. She wobbled in her high-heeled sandals. She couldn't get her balance with Drew pulling her. As she looked back at Matt, their waiter approached the table. He had to be inquiring about the scene that was unfolding. Okay, it was official. This was the worst non-date she'd ever had. Ever.

"Sorry for interrupting your date." Drew let go of her once they were out of the earshot of the other diners.

"Don't be. It's not a date." Despite their screwball performance, Hope was actually relieved by Drew's unexpected arrival. "What's so important you had to track me down?"

"You'll never guess who owns the building Pamela is leasing."

"I'm not in the mood for guessing games."

Drew frowned. "Date not going well?"

"It's not a date. Just tell me who owns the building."

"Lionel Whitcomb. Of course, it's under one of his corporations, but I was able to track it back to Whitcomb."

The information had Hope blinking. The mayor's wife was leasing property owned by the developer who was building all over town, with one of those properties hanging in the balance on a vote by the P&Z Commission. One of those commission members had the spa address in her possession and was the swing vote for the development in question and had ended up murdered. "Coincidence?"

Drew shot her an "are you kidding me" look. "Do you really believe in coincidences? This could explain why Pamela opened the spa in Westport and not Jefferson."

"How do you figure?"

"I dug some more once I found out Whitcomb owns the building. Pamela is paying nowhere near what she should be for rent."

"He's not known to be generous. Why wouldn't he be charging the market rate for rent?"

"I'm thinking Milo promised Whitcomb he would receive the go-ahead for the new development in exchange for a discounted lease on Pamela's spa. Now it makes sense why Pamela kept it quiet. She didn't want to draw attention to the business. This is big news. Local government corruption," Drew whispered. "I can't believe I've cracked this story. Ha!" From the cockiness in his voice, Hope sensed Drew's confidence had returned and if she didn't rein him in, he'd be writing an article heavy on speculation and light on fact.

"You may want to hold off on going to your editor."

"What? Are you crazy? Why? We have what Elaine told you about Lily's vote, and I have the very generous leasing terms for Pamela's spa."

Hope shook her head. "Elaine could retract what she told me. Milo and Pam could come up with some plausible excuses. We need more proof."

Drew sighed as he crossed his arms over his chest. "Then we need to find it fast. I don't want Norrie scooping this story."

"Okay." Hope patted Drew's arm. "We will. I promise."

"I should let you get back to your date." Drew glanced over his shoulder at Matt. "He seems like a good catch."

"He is. For the right person." Hope's voice was wistful as she followed Drew's gaze. "I should get back to him. Let's get together tomorrow."

Drew didn't look happy but nodded in the affirmative. "Enjoy your dinner." He gave Hope a light kiss on the cheek and left the restaurant.

She took a deep breath and mentally prepared herself for the walk back to her table. Surely everyone in the dining room had lost interest in her by now.

"Is everything okay, Miss Early?" Hayley asked as she stepped behind the hostess station.

"Yes. I apologize for the commotion."

"No worries." The petite redhead smiled brightly. "We're getting used to having the press barge in here. Just a few nights another reporter . . . Nora . . . Norrie, yes, Norrie. She breezed in like she owned the place."

Hope wasn't shocked to hear of Norrie's lack of manners. "Who did she come here to see?"

"The mayor. Let me tell you, his wife wasn't happy when the mayor stood and walked out of here with Norrie. They talked for a bit and then she left and the mayor returned to his table."

"It must have been important for Norrie to interrupt the mayor's dinner. Did you happen to hear what they talked about?"

"I don't eavesdrop." The hostess leaned forward and dropped her voice. She certainly wasn't above a little gossip, it seemed. "I think it might have been about the fire on your street. It was on the same night, you know. He threw down a hundred-dollar bill and left shortly after they talked."

"Thanks." She turned and entered the dining room. As she made her way to her table, heads turned and whispers buzzed. They hadn't forgotten.

Before she closed the passenger door of Matt's sedan, Hope leaned in and thanked him again for dinner and for not asking too many questions. When she'd returned to their table after Drew left the restaurant, Matt had probed for answers about the interruption to their meal but Hope had remained tight-lipped. There was a chance she and Drew could be wrong about their theories and spreading gossip about the mayor and Lionel Whitcomb being involved in corruption and murder would be irresponsible of them. Matt had eventually let go of the questions and then moved on to other topics, like how Hope had become a blogger and what had made Matt leave law enforcement to become a lawyer. Even though the night included some embarrassing moments for Hope, it turned out to be a nice evening. Matt said good night and drove away.

She dashed inside her house and was welcomed home by Bigelow, who acted like he hadn't seen her in days. Having him reminded her how lonely her home was before she adopted him. She couldn't imagine coming home to an empty house ever again. After showering him with affection, she headed upstairs to quickly change out of her dress and heels. Bigelow was right behind her and when she wasn't looking, he snagged one of her sandals and used it for a fun toy. She yanked the shoe from his mouth and reprimanded him, but his big brown eyes showed no remorse, just playfulness. She sighed and stashed her shoes in her closet.

Changed into a pair of jeans and a cotton sweater, she grabbed her purse and headed for the back door. Bigelow followed. He looked at her. His big brown eyes had shifted from playful to hopeful. She knew that look and couldn't deny him a car ride.

Within minutes, they were at the police station and the dispatcher was buzzing her and Bigelow into the main office. They made their way to Ethan's office. She rapped her knuckles on the door and he looked up from his paperwork.

"Hey, you got a second?" Hope asked as she led Bigelow into the office.

Not exactly a corner office like the one Hope had managed to snag before her stint on reality television, Ethan's office was modest in size and had a view of the back parking lot. The space was functional, but a few personal touches had been added since he spent so much time there. A long, comfortable sofa lined one wall and on the opposite wall a floor-to-ceiling bookcase held reference books, framed photographs of former colleagues, and sports memorabilia. The only personal item on his cluttered desk was a photograph of his two daughters.

"What's up? And why do you have Bigelow with you?" Ethan set his pen down and swiveled his chair around, clapping his hands and whistling for the dog to come to him.

Hope let go of the leash and Bigelow trotted over to Ethan for pets and a treat. Ethan pulled out a dog biscuit from a box tucked into the bottom desk drawer.

"You shouldn't spoil him," Hope chided.

Bigelow took the biscuit and trotted over to the sofa. He jumped up and settled down to eat his treat.

"Make yourself at home." Ethan laughed. He closed the box and shut the drawer. "So, what's going on?"

"I have some information you should know about." Hope sat on one of the two chairs in front of the desk.

She'd promised Drew they'd meet up the next day and make a plan, but as she ate dinner, she thought the police needed to know what she knew, theory or not. Drew probably was going to kill her, but if what she was piecing together was true, then she was getting way in over her head.

Ethan nodded slowly. "I do appreciate you've come to me. Let's hear it."

"I believe that Milo and Lionel Whitcomb are involved in criminal activity."

"Pretty strong accusations. Do you have any proof to back up what you're saying?"

Hope spent the next fifteen minutes recapping all of the information she'd gathered. When she was done, Ethan leaned back and scrubbed a hand over his face. Day-old stubble and the deep bags beneath his eyes reminded Hope of how many hours Ethan was putting into the investigation. Maybe she should have waited until the morning to talk to him.

"Drew found the records of Lionel's ownership of the building Pamela is leasing."

"Not enough proof. Though, it could be used to start building a case of corruption. But do you really think either man is capable of murder?"

"I honestly don't know. I can't see Milo killing anybody. Lionel? Well, he does have a temper and if Lily flat-out refused to vote his way, I could see him lash out. Look, Ethan, I don't know what any of this means, but I thought you should know."

"I'm glad you told me, even though you weren't supposed to be involved. I'll fill Reid in tomorrow morning."

"Great. I hope it helps with the murder investigation. I guess we should be going." Hope stood and looked at the sofa. Bigelow had finished eating the biscuit and fallen asleep. "Maybe I should leave him."

Ethan chuckled. "I'm not sharing my bed with him."

"You're not going home tonight?"

"Probably not. I have a ton of paperwork. I'll catch a couple hours of sleep."

"You look exhausted. You should go home to a real bed."

"I will. At some point. When this case is closed." Ethan walked around the desk. "I'm going to have Warner escort you home since it's late."

"Why? I have a guard dog." Hope laughed as she nudged Bigelow awake.

The dog yawned widely before jumping off the sofa.

"Some guard dog. He's barely standing up." Ethan walked to the doorway and called out for the officer. He gave his instructions and turned to Hope. "I'll call you tomorrow."

"Okay. Don't work too hard. And make sure you get some sleep." With Bigelow's leash in her hand and him by her side, they exited Ethan's office.

Officer Warner followed behind them as they walked out of the main office. Most of the desks were empty and Hope spied Detective Reid's office, which was dark. He'd probably want to question her about what Elaine told her. Though she'd bet money Elaine would deny what she'd said about her husband, and Hope couldn't blame her. Even if she didn't deny what she had said, Hope wondered if her statement could be used in court because Elaine and Lionel were married.

Passing through the doorway that led to the lobby, she pulled out her cell phone from her back pocket and dialed Drew's number. He was going to burst a gasket when she told him about her visit to Ethan, so she was thrilled to get his voice mail. "Don't be angry with me." Yeah, that was a great way to start a conversation. "I'm leaving Ethan's office now. I told him about Lionel and Milo. I don't know what he's going to do with the information, but you may want to be at town hall tomorrow first thing. Love you." It wouldn't hurt to remind him of her affection for him.

She swiped the phone off and opened the main door and

stepped out into the cool night air. Officer Warner broke away to go to his vehicle while she headed for hers.

Bigelow tugged at his leash as they approached her SUV and her thoughts drifted to Milo. Did she just do the right thing? What if he wasn't involved and the lease on Pamela's spa had nothing to do with improper dealings with Lionel Whitcomb? Any hint of impropriety could damage Milo's reputation. His career. Pamela's career. She could totally be wrong.

Bigelow barked and his haunches raised, prompting Hope to halt. She noticed a figure between herself and her vehicle.

"Good evening, Hope."

"Milo? What are you doing here?" She glanced to the rear parking lot for Officer Warner's car. Where was he?

"We need to talk." Milo stepped forward and Bigelow's bark turned into a deep growl. He bared his teeth.

"Officer Warner will be pulling his car around any second." At least she hoped so. A coldness had lodged deep in her gut. The chance meeting with Milo wasn't a coincidence, and Hope wasn't feeling a friendly vibe from Milo.

"Then I'll make this quick. I don't know what you think you know, but I advise you to mind your own business." An edge had crept into his voice. Gone was the amiable mayor.

"Or what?"

He scoffed. "You've always been a stubborn girl. There are consequences to every action. I'm willing to pay mine. Are you?"

Before Hope could reply, headlights appeared from the back parking lot.

Milo looked over his shoulder and then back to Hope. "Have a nice evening." He strode away toward Main Street and disappeared into the night.

"Everything okay, Hope? Who was that?" Officer Warner asked from his rolled-down window.

"The mayor." Her voice was shaky and her racing heart was pounding. Maybe she and Drew weren't wrong about the mayor.

Warner glanced at Bigelow. "He doesn't seem too happy with the mayor."

*He's not the only one.* The dog was still on alert, his gaze fixated ahead.

She rubbed his head. "Sorry for the delay. It'll take us just a minute."

She tugged on the leash and led Bigelow to her vehicle. She opened the back passenger door and Bigelow jumped onto the seat. Closing the door, she also shut down her doubts.

# Chapter Twenty-Four

Hope and her fellow bloggers were ushered into the community room by Beth Green. There Beth had set up the table and arranged rows of folding chairs for the audience. The space was typically used for functions, like the annual bake sale and speaker events, because of the large audiences they attracted.

Editions of novels authored by town residents were displayed in a tall bookcase hand carved by a local woodworker. Browsing the bookcase was like taking a trip through Jefferson's history. All of Jane's mystery novels were set on a shelf, along with a framed photograph of the town's favorite author. Along the wall several paintings by local artists hung and, on the fireplace's mantel, photographs of the founders of the library were on display.

What started out in the living room of Frieda Bishop's house lending books to neighbors became the town's first library in 1903. Along with two other Jeffersonians, Fred Merrifield and Louisa Dayton, Frieda was able to relocate the library to a small house just north of the existing police department. Over the years, funds were raised to build the current library and it thrived through community involvement and interactive programming.

Hope looked out at the crowd from her seat at the table, where she was joined by Louis, Felicity, and Elena, who eventually showed up, albeit late. Every seat in the audience was occupied, and the attendees listened intently to what the bloggers had to say. A whole bunch of hands were raised once the panel opened the floor to questions.

"How many times do you try a recipe before you write your post?" a woman from the third row asked Felicity.

As Hope had prepared for her day, she had to also prepare for coming face-to-face with Felicity. There were a few ways she could handle the backstabbing blogger from Brooklyn. Some ways, while satisfying, would only serve to hurt Hope in the long run. It was best for her to maintain self-control and take the high road. As her mother always said, "Let them roll around in the gutter while you stand proudly on the sidewalk." Heeding her mom's advice, Hope pasted on her most professional smile and pretended nothing was wrong.

Felicity leaned forward to the mic. "Three times. If it's not successful, I move on. I don't waste my time and I certainly don't want any of my readers to cook a recipe that won't work."

"Thank you," the woman said. "One more question. What's your favorite recipe?"

Felicity flashed a smile as she tilted her head and flipped her hair. "It's so hard to say. I love all my recipes. But my favorite food to eat is mac 'n' cheese. There's so much you can do with mac 'n' cheese. You can add in all types of vegetables and even lobster. Oh, my goodness. Talk about heaven."

The audience nodded in agreement. It seemed Felicity's love of mac 'n' cheese was a shared one. A dozen hands went up to ask a question. Beth, who stood off to the side of the panel, moderated the questions and called upon a library regular, Connie Rydel.

"This is a question for Louis." Connie stood. "Can you expand on the media kit you mentioned earlier? What is it exactly?"

"Great question." Louis pushed his glasses up the bridge of his nose. For the event, he'd managed to look less rumpled. His wrinkle-free navy shirt was tucked into his pressed khakis, and he'd even added a tie.

Hope thought he looked very professional.

"We give them to advertisers or brands we want to work with. What we include is our bio, graphics, which could be some of our best photographs, and some statistics, like page views and unique visitors. You'll also find collaboration options like sponsored posts, giveaways, social media promotion. And then some examples of previous work. It's quite comprehensive."

Beth called on another audience member. "Hope, you mentioned keywords. How exactly do you use them?"

"Not to get too technical—" Hope began.

"We don't want to put anyone to sleep." Felicity giggled and the audience joined in.

Hope silently counted to ten as the audience's amusement died down before she spoke so she wouldn't say something she'd regret later. "Keywords are used throughout a post. In the text, in the title, in the URL, and in the photo titles—something bloggers often overlook. A simple example is the choice between two words that pretty much mean the same thing. An example would be 'frosting' or 'icing.' You do a search to find out which word is searched the most and that would be the keyword you use. Does that make sense?"

The woman nodded. "Yes. Thanks."

Beth called on the man seated next to Drew, who jotted notes and refused to make eye contact with Hope. They'd been friends long enough for her to know Drew was angry with her because of the conversation she had with Ethan the night before. She'd have to find a way to make it up to him.

"Elena, did having your blog help you with your freelance writing or was it the other way around?" the man asked.

"The blog has definitely helped my freelance writing. It's a part of my résumé and gives editors samples of my writing. The blog has definitely opened doors for me." Elena's voice was soft, and she seemed distracted through the presentation.

"So, Hope, it takes you all day to cook a recipe and take photos of it? That's all you do? Sounds like a sweet gig." Jerry Griffin stood.

Hope shifted in her seat. Meg's husband wasn't asking a question. He was making a statement. If he thought he was being original, he was sadly mistaken. Since she went full-time with her blog, she'd been dealing with the same question. What do you do all day long? Even though she and her fellow bloggers had just laid out the major components of blogging and shared that each task took a significant amount of time, Jerry was still under the impression all they did was cook and snap photographs. Answering on the defensive would be handing Jerry exactly what he wanted, a rise out of her so she'd embarrass herself. Since she'd met her quota of embarrassment the day before, she was going to play it cool with Jerry.

"I do have a sweet gig. I earn a living doing what I love and a lot of my day is spent cooking or photographing. I'm blessed." Hope relaxed, satisfied with her response to the rude question.

The audience also seemed to like her response. They smiled and nodded while Jerry slinked back down to his chair. The portly middle-aged man scowled at her and she almost felt sorry for him. After all, he'd been sent by his wife to attempt to publicly humiliate Hope and failed.

"Well, it seems you've found time in your day for some

other activities." Norrie stood up in the back of the room. Like Jerry, she didn't wait for Beth to call on her. All heads swung around to look at Norrie. "Can you comment on your involvement with a person of interest in two murders here in Jefferson?" All heads swung back to look in Hope's direction.

*Good grief.*

Drew crossed his legs and gave Hope a "you're on your own, girlfriend" look while Felicity gave an angry stare at Hope because it appeared the discussion was taking a negative turn. Beth must have thought the same thing because she sprang in front of the table and clapped her hands together to get everyone's attention.

"Hope doesn't have any comments regarding those tragic events. And I think our time is up. There are refreshments in the back. Please help yourselves and our bloggers will be available to answer any more questions on *blogging*. Let's give our presenters a big round of applause for a thoroughly enjoyable and informative talk."

The room broke out in applause, and then the attendees began drifting to the refreshment table. Felicity popped up from her chair and dashed off in the direction of Norrie. Hope tamped down her slow burn and resisted the urge to chase after her. No, she wouldn't engage with Felicity and give Norrie more fodder for a story. Louis was cornered by two women asking how they could earn money from blogging, while Elena quietly slipped away. Hope lost sight of her. Darn.

"So, how did your date go last night?" Claire came up behind Hope.

"Date?" Hope turned around to face her sister. "It wasn't a date."

Claire rolled her eyes. "I know it was a date. So, spill all the details."

"You want details? Here's a little detail." She leaned forward. "Matt's gay."

Claire gasped. "No!"

Heads turned at Claire's outburst.

"Sorry," she murmured.

When the heads turned away, Hope continued, "He's recently broken up with Rodney. They were together for years."

"I had no idea. He never talked about the relationship."

"Well, he did last night after I told him I wasn't sure if I was ready for a relationship with him. And I told him he was sexy for a lawyer." Hope's head hung low with embarrassment.

"No? Oh, how awkward for you." Claire's smirk grew into a full smile and she burst out laughing. "You must have been so humiliated." She laughed harder, so much so she snorted.

"I'm glad you think this is funny." Hope stomped away.

"Hope, come back, I'm sorry." Claire went back to laughing and didn't follow Hope.

"Drew, we need to talk," Hope said, approaching him.

He ignored her as he turned his body to take a photograph.

"Come on. I'm sorry but I had to tell Ethan."

Drew looked over his shoulder and stared daggers at Hope. He wasn't going to make it easy for her.

"You can't really be angry with me. The police needed to know."

"Shush. We can't talk about it with her here." Drew jerked his head in Norrie's direction. "So far nothing's come of your late-night meeting with Ethan. So we need to keep it on the down low."

"Not a problem." Hope let out a big sigh of relief. Her best friend wasn't angry with her anymore. "Something else happened last night after I left the police department."

Drew arched an eyebrow. "I'm listening."

"Milo approached me and told me I should mind my own business."

"He did? Milo usually isn't confrontational. What happened next?"

Hope caught a glimpse of Elena in the hall. "I need to talk to Elena. I'll fill you in on the rest later." She wove through the crowd, promising a few people she'd be right back to talk with them. In the hallway, she spotted Elena about to reach the front exit. "Elena! Wait up."

"I was just going outside to get some air." Then why did she look like she'd been caught with her hand in the cookie jar?

"I won't keep you. And we're expected to mingle with the guests, so I'm going to be direct."

"I have to go."

"This won't take long. You've disappeared several times and you seem distracted. Is everything okay?"

Elena dipped her head. "It's personal."

"If you need help—"

"No, I don't need help." She chewed on her lower lip. "I just don't want what I tell you to become public."

Hope's patience was wearing thin, but when she saw tears in Elena's eyes, her frustration waned. "What's going on?"

"The times I've disappeared I was with Cal."

"Cal? I didn't realize you two were friends."

"We've been more than friends. We had a brief fling after we met at a photo shoot."

"As in an affair?" Hope tried to wrap her brain around Elena's statement. She was the woman Calista referred to the other day when she was talking about Cal's infidelities? Hope's stomach sank. If true, then Cal could've had a motive for murder.

"It ended months ago. We both agreed we didn't have a future. He wasn't going to leave Lily. And I didn't want him to. Please, no one can know." She grasped Hope's arm and squeezed. Her pale green eyes pleaded with Hope. "It'll make him look guilty."

"Hiding the truth will make him look guilty."

"The truth is he wouldn't kill for us because there isn't an *us*. We're just friends now. Please, please, I beg you not to tell anyone." Elena's hold on Hope tightened. Her fear was palpable.

"Hope. Thank goodness you haven't left." Beth rushed across the hall, holding her phone in her hand. "I just heard that Cal Barnhart has been arrested for the murders."

Shock slammed into Hope so hard she wavered. "Arrested? How's that possible?"

"Oh, my God. Someone found out about us." Elena let go of Hope's arm.

Beth looked at Elena with surprise and then back to Hope. "It just happened."

"Gotta go." Drew hustled through the hallway. "Breaking news!"

"Cal was arrested." Hope stopped Drew in his tracks.

"Turns out the police have surveillance footage showing Cal and Lily together later in the morning, the day she disappeared," Drew shared.

Hope remembered the articles she'd read about Lily's disappearance and recalled Cal's original statement that he last saw Lily when she left their house to go to work. He lied?

"And here we thought we'd uncovered a great conspiracy in town and all along it was the husband who did it." Drew turned and rushed out of the library.

"Cal didn't kill Lily. He couldn't." Tears streamed down Elena's face. "Hope, you have to help him."

"I know his attorney. Trust me, he's in good hands." Because he'd been arrested, Hope wasn't in a position to help Cal. "Beth, could you show Elena where the restroom is?"

"Of course." Beth wrapped an arm around Elena and led her away.

Snippets of conversation flowed out into the hall, and as Hope expected, the topic was the breaking news of Cal's arrest. She ducked into the community room and grabbed her purse. No one seemed interested in blogs any longer. No, they had something meatier, juicier to gossip about. Claire was also ready to leave. She wanted to get a briefing from Ethan because she was a mayoral candidate and needed to stay informed on all major events in town. Hope wished her sister luck. She doubted Ethan would share any pertinent information with Claire.

Outside of the library, Hope slogged to her vehicle. She was zapped of every ounce of energy. The news of Cal's arrest hit her hard, and she felt like roadkill. She pointed her key fob at the SUV and the sound of the driver's-side door unlocking was heaven. She'd be home in just a few minutes.

"Hope! The police arrested Cal!" Brenda jogged from the sidewalk to catch up with Hope. When she reached Hope, she was winded from her sprint. "They took him away in handcuffs."

"Did you call his lawyer?"

"Of course. Right away." Brenda closed the small gap between her and Hope. "We have to help him. We're the only people who believe in him."

Hope stepped back, butting up against her vehicle. Brenda required a conversation regarding personal space because she was too much in Hope's face. "He lied to the police about the last time he saw Lily."

"I don't think he lied. I think he was just confused. Neither one of us can imagine what it felt like for him to have his wife missing."

Hope couldn't argue Brenda's point. Though, she did know what it felt like to be lied to. Whether on purpose or by mistake, it didn't matter. A lie was a lie. The thought that a man she trusted and respected was responsible for not only Lily's death but also Peggy's death made her sick to her stomach. Was he the one who nailed the threatening note to her door and sent her the scary text message? Chills skittered up her spine, and she shivered. She'd once again gotten too close to a murderer and didn't see it.

"There's nothing either one of us can do for him now. Let Matt do his job. Good-bye, Brenda." She pulled open the car door and slid in behind the wheel. She drove her SUV out of the parking space, leaving Brenda standing there alone. She hated not being able to comfort the woman, but she had to take care of herself. She was going home to do what she did best and what calmed her mind—cook.

# Chapter Twenty-Five

When Hope pushed open the mudroom door, she was welcomed home by the intoxicating aroma of apple crumble. Looking back at the past few hours, she was thankful she took time to prepare the dessert and leave it to cook in the slow cooker because the apple-cinnamon fragrance enveloped her like the hug she desperately needed. She missed having Bigelow there with his silly greeting, but he was at another playdate with Buddy. She trudged through the mudroom and into the kitchen, where she dropped her purse on the island. She checked on the apple crumble. Bubbly and lightly browned. Perfection. As much as it pained her, she left the dessert on the warm setting while she changed her clothes.

Back downstairs, in a pair of torn jeans and a cotton sweater, Hope checked her social media. There were comments to reply to and some links from other bloggers to share with her followers. She did a quick check of her stats. Traffic was up, the number of comments were about the same, and the shares of her posts were pretty good. All in all, business was going great. She should have been smiling, but all she could manage was a frown.

With her social media checked off her to-do list, next up

was a video shoot for corn chowder. Come August, there would be an abundance of corn from local farms and she wanted to be prepared to share her favorite corn recipes.

A one-woman operation for her blog, she had to find ways to make video shooting work for her. Eventually she figured out how to shoot videos by herself, but it took several hours from setup to editing. It was a painful process, even though she managed to streamline it. Maybe she should consider hiring an assistant.

As she set up the shoot, the events of the past few days kept playing in her mind, with most of her thoughts concentrated on Cal. Adjusting one of the three box lights around the island, she recalled her conversations with him.

He'd told her how much he loved Lily. He feared she was dead and swore he didn't hurt her. Were those lies too? After she got the lights set up, she positioned the camera and tripod across from the island for the first of the two shoots. The first shoot was a full view angle, so she along with all the ingredients would be filmed. The next shoot would be close-ups, so she'd be doing several actions twice or at least not fully complete the first time.

Yes, hiring an assistant would be a smart thing to do; if nothing else, the help with the videos would be a big time-saver.

She positioned herself at the island, with her shoot list off to the side for reference. To prepare, she had created a list of shots she wanted to make sure were in the final video, including B-roll, which were independent video segments she could edit into the video to break up her sometimes lengthy narrative. Rather than have her viewers just look at her when she described how to shuck corn, she could edit in B-roll footage of an ear of corn for visual appeal while she chatted about the process.

She hooked her mic to her sweater, hiding it underneath, and then she tapped on her phone to begin the recording app her mic was tethered to. She then pressed the remote for her camera and waited a minute before saying her introduction.

She lifted her head and smiled into the camera. Her viewers wanted to see a happy blogger and, as much as the expression felt forced, she didn't falter.

"Today we're making corn chowder. This recipe can feed an army or you can freeze batches for some good eating later. You can use fresh corn or frozen. You can even add chicken or crabmeat to this recipe to make it a little heartier. Also consider serving up some buttermilk biscuits. I've added a link for that recipe on my website.

"This is a perfect meal to serve as we transition from summer to fall. Let's get cooking."

Hope continued with identifying each ingredient and demonstrated the steps of making the chowder. She then paused before readjusting her camera for close-ups. The cycle was repeated until the pot of chowder was cooked and she ladled the thick, creamy soup into a deep bowl and sprinkled chopped chives on top. It looked so yummy she couldn't wait to dive in for a taste. She closed her video with a reminder to sign up for her newsletter.

She pressed off the remote to her camera, removed her mic, and ended the recording app on her phone before she grabbed a spoon to taste the soup. Her eyes fluttered shut as she swallowed her spoonful. It tasted as delicious as it looked. She set the spoon down and quickly turned off the three box lights. She scooped up the bowl and spoon and padded over to the table to finish her lunch. The best part of her job was the food. As the soup disappeared down to her tummy, she frowned. A buttermilk biscuit would have been perfect. Then again, it would have meant adding time to her run. So maybe she didn't miss the biscuit too much.

Glancing at her watch, she was reminded Gilbert would be dropping Bigelow off soon so she better clean up her kitchen and put away the video equipment. After she put her bowl and spoon in the dishwasher, she added all of her prep bowls and utensils. With the dishwasher started, she divided the corn chowder into three containers—one for Gilbert, one for Drew when he stopped by later, and one for her. With her nine-quart Le Creuset emptied of the chowder, she filled it with soapy water and let it soak while she reviewed the video footage.

Pleased that she got some good shots, she returned to the sink to wash the pot. Editing the video would wait until after dinner, when she could settle down in her office and work in peace. Bigelow would be in a deep sleep, thanks to his playdate, and she wouldn't have to worry about anyone dropping by so late in the evening. After the pot was rinsed, she hoisted it from the sink to the counter. She loved her enameled cast-iron pots, but they weighed a ton. How on earth had Peggy managed to lift her six-quart pot the other day when she made peppers and onions?

Hope ran a dish towel around the edge of the pot and then carried the hefty vessel to the open shelf, where she displayed her Le Creuset pieces she'd been collecting for years. Memories of good food and good company flooded her. Along with the memory of Peggy's house fire and her ill-conceived idea to try to rescue Peggy. She still didn't know what she was thinking at that moment. She stepped back, her thoughts racing.

She'd brought Peggy's pot home with her the day the smoke alarm went off so she could clean up the mess the burnt peppers and onions had made. It was so heavy, especially for an elderly woman. She'd noticed some other, lighter weight pots in Peggy's kitchen. So why had Peggy cooked in her Le Creuset pot?

Something about Peggy's fire wasn't sitting right with her, and it kept poking at her brain. The night of the fire,

Ethan had asked Everett to walk her home. No doubt he wanted to make sure she didn't do something else stupid. On the walk back to her house, Everett had made a comment about Peggy falling asleep again cooking.

Falling asleep again.

*Again?*

How had Everett known about the previous incident with Peggy's stovetop fire? Hope hadn't told him. She had told Gilbert, and Claire when she returned home with the pot. Then she told Ethan. But not Everett.

She shook her head and rolled her eyes at how suspicious she was being. Neighbors talked and there was a chance Gilbert or Mitzi had mentioned the incident to Everett in passing.

Hope returned to the island and gave it one final wipe down before checking her Facebook page. Settled at the table and her laptop open, she checked her page engagement. The numbers looked good. Her Facebook page was all about creating relationships so she liked to keep the conversation light and filled her page with photos of food and Bigelow. Her pleasure with her statistics didn't last long.

Her mind fixed on Everett's words and wouldn't let go. He wasn't really a part of their close-knit neighborhood. He didn't volunteer to get Peggy's mail or do her yard work when she was in rehab and he certainly knew about her hospitalization because Dorie had gone door-to-door one weekend to have all the neighbors sign a get-well card. Hope remembered Everett's generic "feel better soon" message scribbled beneath Mitzi's heartfelt mini-novel. For weeks all everyone talked about was Peggy's recovery and Lily's disappearance. Everyone except for Everett.

So how did he know about Peggy's cooking mishap?

Hope closed her Facebook page and stared at the blank screen. She didn't know Everett very well. He was either at his shop or inside his home. He didn't putter outside.

Rather, he had a lawn service. He didn't accept invitations to backyard barbecues. He didn't walk the street like Dorie or Leila. There was so much she didn't know about Everett.

What she did know was Everett directed her to Hans Vogel by giving the hoarder a motive for murder and then Hans had ended up dead.

Before she could stop herself, her fingers were tapping on the keyboard and she was doing an Internet search on Everett Cranston. Results immediately came up. She clicked on one link and then another and began piecing together who the man was. She wasn't sure what that said about the world today when you could easily piece together a person's life one click at a time.

He'd owned an antique shop in Fairfield, Connecticut, before moving to Jefferson. A few more clicks gave Hope a better understanding of the shop and why it closed. The building, which Everett owned, burned in a fire. Wait. Gigi from Pamela's spa mentioned her favorite antique shop in Fairfield closed because of a fire and relocated to Jefferson. Could they be one in the same?

Hope continued reading. At first the fire was labeled suspicious but, after an investigation, there was no evidence the fire had been intentionally set and he collected a significant amount of money from his insurance company.

Hope took in all of the information and reviewed what happened in Jefferson recently. Lily Barnhart disappeared, then was found dead in Peggy Olson's house after a fire was intentionally set. Lily Barnhart, by all accounts, was not in favor of Lionel Whitcomb's proposed commercial development. According to Elaine, Lionel was assured Lily would vote in his favor. Hans Vogel had an angry outburst directed at Lily and was later found dead. Everett was on the P&Z Commission and led Hope off in the direction of Hans. Everett was a guest at the country club the same day Lionel Whitcomb was there.

And then there was Milo. His wife had a sweet leasing deal with Lionel Whitcomb, and he had given Hope a veiled threat to back off the investigation. As mayor, he worked closely with Everett and the P&Z Commission. The other day she interrupted a serious discussion at the antique shop between Milo and Everett.

Could it be possible Everett was behind all of this?

The mother of all headaches was ramping up. She rubbed her temples, but there was no relief forthcoming.

She needed a mindless distraction. A quick visit back to Facebook provided her with some needed comic relief. A silly cat video. She loved them. She laughed as a fluffy gray kitten batted a Great Dane with its teeny-tiny paw.

*The cat.*

Dorie had told Hope she'd been taking care of Peggy's cat and her house had been broken into around the time of Lily's disappearance. Hope reached for her cell phone and called Dorie. She picked up on the third ring.

"Hi, Dorie. Sorry to bother you. I have an odd question. Do you have a key to Peggy's house?"

"Of course. I watered her plants while she was in rehab. What's going on?" Dorie asked.

"Nothing," Hope lied. "Thanks." She ended the call with a promise to bring over some corn chowder later. Could something have been taken and later returned? Like Peggy's house key? The intruder could have stolen the key and used it to enter Peggy's house and hide Lily's body.

A sinking feeling settled in Hope's stomach. Everett might not have been the most involved neighbor on the street, but he was observant. He could have easily known Dorie had a spare key to Peggy's empty house.

She set her phone on the table, remembering Everett had an alibi for the night of the fire. He'd told her that night he'd been on the phone for an hour with Milo.

But the hostess at the Avery Bistro said Milo had been

there having dinner with his wife and then talking to Norrie. So how could he have been on the phone with Everett at the time of the fire?

Everett could have been the person who assured Lionel Whitcomb that Lily's vote in favor of his development was a done deal. But when Lily refused, she might have threatened to go to the police and Everett had no choice but to kill her and dispose of her body.

Hope shivered.

Everett needed somewhere to hide Lily. He knew Peggy's house was empty. She didn't have any proof. Only snippets of conversation on a very hectic and stressful night.

Even so, she needed to let Ethan know there might be another avenue to investigate. The police might have the wrong man in custody.

The chiming doorbell broke her concentration. She glanced at the time on her phone.

*Oh, no!*

She'd forgotten Everett would be delivering the table today. How did the appointment slip her mind? She stood. Maybe it was Dorie or Leila again or some kid selling cookies. Could she be that lucky? Passing through the living room, she caught a glimpse of Everett's black van out the window.

She considered not answering the door, but the thought of cowering in her home angered her. She wasn't about to hide from anyone and, besides, she had no proof Everett was involved in any wrongdoing. For all she knew, he could have been duped by Lionel Whitcomb or even framed. She also couldn't forget that Kent Wilder had a motive to murder Lily. He and Whitcomb could have worked together with the intention of steering the suspicion in Everett's direction.

The doorbell chimed again and her stomach lurched.

She drew in a calming breath. She'd play it cool. Allow Everett to make his delivery and then shuffle him out as quickly as possible, and then lock the doors and call Ethan. She just needed to stay calm and Everett wouldn't suspect anything.

Her shaky hand twisted the doorknob and she opened the door. "Hey, Everett. Thanks for coming by with the table. I do have a conference call with my agent in a few minutes." She hoped the lie sounded believable as she hid her still-trembling hand behind her back.

"No problem." He gave a toothy smile. "Where should I put the table?"

At the moment, she wanted the table and Everett far away from her house. "The dining room for now. I'll prop the door open while you go get the table."

"Let me see where it's going first." Everett walked past Hope and dropped a black backpack on the floor beside the staircase. He must've noticed Hope's stare. "When I make deliveries, I bring some tools of the trade."

"For delivering a table?"

Everett's toothy smile broadened. "A few furniture slides so I don't damage hardwood floors, some dustcloths and polish." He headed for the dining room.

*Shoot.*

Hope chased after him. When she caught up with him, he was standing in the middle of the room. Remodeling clutter ate up most of the square footage. Chair railing was piled in a corner and a white sheet covered an antique chandelier she'd found at an estate sale weeks ago. For now, the antique table would be stored there until she found a permanent place in the house for it.

"I don't mean to rush you, but I do have a conference call."

"Sure thing. I'll bring the table right in." Everett's gaze swept the room and landed on Hope. "Everything okay?"

She nodded. "Yes, of course. It's just a hectic day."

"Let me get the table." Everett gestured for Hope to lead him out of the dining room.

Hope breathed a sigh of relief. He looked like he didn't suspect anything. Just a few more minutes and he'd be gone. She turned and walked out to the hall.

"I saw a couple of vases in your shop I want to get for the living room." She hoped a little chitchat would keep the mood light.

"Stop by when you have a chance." Everett paused to pick up his backpack and slung it over his shoulder.

"I will." The chitchat was working. Just a little bit longer. Hope reached for the open front door but before her hand could reach the knob, she was grabbed and jerked back.

Everett's free hand clamped down over her mouth. "You just had to stick your nose where it didn't belong. Now I have to get rid of you, too." He stretched out a leg and kicked the door shut. He then dragged Hope farther into the house.

Hope cried out in pain, his grip crushing her ribs, but her voice was stifled because Everett's hand covered her mouth. Panic and fear exploded inside of her. Her brain scrambled to come up with an escape plan. But first, she needed to break free of his hold. She struggled to breathe. Part of his hand pressed against her nose. She shook her head, trying to loosen his hold on her. All she was doing was exhausting herself.

He wasn't letting go.

The more she struggled, the tighter he squeezed.

In the family room, he let her go and pushed her so hard she fell to the floor. Her head struck a corner of the coffee table and a sharp pain disoriented her. She cried out again.

She slapped her hand on the coffee table and used the leverage to try to rise, but Everett pressed his foot on her back. The sole of his hiking boot forced her down. Her head banged against the knotted pumpkin pine floorboards. A moment of darkness was shattered by a mini-explosion of bright lights. Her eyes fully opened in time to see Everett pull out a length of rope from his backpack.

She shoved down the sobs lodged in her throat. She wouldn't give him the satisfaction of seeing her cry or having her beg. "Why are you doing this?" Her voice was uneven and she willed it not to crack. "You won't get away with this."

Smirking, he squatted down and straddled her. "You know too much." He yanked her hands behind her back. He tied them together with the rope. He rolled her over onto her back.

She stared at him through teary eyes. What happened to the mild-mannered antiques dealer she knew? Her mind whirled with questions, but her head throbbed. Everett became blurry.

"Why? Why did you kill Lily?"

He sneered. "Still with the questions." He rested his hands on his thighs. "I guess there's no harm in telling you since you won't have the chance to tell anyone else." He leaned down farther. "For the money." His smirk bloomed into a smile and a deep bout of laughter oozed out of him. His deep, chilling laugh made Hope's skin crawl and tears streamed down her face.

*Damn it.* She didn't want to cry in front of him.

"Milo paid me to persuade Lily to vote in favor of the development. He and Lionel have an arrangement. But you know about that, don't you? Your visit to Pamela's spa wasn't just for a facial, was it? Lily wouldn't listen to reason. Too bad for her, she had morals."

Hope fought back a whimper. The rope cut into her wrists and her head pounded. Everett seemed to sway, but when she blinked, he was perfectly still. "What does Milo get out of it?"

"Money. It's all about the money, *honey.*" The word *honey* dripped out of his mouth with disdain.

His menacing eyes bore down on Hope. She'd find no compassion in him so begging for her life would be futile. She had to maintain her strength if she was going to escape.

First, she had to distract him.

"You abducted Lily when she was on her way to work and killed her. Then you hid her body in Peggy's house because you knew she was in rehab. You broke into Dorie's house to get Peggy's key. Where did you hide Lily's body? The basement?" Keeping him talking bought her time. Time to devise a plan. Time for someone to come and discover she was in trouble. Big trouble.

His gaze hardened. "Right up to the end you're full of questions. I'm happy to indulge because you have just a few more minutes to live."

Hope grimaced. Her head pain intensified, spreading from her forehead down to the base of her neck. Her eyelids started to close. *No!* She forced them to open and stared at Everett. How was this the same man who was so pleasant and amiable just the day before?

"In the basement." Everett straightened and propped his hands on his hips. "That's where I put her, all wrapped up because I didn't know how long she'd have to stay hidden. You know, I didn't plan to kill her, but when we met, she argued. Her death was an accident. No one would believe me once they found out what we were discussing. I looked guilty no matter what.

"I had to hide her while I figured out what to do next. I tried to move her, but there were always people around. Walking, gardening, chatting . . . what the hell is it with you people?" Everett shook his head. "Then the old lady came home quicker than any of us thought. And then it hit me. Having the old lady back home was a blessing . . . for me at least. Old and still recovering from whatever ailment she had. I knew I had the perfect way to dispose of Lily's body."

"The fire. You intended it to look like Peggy accidentally

set fire to her house while cooking. You burned those peppers and onions the other day?"

Everett nodded. "You're pretty good at this detective stuff, too bad for you. Yeah, I'd made a copy of her house key after I stole it from Dorie and snuck in while she was napping and cooked up the peppers and onions. They were out on the counter. I set the pot on the stove and then I locked up on my way out."

"How could you? She was an innocent old woman who never hurt anyone."

Everett scoffed. "What do they call it? Ah yes, collateral damage."

Hope's stomach rolled with nausea. She was looking at pure evil. "But what about the gasoline container? You used gasoline to set the fire? It seems like your last fire was better planned out."

Everett cocked his head to the side. "You know about the shop in Fairfield? Impressive. If you were going to live you might have wanted to make a career change."

"You don't have to do this."

"I don't have a choice. And yes, not everything went as planned the night of the fire at Peggy's house. As I mentioned, this street has a lot of activity on it. Now, I think I've answered enough questions. I'm going to tie your feet up and then get the gasoline. By the time the fire department arrives, I'll be heading for the New York border. Sorry it had to end this way, Hope. I really did like you."

Everett tied Hope's feet together and then straightened up. "Don't go anywhere," he said in a mocking tone before he stomped out of the room.

Hope struggled, trying to untie her hands, but she couldn't. Her breathing was ragged. Her chest hurt on every inhale. He must have broken a rib or two when he grabbed her. Fighting through the pain, she wiggled and shifted to make herself upright, but she didn't have the strength.

She had to get up. One more push of momentum and determination and she was sitting up.

Great. *Now what?*

The room spun and the blurriness came back, along with a heavy dose of drowsiness. She wouldn't surrender. She wouldn't give up. She'd power through the pain and dizziness.

*Come on, Hope, you can do it!*

Nausea rolled through her as the spinning in her head became faster. *Oh, God.*

As she succumbed to her heavy eyelids closing, her body fell back to the floor. Her last thought as she drifted into unconsciousness was she was grateful Bigelow wasn't home.

Her dog would be safe.

# Chapter Twenty-Six

Hope's eyes opened and she moaned. Why was she on the floor? What happened? Her hands were bound. And her feet, too.

Why?

Snippets of recall flashed. She'd hit her head.

Her eyes opened wider as her memory trickled back. She'd hit her head after she was pushed. She must've been knocked unconscious. How long was she out? Who pushed her?

Too many questions for her throbbing head to wade through but . . . what was that smell? Her nose sniffed harder.

Smoke!

*Everett.*

All the memories came crashing back.

Everett had thrown her on the floor. Tied her up. Laughed. There wasn't any pity or remorse, just his arrogant confession of murder and arson. She twisted her head to look over her shoulder. Every inch of her body was sore.

Her eyes widened in terror at the sight of smoke billowing out from the front of the house.

Her house was on fire!

She coughed violently. The smoke was filling up her lungs. It was so hard to breathe.

She struggled to right herself but couldn't. She was tied too tightly. She couldn't get enough leverage to lift her body up. Damn.

*No*. She wasn't going to die in a fire.

She worked the rope around her wrists, but they were tied so tightly they cut into her skin. The blood was sticky on her fingers. Tears welled in her eyes. Defeat threatened to overwhelm her.

More thick smoke filled the room. The heat from the fire intensified. It was getting closer to her.

She couldn't untie herself, but maybe she could inch her way to the French doors and kick out the glass.

With every ounce of strength she could tap into, she pushed herself along the floor. She willed herself to stay positive. She concentrated on getting out, seeing Claire, and hugging her niece and nephew. Her belly glided across the floor. Slow. So slow. She barely had any energy left. She couldn't go on.

Her head hit the floor. She'd barely made it to the end of the sofa. To get to the doors, she needed to turn her whole body around the end of the sofa. She couldn't do that. Tears streamed down her face. Was this how it was going to end? She coughed again. Smoke was overtaking her and her eyes began to close again.

"Hope! Hope!"

*Ethan?*

"Hope! Are you in here?!"

Hope's eyes closed. Her coughing and her fight succumbed to the smoke.

"Oh, God! Hope!"

*Love you, Ethan.*

"Hang on, honey. Hang on." His voice was raspy and he coughed. "I've got you now."

*No. Save yourself.*

"I'm going to get you out of here."

*Fire! Leave! Save yourself!*

"Can you hear me?"

She wanted to answer him, to wrap her arms around him, but all she could do was lie there on the floor. *Wait.* She was being lifted, scooped up. What was going on? Her body bounced, like it was running. But she wasn't. Her head bobbed. Her neck was sore. Air. Fresh air hit her, but there wasn't any room for it in her lungs. She was too weak.

"Breathe! Hope, breathe, damn it!"

Was she outside? Out of the fire? She was able to drag in a small breath. *God that hurt.* She smelled freshly cut grass. Under her body, she felt the softness of the ground. Her hands weren't restricted anymore. Her feet were freed too. Another breath. Another cough. More fresh air.

"You're safe, Hope. Can you hear me? You're safe."

Hope's eyes opened. Was she dreaming? Was Ethan really leaning over her? He swept back the hair off her face. He was real. Her hero. Her handsome, rock-solid hero. Though, he was blurry. She couldn't focus on any of Ethan's features. She coughed, ragged and deep. Her lungs burned. Her throat felt raw and her head spun with confusion.

Sirens blared in the distance.

Ethan straightened. "Over here."

Hope threw up an arm and grabbed him. He couldn't leave her. She was too scared to be alone.

"Hey, I'm not going anywhere."

"Prom . . . promise?" Her voice sounded so small to her ears.

He nodded. "Promise." He removed her hand from his arm and held it firmly in his hand. He kissed her palm lightly.

The blurriness lingered and she barely made out dark shoes approaching before two men dropped down to their knees. Her body tensed. Who were they? She heard their voices but she couldn't make out what they were saying. One positioned an oxygen mask over her face. Oh, they were paramedics. Ethan answered their questions and walked beside the stretcher to the ambulance. The paramedics lifted the stretcher into the ambulance on the count of three and Ethan climbed in, sitting on the bench.

"Who did this? Can you tell me?" he asked.

"Ev . . . Ev . . ." She squeezed her eyes shut, frustrated she couldn't say one simple name. "Et . . . Ev . . . Et."

"Are you trying to say Everett?"

Hope nodded. Panic surged through her body. A flash of being yanked back from the front door hit her hard. "Yes. Him."

"We need to get going, Chief," one of the paramedics said.

"Hope, you have to go to the hospital, and I need to get my men looking for Everett. I promise I'll be at the hospital in a little while. Okay?"

Fear rippled through her.

He must have seen it in her eyes. "Hey, you're safe now. Nothing is going to happen to you. You have my word. Have I ever let you down?"

"No," she whispered.

She lifted her hand and touched Ethan's face. Day-old stubble pricked her fingers. He needed a shave. She smiled. He took her hand into his and kissed it lightly.

"See you soon." He let go of Hope's hand.

"Okay," she murmured as her eyes closed.

Ethan exited the ambulance and then closed the doors.

She looked to the paramedic next to her. "Guess I'm lucky."

The paramedic nodded. "I'd say."

"How bad is my house?"

"Don't worry about your house. We're going to get you to the hospital. You're going to be fine."

The motion of the ambulance speeding away with sirens left Hope desperately wanting to go back to see her house. To see how much damage was done by Everett. Her heart sank. All the work she'd done to restore the home was now for naught. Like Peggy's house, it too was destroyed. As the ambulance made a turn, she wondered if she had the strength to start over again.

# Chapter Twenty-Seven

The beautiful Saturday afternoon brought people out looking for treasures and bargains, like the group of women walking ahead of Hope. They were more interested in antiquing than the recent events in Jefferson, which were murder and arson. The shoppers were dressed in comfortable walking shoes and each carried a large tote bag. Hope envied their "not a care in the world" swagger. She glanced at Bigelow, who walked beside her, and he looked up to her with his big brown eyes filled with unconditional love.

A pain stabbed at her heart. She had been so close to never seeing him again.

A chorus of loud disappointment drew Hope from her "what might have been" thoughts to the group of shoppers ahead. They'd stopped at the Red House Antique Shop and stared at the CLOSED sign on the front door. Little did they know the shop was closed because its owner was a wanted man in two murders, one attempted murder, and three arson cases. They sucked up their disappointment and continued a few feet to another antique shop, while Hope and Bigelow remained in front of Everett's former business.

She looked into the shop's window. Not too long ago she'd stood in there talking with Everett and handing over her credit card for the table. Had she only known she wasn't talking to a friend, maybe she wouldn't have almost ended up dead and her beloved home would have been spared being set on fire.

Bigelow barked. She looked at the little guy and was so grateful he'd been out on a playdate with Buddy when Everett revealed his true colors and doused her house with gasoline. She couldn't bear losing Bigelow.

Tears filled her eyes. Again. She'd been on an emotional roller coaster since being released from the hospital a day after the incident. With smoke inhalation, combined with a concussion and bruised ribs, the hospital kept her for observation. Normally, she balked at being kept confined, but for once she didn't put up an argument. Her body needed to heal and her mind had to sort some things out. She seemed to be crying at the silliest things and was guarded around those closest to her. How could they understand what she was going through when she couldn't? Time. Maybe she just needed time.

She sipped her coffee. Bless Kimberly, the co-owner of the Coffee Clique, for "not seeing" Bigelow when Hope popped into the shop for her much-needed caffeine. Hope didn't have clearance to drive yet from her doctor, so Claire had driven her sister into town, then dashed off for a house showing. Hope planned on visiting Sally and Jane and was headed in the direction of the inn.

The Merrifields had been so kind, visiting her in the hospital and then checking up on her since her release. Because of the damage done to her house by the fire, she'd been staying with Claire. She took another sip of her coffee. Her niece and nephew loved having Bigelow stay with them. Claire? Let's just say it was an adjustment. It seemed that four thousand square feet of living space wasn't big enough for both Claire and Bigelow. She hoped the fire restoration company she hired would make quick work of getting her home back to the way it was before the fire.

"There you are, dear."

Hoped turned at the lyrical sound of Jane's voice. As always, a smile covered her face and her blue eyes twinkled with delight. Her soft pink floral dress flitted in the light breeze as she walked toward Hope.

"I was just on my way to see you and Sally." Having another near-death experience reminded Hope of how important friends and family were to her. In those dark moments, when she didn't believe she'd make it out of her house alive, she thought about never seeing those she loved. That pain was more excruciating than whatever physical pain she had been in. And now the memory hit her hard, causing her heart to ache all over again.

"It's a lovely day for a walk. You need all the fresh air you can get." Jane came to a stop and reached down and patted Bigelow on the head, which he accepted graciously.

Hope said a silent thank-you to the dog-training gods because he didn't slobber Jane's hand with his excited kisses.

Jane straightened and set her gaze on Hope. "How are you feeling?"

Truthfully, Hope didn't know. It had only been five days since her release from the hospital. Some days her chest hurt because of something as simple as breathing. Her head sometimes spun and a wave of nausea hit her. Other times her throat was so scratchy she didn't think it would ever heal. The ups and downs of recovery, she guessed.

"A little better. My throat still hurts and so do my ribs. And my head, actually. But each day it's a little less discomfort." She hated not feeling well. She hated having a laundry list of ailments or complaints. Most of all, she hated people feeling sorry for her.

Jane's smile widened. "In no time you'll be back to your old self." Her gaze drifted to the closed shop and her smile slid into a frown. She was probably thinking what every other person in Jefferson was thinking—how was it possible that the mild-mannered Everett Cranston was an arsonist and murderer? Hope knew how. He was a psychopath.

"You did a wonderful job uncovering him as the killer. Though, you did find yourself in a very dangerous situation."

A rueful laugh escaped. Talk about an understatement.

"I'm very glad you weren't seriously hurt." Jane's eyes cast down. "Or murdered."

So was Hope.

"However, on the bright side"—Jane glanced back to Hope—"you're very good at being an amateur detective. You have a mind for murder."

Hope wasn't sure if she wanted a mind for murder since it'd almost gotten her killed twice in as many months. Though, both times she did manage to escape with just a few minor injuries. It probably was just luck and how long could she rely on luck to keep her alive if she kept playing detective?

"I'm not Barbara O'Neill," Hope said. Jane's fictional detective was far braver and always seemed to get away unscathed.

"I know that, dear. You're a real person I care deeply about. I'd never want to see you hurt, and it saddens me that you were." Jane's soft voice was sincere. "But, when you have a gift like you do, you must use it. You helped solve two murders. I envy you, dear."

She envied Hope? No one should envy the foolish choices she'd made. While she might have a penchant for investigating and she did find it a little exciting, okay, very exciting, she put herself in danger. "The next murder mystery is all yours."

Jane laughed as she reached out and patted Hope's arm. "Enough of this. Let's go to the inn so Sally can see for herself that you're on the mend. And we can indulge Bigelow with some peanut butter cookies from that adorable little pet boutique."

"Sounds good to me." Hope looped her arm into the crook of Jane's, and the three of them started walking toward the inn. Bigelow walked obediently by her side, his eyes wide open, looking at everyone they passed. Hope was very pleased with him. He was getting better on the leash and his manners were improving. Maybe hiring a trainer wouldn't be necessary. They walked by shops and a few private homes on their way to the inn. Abundant flower-pots were set outside the front doors, and many of the shops had benches set out for people to sit and relax. Main Street was idyllic and gave no hint to the horror that played out recently. People chatted as they walked by and the birds chirped. She could see how special Jefferson looked to visitors.

"Your blogging friends have left. They were an interest-ing bunch. I can't believe sweet Elena had an affair with Cal. Foolish girl. Those things never work out."

"I'm going to miss Louis. He was fun." Hope enjoyed his company and laid-back attitude, but most of all she loved his passion for blogging. It was refreshing. She intended to stay in touch with him. Who knew, maybe they could part-ner up for some projects.

"Felicity was a piece of work."

"Tell me about it. She's the one who took the photo of Cal and me and sent it to Norrie."

Jane stopped walking. "She did?"

Hope nodded. "Felicity has a competitive streak. I saw it at the audition and at a few blogger conferences we both attended." She understood Felicity's ambition. Blogging wasn't easy. With over seven million blogs on the Internet, few bloggers made a livable income from their blog. So, any type of exposure, from a television show to a brand endorsement to a magazine article, was coveted.

"She should be ashamed of herself. She put you in an awkward position."

Hope couldn't argue that point. But compared to what happened with Everett, it really was nothing. There was a good chance she'd run into Felicity at a future blogger conference and she'd deal with the conniving blogger then.

The front door of Hair-O-Rama, Jefferson's popular hair salon, opened, and Maretta stepped out into the sunshine. She stopped short when she saw Hope and Jane and the look on her face soured just as Hope's mood did. They hadn't spoken since Maretta announced her bid for mayor a week ago. Though, Maretta and Alfred did send her a lovely flower arrangement with a note wishing her a speedy recovery.

The three women stood looking at one another in an awkward silence. Hope really didn't have anything to say to Maretta other than thank you for the flowers. And Maretta didn't indicate she'd be uttering any words, preferring to glower at Hope instead.

"It's a lovely day, isn't it?" Jane broke the ice. She glanced at Hope and the look on her face was very readable. She wanted Hope to say something. Anything.

Hope did her best to keep from rolling her eyes because she adored Jane and would do anything for her. "Thank you for the flowers. They're very pretty."

Maretta lifted her chin and her judgmental brown eyes fixed on Hope. "What happened to you shocked us all. Though, you really couldn't have been too surprised you'd gotten yourself into another mess by sticking your nose where it didn't belong. You're lucky the neighbors called nine-one-one right away."

Hope bit her tongue. To engage with Maretta meant she'd

have to stoop down to her level. And quite frankly, Hope didn't have the dexterity or desire to do so. "I'm fortunate to have good neighbors."

"If it weren't for Hope, Everett might have never been identified as the killer." Jane squeezed Hope's hand for added support. "We should all be thanking her for what she did and not blaming her for the unfortunate incident at her house."

Unfortunate incident? Another understatement.

"It figures you'd take that view, given you're the one who's encouraging her to be an amateur sleuth or whatever you call it. Now it appears, when I'm elected mayor, I'll have my hands full cleaning up the town corruption."

"My sister is still in the race." Hope always supported whatever her sister wanted to do, but now she intended to not only jump on board the bandwagon of the mayoral race, but be leading it to victory. She'd brainstormed ideas for events and rallies and would use every trick she ever learned about public relations to help her sister beat the support hose off Maretta.

"I really don't have time to chat. I have a campaign to manage." Maretta briskly walked past them and eventually disappeared inside her husband's real estate office down the street.

Jane smiled. "Her feathers are definitely ruffled."

Hope laughed. It felt good to laugh, even though her ribs hurt. "When aren't they ruffled?"

They continued their walk again. The warm sun felt good on her face and walking with a friend lifted her spirits.

"It's a shame you missed Lily's funeral. The readings Cal selected were so beautiful and poignant," Jane said.

Before Hope's doctor cleared her for minimal activity, like she was doing now, Cal had the funeral for his wife. She hated missing the service and called Cal to express her condolences. He thanked her for finding Lily's killer and told her he'd be leaving Jefferson for a while. She understood and wished him well.

They'd almost reached the inn when a honking car drew their attention to the curb. She recognized the car immediately. Detective Reid.

"Wonder what he wants," Jane whispered as Reid exited his vehicle and stepped up on the curb.

Hope shrugged. She'd given her statement once the emergency room doctor declared her stable enough to talk. What he wanted now was a mystery.

Bigelow growled as his haunches raised. He shifted from laid-back, easygoing to fierce protector. He definitely deserved an extra biscuit when they reached the inn.

"How are you feeling, Miss Early?" He glanced at Bigelow, who'd positioned himself between Reid and Hope. The detective looked relaxed. Either it was casual day at the police department or he was off duty because gone were his blazer and dress pants. Instead, he sported a polo shirt and a pair of dark gray cargo pants. His polished oxford shoes were replaced by a pair of canvas slip-on sneakers.

"Better. Thank you." Not knowing what he wanted to talk to her about put Hope on edge a bit. Since the fire, she'd become very aware of her body and her pulse rate picked up.

"Is there something we can help you with, Detective?" Jane must have sensed Hope's discomfort. "We're just on our way to the inn."

"I won't keep you then. I just wanted to let you know we have Cranston in custody. He was apprehended in Ohio and is being returned as we speak. He's confessed to the murders and arson."

Hope's throat got tight with emotion. She'd been looking over her shoulder for Everett since the day he set fire to her house and left her to die. She worried if he learned she was still alive he'd return to finish the job. Now she could stop worrying and maybe now the nightmares that plagued her would end.

"It's about time. I can't believe he's been on the run for so long." Jane patted Hope's arm. "It's over now."

"Yes, it is," Hope managed to say.

Reid rubbed the back of his neck. "Unfortunately, not all crimes are wrapped up as quickly as television portrays. Cranston's confession has also led to an investigation into Milo Hutchinson and Lionel Whitcomb. We're not sure where it will lead at this juncture."

"How long has this corruption been going on right under the noses of you and the rest of your colleagues?" Jane wasn't about to let Reid off the hook just yet.

"I assure you that if there'd been any prior allegations of impropriety, we would have conducted a thorough investigation."

Hope had to give him credit for not sounding defensive at Jane's very direct question.

Jane let go of Hope's arm and stepped forward. She looked up to Reid. "The reality is you needed to have the case handed to you on a silver platter. I dare say, Hope is owed a deep appreciation by your department for the work she's done. She solved the murders of three people."

Reid shoved his hands into his pants pockets. There was a small part of Hope that enjoyed seeing him squirm.

"On behalf of the Jefferson Police Department, please accept our appreciation for your assistance in this matter."

Hope wondered how much that hurt Reid. "You're welcome."

"However, there were two murders. Hans Vogel wasn't murdered," he informed them.

"He wasn't?" Hope and Jane asked together.

"His autopsy came back and his cause of death was a heart attack."

"Poor man." Jane lowered her gaze for a moment.

"Miss Early, I'm sorry about your house. I know how much it means to you."

He actually sounded sincere. "Thank you. The damage can be repaired." She had her contractor, Liam Ferguson, on the job, and he was working hard to get her back home as soon as possible.

"I'll let you two continue on your way. Have a nice day." He turned and went back to his vehicle.

"Come on, dear. Sally is waiting for us." Jane started walking. "You know, you should receive a medal for what you did."

Hope didn't want a medal. She didn't want a ceremony. She didn't even want an article in the *Gazette* written about her. She just wanted her home put back together. And maybe a soak in a hot bath. She and Bigelow caught up with Jane. Until she could climb into a tub, having tea with two friends would be good.

"I'm pushing my guys as hard as I can so you can get back home soon." Liam Ferguson wiped his sweaty forehead with a bandana. The sixty-something contractor had been by Hope's side since the day she closed on her dream house. While she did a lot of the work herself, there were some things she needed to outsource, like the kitchen remodel and the building of the garage.

"I appreciate all of the hard work." Hope stood on her lawn, riveted by the sight of her farmhouse. Her lower lip quivered at the sight of the damage caused by the fire. Her first visit back to the house three days earlier overwhelmed her and she cried for most of the day. Now, standing there, she had more resolve, but it was still difficult.

She remembered the first time she saw her house. It was a wreck. Neglected and unloved, it's charm long gone. But she saw potential. Yes, potential was a real estate buzzword to sell money pits, but that wasn't the case with the farmhouse on Fieldstone Drive. It wasn't going to be a complete money pit. It had good bones. The structure of the house was sound and so was the foundation and roof. What was needed was a complete gut job on both floors and the front porch needed a good cleaning, the floorboards refinished and a new coat of paint. She was willing to roll up her sleeves and put in the countless hours of work to make the home shine again.

And once again, the house needed to be made shiny again. Luckily, the fire department responded quickly, so her house wasn't a total loss, like Peggy's beloved home. The fire didn't have time to spread throughout her house but enough damage was done to force Hope to move out.

"There's no sign of structural damage." Liam shoved the bandana into his pants back pocket. "We're replacing the insulation and drywall. And you see my guys up on the roof?" Liam pointed to the front part of the roof past the covered porch. His leathery, tanned skin gave testament to his countless number of hours on roofs over the years. "A section needed sheathing and shingles."

On her previous visit, Hope was allowed inside the house to do a quick tour. Her heart sunk when she saw all the caked-on smoke damage. The walls, fixtures, floors, and ceilings were all black. Luckily, Claire was with her and gave her a quick pep talk, reminding Hope the damage could have been a lot worse. And she could have died. So, a little soot wasn't the end of the world.

"It's a miracle," she said.

"I'd say so." Liam looked down the street. "Tomorrow we're knocking down the Olson house completely. Shame. It was a beautiful house."

The news hit Hope like a punch to the stomach, and she flinched. She couldn't imagine losing her house completely. She turned her head and followed his gaze down the street. Tomorrow there would be a pile of rubble where the once-spectacular Victorian house stood. Sadness sagged her shoulders. "I should let you get back to work. Thanks for the update."

"I promise you it'll look like it did before. Trust me." Liam squeezed Hope's shoulder to reassure her and then walked back to the house, his limp from a fall off a roof years ago prominent. He shouted out something to one of his workers that she couldn't make out.

"This is so unreal. I can't believe all of this happened right here on our quiet little street." Dorie Baxter approached Hope with a pet carrier.

Hope turned, raising her hand to shield her eyes from the sun. No doubt Dorie's shock was shared by all of the residents on the street. She stepped forward and met Dorie halfway.

"How are you doing?" She wrapped her free arm around Hope and hugged her tightly. A soft meow came from the carrier.

"I'm good." Hope sucked in a breath. Even though she knew what she'd find when she arrived at her house, she was still overwhelmed by the sight. "Thanks for asking."

Dorie let go of Hope. "Hon, you know I'm always here for you. Now, are you sure you want to take the cat?"

Hope looked at the carrier. Fluffy little Princess was homeless. Her owner was dead. Her caretaker's husband was allergic to her, and so was Meg. The cat had nowhere to go except to the animal shelter if Hope didn't take her.

"I feel so bad not being able to keep her." Dorie lifted the carrier to bring Princess to eye level. "She's such a sweet girl."

Hope peered into the carrier. Princess was a ball of fluff curled up with her eyes wide open. She looked nervous. Poor thing. Like Hope, she'd been through a lot, and Hope couldn't let her go to a shelter. "I didn't know Meg was allergic to cats."

Dorie slid a dubious look to Hope. "Neither did I."

Hope wouldn't be surprised to find out Meg suffered from no allergies. Hope hated to think the worst of Meg, but she was confident the only inheritance the woman wanted from her aunt was the insurance money on the house, not a cat.

"You know I don't like to pry, but I have to ask you. Has Meg thanked you for discovering the person responsible for her aunt's death?" Dorie handed the carrier to Hope.

"She sent me a text message a couple of days ago and thanked me."

"A text? Nothing else?"

Before she could reply, Drew drove up to the curb. "Are you ready?" he asked after the passenger window lowered.

"Yes, we are. Dorie, I'll see you in the morning when I come by to feed the chickens." The barn wasn't damaged, so relocating the chickens wasn't necessary. Ethan had volunteered to take care of the chickens until she got the all-clear from her doctor. She owed him big-time and not just for feeding her chickens, but for everything he'd done for her since moving back to Jefferson. Hope opened the back passenger door of Drew's car and set the carrier on the backseat. She waved good-bye to Dorie and slid into the front passenger seat.

"We need to go to the pet shop to get some things for Princess."

"Did you tell Claire you're bringing the cat to her house?" Drew pulled his car from the curb and headed in the direction of Main Street.

"No, not yet. But it shouldn't be a problem. Princess is so little. And she's a cat who lived with an elderly woman. She's so docile. She won't be any problem."

"Are you sure about that?"

"Yes." Hope was confident Princess would behave. Rather, she was worried about Bigelow. She didn't know how he'd react to a cat. He was okay with the chickens, so she was hopeful he'd get along with Princess.

"What's going on with the cookbook? Have you spoken with Calista yet?"

"I did. I have an extension due to what happened. Since I'm feeling better, I'm going back to work tomorrow." Not having the pressure of a looming deadline was a big help with her recovery. Her doctor wanted her to remain as stress free as possible. As for her blog, she had several weeks of content in queue while she recuperated. "How's it going at the newspaper with Norrie?"

"She's all over this corruption story now. I almost feel sorry for Milo and Lionel Whitcomb." Drew laughed. He reached a stop sign and waited while another car made a turn. "Do you think next time you could sit the investigation out and let me handle it?"

"Are you still upset by what Norrie said?" Inwardly Hope cringed when she remembered Norrie's sharp words about Drew tagging along with his friends to get a story. "It was you who broke the story on the bookkeeper who embezzled church funds and because of your reporting about the volunteer thrift store, enough money was raised to repair the shop's roof. You're a good reporter."

"A good investigative reporter is only as good as his last story."

"If there's a next time, it's all yours." God willing, this last adventure into amateur sleuthing would be her last.

"Much appreciated." Drew perked up. He flicked on his

turn signal and waited to make a left turn into the parking lot behind the pet shop.

"I have a list on my phone of everything Princess needs." Her phone rang and she pulled it out from her purse. The caller ID said it was Ethan.

"Hi," she said after swiping her phone on.

"Where are you?" Ethan asked.

"Drew and I just arrived at the pet shop. I need to pick up things for Princess. I heard about Everett."

"He's going away for a long, long time."

"He should rot in prison."

"He will. I was calling to see if you wanted to have dinner tonight."

"Dinner? Sure. Claire won't mind if I cook tonight. Actually, I'd kind of like to cook."

"No, that's not what I had in mind."

"What were you thinking?"

"I was thinking of taking you out to a nice restaurant."

*Is he talking about a date? Keep calm and don't jump to any conclusions. Remember the last time I suspected I was on a date.*

"Sounds nice. What time?" Hope asked.

"I'll pick you up at seven. Oh, one more thing. You looked beautiful in that dress the other day. See you later."

Her breath caught as the call disconnected. *I looked beautiful.* Butterflies swirled in her stomach. *It has to be a date.*

"What's going on?" Drew asked.

A slow smile eased onto her lips. "Dinner."

"It's more than dinner. I can tell by the look on your face."

"Just dinner." Hope opened the door and stepped out of the car. She then opened the back door and grabbed the carrier. "I don't have all day." She had to prep for a date with Ethan.

"A-ha. You know I'm going to find out." Drew followed Hope into the store. "I'm a highly skilled investigative reporter."

Hope opened the door of Claire's house and found Ethan on the front step, dressed up and more handsome than ever. She wasn't used to seeing him outside of his uniform or jeans. Boy, did he clean up nicely. Her insides got all warm and fuzzy.

For the first time since Everett tied her up and set her house on fire, her nerves settled and she felt she could breathe again. While she had been busy preparing for dinner, all of her aches and pains seemed to vanish. She had been more consumed with finding the right dress to wear from Claire's closet. Luckily, they wore the same dress size and shoe size, so she'd selected a pale coral sheath dress and a pair of nude heels. She'd snagged one of Claire's designer clutches and swept her hair into a French twist. She'd added her gold stud earrings and a simple heart necklace and was ready to go as soon as she grabbed a wrap.

"You look beautiful." Ethan held out his hand for her.

Her cheeks warmed as she placed her hand into Ethan's. He'd traded in his pickup for his sleek black convertible for the evening.

"Thank you." She adjusted the sheer wrap around her shoulders.

"Is everything going well with Claire? She's okay with the cat and dog?"

"Of course she is."

It was a slight fib. Claire was willing to tolerate Bigelow because his manners showed a hint of improvement. The cat? Well, she wasn't thrilled Princess used one of her upholstered armchairs as a scratching post. Hope had to tack the cost to repair the damage to the chair to her renovation budget. Maybe Princess would eventually use the new scratching post Hope introduced her to. Or else she'd be paying for a lot of furniture repair.

"I sense you're leaving something out."

"Princess is settling in. It's all new to her." A loud bark sounded from the back of the house. Really loud. Then she heard Princess's piercing screech followed by something crashing to the floor. She winced. Then she heard Claire's shrill voice.

"Oh, boy. We better get going." She pulled the door shut and hustled down the front steps, pulling Ethan behind her. She dragged him in a mad dash to his car. "Get in!"

He attempted to open her door, but she shooed him away. "Get in and drive!"

Just as Ethan turned the ignition on, the front door opened and Claire came running down the front steps.

"Hope! Get back in here and manage your zoo!"

Ethan drove the car to the end of the circular driveway and Hope looked back, waving to her sister. As they passed through the gate at the end of the property, Hope leaned back into the car seat and looked over at Ethan. He returned the look and smiled. He reached out his hand and took hers to hold tightly.

She was going on a date with Ethan.

Recipes from Hope's blog,
*Hope at Home*

# LEMON RICOTTA COOKIES
*posted by Hope Early*

I'm in love with the brightness lemons bring to any dish but
when you make it a central part of a cookie and add in a
sweet and tangy glaze you've baked an irresistible cookie
that is delightful year-round.

Yield: about 3 dozen

**Ingredients:**

2 cups granulated sugar
2 lemons, zested
2½ cups all-purpose flour
1 teaspoon baking powder
1 teaspoon salt
1 stick unsalted butter, softened
2 large eggs
1 container (15 oz.) whole milk ricotta cheese
3 tablespoons lemon juice, freshly squeezed

For the glaze:
1½ cups confectioners' sugar, sifted
3 tablespoons lemon juice, freshly squeezed
1 lemon, zested

**Directions:**

Preheat oven to 375 degrees.

Line baking sheets with silicone mats or parchment
paper.

In a medium bowl, combine sugar and lemon zest
until the lemon sugar is fragrant. Set mixture aside.

Cream together the butter and lemon sugar with electric mixer until light and fluffy, about 3–5 minutes.

Reduce the speed of the mixer and add in the eggs,
one at a time until fully incorporated. Add in the

ricotta cheese and lemon juice and mix until well combined.

Gradually add the dry ingredients until just combined, being careful not to overmix.

Scoop the dough, about two tablespoons for each cookie, onto prepared baking sheets.

Bake for 13–15 minutes until slightly golden at the edges. Remove from oven and leave on baking sheet just long enough for cookies to set up before moving to cooking rack.

When cookies are completely cooled, drizzle with lemon glaze.

### Directions for the Lemon Glaze:

In a medium bowl, combine the powdered sugar, lemon juice, and lemon zest. Whisk until smooth.

Dip the top of each cookie into the glaze and then place the cookies on rack or wax paper. Glaze will harden.

# CHICKEN WILD RICE CASSEROLE
*posted by Hope Early*

After a long, exhausting day when I needed comfort, I tied on my apron and made my tried and true Chicken Wild Rice Casserole. Simple, hearty ingredients combined into a baking dish and baked for twenty minutes definitely soothed my soul and made my tummy very happy.

Yield: about 6–8 servings

### Ingredients:

3 tablespoons unsalted butter
1 cup diced onion
½ cup diced celery
¼ cup all-purpose flour

2½ cups chicken stock
2 cups crème fraiche*
2 tablespoons sherry vinegar
1 tablespoon soy sauce
1 tablespoon roasted garlic paste or homemade roasted garlic
2 cups shredded chicken breasts
3 cups cooked wild rice
2 cups chopped broccoli rabe
1 tablespoon rosemary leaves, chopped
½ teaspoon liquid smoke
¼ teaspoon red pepper flakes
8 oz. Swiss cheese, grated
½ cup sliced almonds

### Directions:

Preheat oven to 375 degrees.

In a large skillet that is oven-safe melt butter over medium-low heat. Add onions and celery and sauté until tender, 5–7 minutes. Stir in flour and cook, continuing to stir, about 3 minutes.

Whisk together chicken stock, crème fraiche, sherry vinegar, garlic paste, and soy sauce in bowl. Slowly add mixture to the onion and celery mixture. Continue to whisk and any lumps will go away.

Let cook until the sauce simmers and is thick enough to coat the back of a spoon. Then add in chicken, rice, broccoli rabe, rosemary, liquid smoke, red pepper flakes, and cheese.

Top casserole with sliced almonds and bake until golden brown, about 15–20 minutes.

Remove, let set for about 10 minutes, and serve.

*Cook's Note: In a pinch, I've used sour cream or plain Greek yogurt in place of crème fraiche.

# OATMEAL RAISIN COOKIES
*posted by Hope Early*

The best thing about this cookie is that it's not fancy or complicated; it's just pure homemade deliciousness. There's no fuss in baking this cookie and it pairs well with a cup of milk or a cup of tea. Wrap a couple in parchment paper and drop into a lunch bag or fill up a plate for an impromptu get-together. Just be warned, you may want to make a second batch of this dough because I've yet to fill up a cookie jar with any leftovers.

Yield: about 2 dozen

**Ingredients:**

1½ cup old-fashioned rolled oats (do not use quick cooking oats)
½ cup all-purpose flour
½ cups raisins
½ teaspoon baking soda
½ teaspoon salt
6 tablespoons unsalted butter, room temperature
⅓ cup packed dark-brown sugar
¼ cup granulated sugar
1 egg
1 teaspoon vanilla

**Directions:**

Preheat oven to 350 degrees.

In medium bowl, whisk oats, flour, raisins, baking soda, and salt together. Set aside.

With electric mixer, cream together butter and sugar until light and fluffy, scraping bowl as needed. Add egg and vanilla and beat until combined. Gradually add in oat mixture and beat until well combined.

Drop dough by rounded tablespoons, 2 inches apart, onto baking sheets. Bake until cookies are golden brown but still soft, 12–16 minutes, rotating sheets halfway through. Cool cookies on sheets for about 5 minutes, then transfer to a cooling rack to cool completely.

# MEATBALL SUB CASSEROLE
*posted by Hope Early*

This recipe is a meatball lover's dream come true and then taken to a whole new level with a thick layer of garlic bread and a generous topping of mozzarella cheese. When you want a satisfying meal but are short on time this dish will be your best friend. It's because of this dish I keep extra meatballs in my freezer.

Yield: 4 servings

**Ingredients:**

1 loaf garlic bread, cut into 1-inch thick slices (recipe follows)

2 cups shredded mozzarella cheese, divided

1 pound meatballs (if using frozen make sure they're thawed)

1 28-oz. jar pasta sauce, or homemade equivalent

**Directions:**

Preheat oven to 350 degrees.

Arrange bread slices in a single layer in an ungreased 13" x 9" baking pan and sprinkle with ½ cup cheese; set aside.

In a bowl, mix together meatballs and pasta sauce, and spoon over cheese and bread. Sprinkle with remaining cheese.

Bake, uncovered, for 25–30 minutes, until meatballs are cooked and cheese is bubbly and melted.

# GARLIC BREAD
*posted by Hope Early*

Let me tell you, it doesn't get much better than a warm slice of cheesy garlic bread straight from the oven. It's one of life's simple eating pleasures. And luckily for us, it's one of the easiest things to whip up in the kitchen.

Yield: 4–6 servings depending how thick your slices are

## Ingredients:

1 loaf Italian or French bread
½ cup unsalted butter, softened
2 large garlic cloves, smashed and minced
1 heaping tablespoon freshly chopped parsley
¼ cup freshly grated Parmesan cheese (optional, but why wouldn't you?)

## Directions:

Preheat oven to 350 degrees. Slice bread in half, horizontally.

Combine butter, garlic, and parsley together in a small bowl. Spread garlic butter mixture over both halves of the bread.

Place bread halves on baking pan and heat in the oven for 10 minutes.

Remove pan from oven. Sprinkle Parmesan cheese over bread. Return to oven on the highest rack and broil on high heat for 2–3 minutes just until the edges of the bread begin to toast and the cheese bubbles. Don't leave the oven as the bread can go from toast to burnt quickly.

Remove from oven, let cool for a minute, remove from pan, and slice.

# APPLE CINNAMON MUFFINS
*posted by Hope Early*

Biting into a warm Apple Cinnamon Muffin is a perfect way to start your morning. These muffins pack a big punch of apple flavor with a cinnamon-sugar crunch on top. These are my go-to in apple season but there's never a wrong time to bake a batch of these muffins.

Yield: 12 muffins

**Ingredients:**

2 cups all-purpose flour
1 cup sugar
3 teaspoons baking powder
1¼ teaspoons ground cinnamon
½ teaspoon baking soda
½ teaspoon salt
2 eggs
1 cup sour cream
¼ cup butter or margarine, melted
1½ cups chopped, peeled tart apples

For topping:
3 tablespoons all-purpose flour
¼ cup sugar
¼ teaspoon ground cinnamon
2 tablespoons cold butter or margarine

**Directions:**

Preheat oven to 400 degrees. Line a 12-cup muffin tin with paper liners or spray with nonstick coating.

In a large bowl, combine dry ingredients.

In medium bowl, beat the eggs, sour cream, and butter. Stir into dry ingredients just until moistened. Fold in apples.

For the topping, in a small bowl, combine sugar, flour and cinnamon. Cut in butter until mixture resembles coarse crumbs.

Fill muffin cups to the top and sprinkle with a rounded teaspoon of cinnamon topping over each muffin.

Bake for 20–23 minutes, or until cake tester/toothpick comes out clean. Cool for 5 minutes before removing to a cooling rack. Serve warm.

To store: Place in an airtight container in the refrigerator. Reheat one muffin in the microwave for 10–15 seconds, if preferred warm.

# Connect with Us

Visit us online at
**KensingtonBooks.com**
to read more from your favorite authors, see books
by series, view reading group guides, and more.

for sneak peeks, chances to win books and prize packs,
and to share your thoughts with other readers.

**facebook.com/kensingtonpublishing
twitter.com/kensingtonbooks**

## Tell us what you think!

To share your thoughts, submit a review,
or sign up for our eNewsletters, please visit:
**KensingtonBooks.com/TellUs.**

# Grab These Cozy Mysteries
## from
# Kensington Books

| | | |
|---|---|---|
| Forget Me Knot<br>Mary Marks | 978-0-7582-9205-6 | $7.99US/$8.99CAN |
| Death of a Chocoholic<br>Lee Hollis | 978-0-7582-9449-4 | $7.99US/$8.99CAN |
| Green Living Can Be<br>  Deadly<br>Staci McLaughlin | 978-0-7582-7502-8 | $7.99US/$8.99CAN |
| Death of an Irish Diva<br>Mollie Cox Bryan | 978-0-7582-6633-0 | $7.99US/$8.99CAN |
| Board Stiff<br>Annelise Ryan | 978-0-7582-7276-8 | $7.99US/$8.99CAN |
| A Biscuit, A Casket<br>Liz Mugavero | 978-0-7582-8480-8 | $7.99US/$8.99CAN |
| Boiled Over<br>Barbara Ross | 978-0-7582-8687-1 | $7.99US/$8.99CAN |
| Scene of the Climb<br>Kate Dyer-Seeley | 978-0-7582-9531-6 | $7.99US/$8.99CAN |
| Deadly Decor<br>Karen Rose Smith | 978-0-7582-8486-0 | $7.99US/$8.99CAN |
| To Kill a Matzo Ball<br>Delia Rosen | 978-0-7582-8201-9 | $7.99US/$8.99CAN |

*Available Wherever Books Are Sold!*

31901064671276

Visit our website at **www.kensingtonbooks.com**